Heartache. Betrayal. Fo[...] *time to head back to Magda[...]* *little time with the people we l[...]* *love to hate.*

They should have been married and working on their "happily-ever-after" but fate intervened and stole their chance. Can the residents of Magdalena help them get it back and give them a second chance?

On the day Michael Androvich stands at the altar before family, friends, and most of the town of Restalline, Pennsylvania, he's prepared to pledge his life, love, and fidelity to the woman who owns his heart. There's only one thing missing—the bride.

Elise Pentani loves Michael Androvich truly and completely, but there's a tiny piece of her that believes he'll fall back into his "bad boy" ways. When a threat from his past visits her, Elise lets doubt rule and skips her own wedding.

Nursing a broken heart and determined to forget the woman he can't forget, Michael heads to Magdalena, New York, to secure a business deal for his family's lumber company. He's not prepared for the endless questions and inquisitive nature of the residents who remind him an awful lot of his hometown.

Just when Michael has gotten the town to accept the fact that he's not talking about his past or the reason for his surly disposition, his ex-fiancée shows up with an apology he doesn't want to hear and certainly doesn't want to believe. So much for the town leaving him alone; everybody has an opinion and they're all more than anxious to share it.

There's no way the residents of Magdalena can ignore

these two broken-hearted souls. Michael and Elise have "need help" and "belong together" stamped all over their sad faces. Add that to Pop Benito's determined matchmaking skills and Lily Desantro's clever curiosity, and this couple might just get that second chance…

Note: Michael Androvich and Elise Pentani are secondary characters in *Simple Riches*, Book Three of *That Second Chance* Series. If you haven't read *Simple Riches*, you won't want to miss getting to know this couple or the Androvich family and the small town that is an awful lot like Magdalena.

Other secondary characters from *That Second Chance* series will also be visiting *A Family Affair*'s Magdalena in future books:

Grant Richot from *Pulling Home*, Book One
Angie Sorrento from *The Way They Were*, Book Two
Adam Brandon from *Paradise Found*, Book Four
See you in Magdalena!

Truth In Lies Series:
Book One: *A Family Affair*
Book Two: *A Family Affair: Spring*
Book Three: *A Family Affair: Summer*
Book Four: *A Family Affair: Fall*
Book Five: *A Family Affair: Christmas, a novella*
Book Six: *A Family Affair: Winter*
Book Seven: *A Family Affair: The Promise*
Book Eight: *A Family Affair: The Secret* (TBA)
Book Nine: *A Family Affair: The Wish* (TBA)

If you love to read about second chances, don't miss:
That Second Chance Series:
Book One: *Pulling Home* – (Also prequel to *A Family*

Print ISBN: 978-1-942158-04-2

A Family Affair: Winter

Truth in Lies, Book Six

by
Mary Campisi

Dedication

To Noël—editor, friend, and fellow dog lover. Thank you for making my books better.

Who's Who in *A Family Affair: Winter*

Michael Androvich: *Intended husband of Elise Pentani*
Kevin & Sara Androvich: *Michael's children*
Dr. Nick Androvich: *Michael's older brother*
Alexandra (Alex) Androvich: *Nick's wife*
Gracie Androvich: *Nick and Michael's younger sister*
Rudy Romanski: *Husband of Gracie*
Stella Androvich: *Matriarch of the Androvich clan*

Elise Pentani: *Michael Androvich's bride-to-be*
Dominic Pentani: *Elise's father*

Bree Kinkaid: *Wife of Brody*
Brody Kinkaid: *Works for Bree's father*
Rex & Kathleen MacGregor: *Parents of Bree Kinkaid*
Georgia Kinkaid: *Brody's mother*

Pop Benito: *Beloved "Godfather of Magdalena"*
Lucinda (Lucy) Benito: *Pop's deceased wife*
Lucy Benito: *Pop's granddaughter*
Tony Benito: *Lucy's father*

Nate Desantro: *Husband of Christine Blacksworth*
Christine Desantro: *Daughter of Charles & Gloria Blacksworth*
Lily Desantro: *Daughter of Charles Blacksworth & Miriam Desantro*
Miriam Desantro: *Mother of Nate & Lily*
Harry Blacksworth: *Christine's uncle*
Gloria Blacksworth: *Deceased widow of Charles Blacksworth*

Daniel "Cash" Casherdon: *Nephew of Ramona*

Casherdon

    Tess Casherdon: *Married to Cash*
    Ramona Casherdon: *Premier cook in Magdalena*

    Ben Reed: *Husband of Gina Servetti*
    Gina Reed: *Daughter of Carmen and Marie Servetti*

    Mimi Pendergrass: *B&B Owner, Mayor of Magdalena*
    Jeremy Ross Dean: *Chef at Harry's Folly*
    Phyllis: *Waitress at Lina's Café*
    Barbara Germaine: *Owner of Barbara's Boutique and Bakery*

Chapter 1

Michael John Androvich glanced at the crowd gathering in the pews of St. Stanislaus. Had the whole damn town come to watch? And the music? He was a straight rock 'n' roller, not a flute and high-pitched soloist kind of guy, but he'd done it. He'd agreed to the suit, too, *and* the tie, *and* the church wedding, and... Who was he kidding? He would have agreed to whatever Elise wanted, so long as *she* agreed to spend the rest of her life with him.

Now that was interesting, coming from him. He'd never thought of himself as a one-woman, happily-ever-after kind of guy, even when he'd married the first time. But that was different. *He* was different. And it all had to do with Elise Pentani. His soon-to-be wife made him better, made him *want* to do better, and he didn't even mind the damnable suit or the other trappings she chose for her fairy-tale "I do." As long as he could be her prince, and she'd called him that more than once, then what the hell, a haircut and shave weren't the worst things in the world. If it hadn't been for her old man's emergency stent operation two days before Christmas, they would be married by now, cuddled before the fire in his log cabin—naked—oblivious to the February snow and bitter cold.

Still, what did a month or two matter? They had their whole lives to spend together, starting with a honeymoon trip to that little bed and breakfast in Magdalena, New York. He'd take care of company business a few hours a day and then he'd take care of his wife, a few hours a night...or maybe several hours a night... What better way to start a marriage?

"Hey, wipe that smile off your face and sanitize those thoughts. You're in church."

Michael turned toward his brother, Nick, and the smile

spread. "Got to find something to pass the time, don't I? How much longer before this shindig gets started?" He glanced at his watch. "It's almost 2:00 p.m. and I'm getting claustrophobic in this damn tiny room."

"Relax." And then, "I never thought I'd see my little brother this anxious to tie the knot."

"Shut up, or I'll tell that wife of yours you aren't the god she thinks you are. Not that she'd believe me, but I'd give her a story or two to make her wonder."

"You do that." Nick stared him down, but Michael didn't miss the half smile his brother tried to hide. "How about you concentrate on your own wife and leave mine alone?"

"Now that's an idea I like." *Elise Androvich.* Yeah, he liked the sound of that. "You know I hate waiting, and this whole hoopla is not my deal."

"I know. You'd rather exchange vows in jeans and flannel in the middle of the woods. Maybe shorten the vows to *I do*?"

"Pretty much." Michael yanked at his tie. He was used to working outdoors, fresh air and trees surrounding him and nothing more constricting than the zipper on his jacket. This indoors-dress-up was not his style, but Elise didn't like the idea of getting married in the woods, with the leaves underfoot and a tree stump as an altar.

"Yeah, well, it'll all be over soon enough and then you won't need a suit again until the christening."

"What? Is Alex pregnant?" Damn, but his brother and Alex had only been married a month. Talk about fast work.

"No, idiot. I'm talking about you and Elise."

"Right. I'll keep you posted." That was a subject he was not going to discuss with Nick or anyone but Elise. They'd talked about having a kid or two, but she wanted to make sure Kevin and Sara were okay with the new family dynamics before they added another one. Not that his kids wouldn't be, because they loved Elise, wanted to call her "Mom," but still, they hadn't all lived in the same house, shared the same bathroom in the morning, the I-can't-sleep in the middle of the night. That would all be an adjustment. Plus, he wanted his wife to himself for a while.

"Here comes Mom with Rudy." Nick slapped Michael on the back. "Show's about to start. Don't mess up your lines."

Stella Androvich moved down the aisle, decked out in a long silver dress with sparkles, the same one she wore for Nick and Alex's wedding. Come to think of it, she might have worn it at Gracie's wedding, too. Hard to remember since their little sister acted like she'd been married her whole life and not in a complaining manner either. She and Rudy were the perfect couple; add in a couple of rugrats and they were the ideal family. That didn't mean Rudy hadn't been squawking lately about washing too many dishes or changing diapers, but with Gracie running Androvich Lumber the past few months, that was part of his new job. Compromise, Gracie called it. Crap, he did not look forward to that kind of compromise, but he supposed he could wash a dish or two. Maybe even change a diaper. Michael swiped a hand over his face and pushed dishes and diapers from his brain. One thing at a time, like the vows and the honeymoon.

"Come on, you're up." Nick motioned toward the altar. "Let's get you married."

Michael sucked in a deep breath, nodded, and followed his brother to the front of the altar. It was one thing to be an observer in the background, but to be thrust center stage and become the observed, without benefit of a ball cap, sunglasses, or Elise to soften the glare? Well, that was just plain uncomfortable. He squared his shoulders and stared toward the pews, seeing everyone and no one. Was that Bernie and Alice from Big Ed's? Was Edna Lubovich actually wearing a pink polka dot hat? And how about Uncle

Frank in the third row, decked out in a three-piece suit and tie? Michael would bet the last time he'd worn a suit was at their father's funeral. His gaze drifted further back, settled on Norman Kraziak and his wife. And beside them was Cynthia Collichetti. What the hell was she doing here? It wasn't like a person needed an invitation to attend a wedding ceremony, but why would a woman who'd shared a past with the groom—and not a take-you-on-a-date past but a have-sex-and-out-the-door past—want to witness him get married? The woman must have a sick need for punishment.

The music shifted and the flute picked up, signaling a change in the agenda. Michael glanced at his mother, noted the smile on her face, the small nod of her dark head. Finally, he'd done something right.

The Androvich side of the church was packed with friends, relatives, business and work associates. He could swear he spotted Walter Chamberlain, Alex's uncle in one of the pews. It was hard to miss a Dapper Dan like that guy, but ten months ago, the man would not have been caught in the same town as the Androvich clan, unless it was to tell them he'd bought up their land. Yeah, like any of them would have let that happen. Good thing the old man realized he'd lose his niece if he didn't change his thinking. And good thing Alex and Nick realized people sometimes hurt the ones they loved the most. He'd learned a helluva lot these past months, all because of Elise and her ability to get him to open up, trust, take a chance. On her. On life.

Nick nudged him, leaned over, and whispered, "Elise and her father are coming together, right? Nobody was supposed to pick them up?"

Michael shook his head. "No, she said she wanted to be with him this one last time." Personally he'd thought it was a bunch of bull, but Elise was big on tradition and the church. Plus, it had been her and her father for a while now, so he got it, especially after the close call with the old man's heart. "Are they not here?"

"Not sure, but something's up. Check out Rudy, in the vestibule, waving his arms like a crazy man."

Spurts of panic shot through Michael, filled him with dread and worry. Had something happened to Elise's father? Dominic Pentani was a spry old bugger, but he had a dicey heart and stents or no, the man did not know the meaning of *slow down*. Or maybe they'd had an accident on their way to the church. The roads were slick and he'd wanted to get Elise new tires two weeks ago, but she'd put him off, said they'd have plenty of time after the wedding. But what if they didn't? What if not changing those tires stole their time, erased it, erased *her*, too? She wasn't the best driver, hell, she was barely an adequate driver...and those tires... "Something's wrong."

"Try to relax and give them a few more minutes. I'll see what's going on with Rudy."

"No. I'll go." Michael pushed past his brother and made his way down the aisle, ignoring the curious looks that followed him. When he reached Rudy, his brother-in-law shook his head and said, "Gracie's been trying to call Elise but there's no answer. I was getting ready to head over there now."

"I'll go." If something had happened to her father, he needed to be there, not Rudy. And if anything had happened to Elise... He refused to consider that possibility as he opened the church door and caught a blast of cold air before pushing past it to make his way toward his truck. *Dear God, let them be safe. Please, let them be safe.*

***

Michael traveled the route Elise would have taken to reach St. Stanislaus and spotted no signs of a car in a ditch. Thank God for that. He'd make damn sure nobody drove that car again until there were four new tires on it. As he turned onto the Pentanis' street and spotted the small white house with the blue shutters, he blew out a long breath. Elise's car was parked in its usual spot at the top of the drive. Snow covered the roof and windshield, a clear sign that she hadn't moved it today. Michael pulled into the driveway and hopped out of the truck, his thoughts on Dominic Pentani and his bad heart.

He rang the doorbell and just as he was about to try the door, it creaked open. His future father-in-law stood before him, no apparent distress on his face, unless a person counted the narrowed gaze and the dark scowl. Or maybe the clenched fists indicated a not-so-happy man. Clearly, the guy was ticked about something.

"Dominic? What's the matter?" Michael took in the old man's flannel shirt, the high-waisted corduroys, the slippers. Not wedding gear, even by Michael's standards. "Why aren't you at the church? And where's Elise?" Dominic was old school, a man of manners and superstition, but he'd seemed to like Michael, welcomed him into the family, even baked him his favorite sourdough bread every Monday. But the man staring him down did not look as though he'd be making bread for Michael anytime soon, unless it had a touch of poison in it.

"You. Why do you break my daughter's heart?" He shook a clenched fist at Michael. "Why you no can keep the pants zipped?"

"What are you talking about?" What *was* he talking about? And then, "Where is she? Where's Elise?"

"She no want to talk to you. Leave her alone." He cursed in rapid Italian, lifted the other fist and shook it at Michael. "She never forgive you for what you do."

Michael stepped past him and entered the house. There was enough room to turn around twice and that was it. He bounded up the stairs, reached the first bedroom on the left, and thrust open the door. "Elise?" The blinds and curtains were closed, casting a grayness into the room as though it were dusk and not midafternoon. A long white dress wrapped in plastic hung from the top of a closet door: Elise's wedding gown. He moved toward the bed where his fiancée huddled under a massive floral comforter, head bent, hair tumbled about her. He sat on the edge of the bed, reached out to touch what he thought might be her shoulder beneath the comforter. "Babe?" He kept his voice soft, gentle. "Why aren't you at the church?"

That was the wrong question. His bride-to-be flung back the covers and lunged at him, beating his chest, trying to scratch his face. "Damn you, Michael Androvich! Damn you and your lying, cheating self to hell!"

"Hey!" He grabbed her arms, tried to hold her still, but she fought him, clawed his chin and drew blood. "Stop it. Settle down. Elise! That's enough!"

She stilled, her eyes wild and bloodshot, mouth quivering, nose red and swollen, hair a tangled mess. When she spoke, her voice turned whisper-soft and he had to lean closer to hear. "How could you?"

"How could I what? What did I do?" He'd been accused of a lot of things in his life, many of them true, but that life was gone, replaced with the love of a decent woman, a second chance to do the right thing, and hope. Lots of hope.

"You and Cynthia Collichetti." She sniffed, sniffed again.

Damn. "You knew about her." He wished he could erase every minute he'd spent with that woman, but he couldn't, nor could he lie to Elise about it.

"Did I?" The softness in her voice turned cold, shifted to downright frigid. "Did I know all of it, Michael, or only the parts you wanted me to know?"

What the hell did that mean? She wanted a play-by-play

of a time and a woman he would rather forget? He cleared his throat, tried to keep his voice calm. "I stopped seeing her the afternoon you came to my house and you know that." Elise had brought dinner for him and the kids, only the kids hadn't been there; Cynthia Collichetti had. Elise had cursed him out, told him to go screw himself, though she'd used more graphic terms. It had taken an accident with his saw to make him realize he was in love with Elise Pentani, and once they'd both owned up to the truth, they'd been inseparable. He'd transformed into a decent, committed, dependable guy who was actually happy with his life and it had all been because of her. Today was supposed to be their wedding day, only it didn't look like the bride was ready or interested in a wedding, especially not to him.

"That's not what Cynthia told me."

"What? When did you talk to her, and hell, *why* did you talk to her?" Why were they even talking about this woman? Men didn't spend time with that woman because they wanted her recipe for blueberry muffins and Elise knew that. Cynthia Collichetti was a quick, easy lay who didn't nag or expect a commitment. Hell, she didn't even expect a relationship. A good, hard screw, that's what she wanted and most of the time that's exactly what she got. "What the hell is this all about and why aren't you and your father dressed and at church?"

Her eyes narrowed and glittered like she might shoot sparks from them. "Cynthia stopped by this morning. I'd just taken a shower and was packing the nightgown Gracie gave me." Her voice dipped, shifted lower. "Black satin, low neckline. She was sure you'd like it." She shrugged, looked away. "Guess we'll never know."

Michael grasped her chin between his fingers and forced her to look at him. "Stop it. I can't undo what happened between me and Cynthia, and it's not something I'm proud

8

of, but that's been over a long time. Come on, Babe, you're all I want." Maybe this was what they called wedding jitters and she needed reassurance. Even though the church must have emptied out by now and the food at the reception would end up wasted, which would truly disappoint his mother, what did it matter? They could still grab the priest and say their vows, and then—

"Cynthia's pregnant."

"What?"

"Cynthia Collichetti's pregnant." The words fell from Elise's lips as though she didn't recognize them. "She says you're the father."

"Bullshit."

She shrugged. "The woman can be pretty convincing. Says she's three months pregnant."

"Are you serious? You really think I could be the father?" Her silence pissed him off. "Do the math. We've been together since July. This is February."

"I know." She swiped at a tear. "That's what's breaking my heart."

Michael stared at her. "You think I cheated on you?" More silence. "Cheated on you and got another woman pregnant. Wow." He released her, stood, dragged a hand over his face. "You really have a high opinion of me, don't you? And all this time I thought we were building toward something, like a family, and trust, even a little bit of that happily-ever-after crap."

"We were."

"Until I cheated on you, right?" Oh, now he was past pissed. "What have we been doing all these months? Was that just pretending? Play-acting? Let's have a relationship, fall in love, build a family together? I don't know what you were doing, but I wasn't playing. I was in it for real, and I was in it for good." He paced the small room, wishing he were deep in the woods so he could throw back his head and yell until he grew hoarse. She didn't trust him, didn't believe in him, *didn't love him enough.*

"She said you'd deny it."

"Yeah, I'll deny it all right, because it isn't true." He advanced on her, stopped when he was inches from the bed. "But the truth doesn't really matter, does it? Not that truth anyway. You'll find out soon enough that she lied for whatever reason she might have had. Maybe she was pissed I wasn't interested in her anymore, or maybe she didn't want anybody to be happy. Who knows? I'll bet she's not even pregnant." He let out a cold laugh. "Yeah, that's what I'll bet."

Elise pushed back a tangle of hair and studied him. "Would you agree to a paternity test?"

"A paternity test. Oh, that's just great. I'll get a paternity test and if I pass, you'll marry me, right?" He didn't expect an answer this time, but damn if she didn't give him one.

"Yes."

"Huh. You know, I don't have a degree in psychology, but this is really screwed up. Do you not see the trust issues here? Hell, if I can see it, that's pretty sad." *This is what opening up to another person gets you, stabbed in the heart, left to bleed out. At least he could crawl away with a little dignity and die in peace.* "I guess Cynthia's lie saved us both from making a huge mistake."

"So, you won't get the test?"

"Oh, I'll get it all right. I'm going to find my brother right now and see if he's got a kit in his office. Is that fast enough for you?" He ignored the pain on her face and pushed on, desperate to finish while he still had breath in his lungs. "What are you going to do when you realize you were wrong? That you gave up on me, gave up on *us*, and everything we were supposed to be building for, because you were too scared to trust me, to believe in us? What are you going to do then?" He walked to the door, turned, and forced out his next words. "Good-bye, Elise."

Chapter 2

Elise Antonia Pentani had spent her entire thirty-one years thinking of others. She'd gone to nursing school because it was the selfless thing to do. She'd moved back home to help care for her mother when Rosetta Pentani was diagnosed with a bad heart. She'd filled in at the family bakery when her father needed an extra three dozen cupcakes for a party or deliveries for graduations, communions, weddings. She gave and gave, never thinking of herself or what she might want, because she had *no idea* what that might be. The years passed and she turned thirty, imagining she was in love with a man who didn't know she existed. It was easy to think herself in love with Nick Androvich, the doctor-boss she worked for, the widower and father with the kind heart and wounded soul. But it had all been a one-sided dream because once Alexandra Chamberlain walked into town, Nick's heart and soul belonged to Alex.

And then Elise met Michael John Androvich. Oh, she'd known him since they were kids. He was a few years older, the bad boy to his "hero" older brother. Michael had a less than respectable past, an ex-wife he only married because she was pregnant, two children he didn't spend enough time with, and a penchant for drinking and bad girls. She was the Goody Two-Shoes, the one who followed the safe course in life and shied away from anything hinting at reckless. Certainly she would never consider a bad boy like Michael Androvich, with his crude language and looks that stripped a girl of her clothes and her will in the time it took to finish a drink.

But the more she was around Michael, the more she saw that his bad-boy act was just that, an act to hide behind so people didn't expect too much, if anything, from him. Not even his kids. Elise recognized the need in him, the desire to belong, the vulnerability, and she also recognized the fear, though she didn't tell him that until the day she exploded and yelled words at him she'd never used in her entire life.

It would take a bit more time and an accident to make Michael and Elise realize they loved each other and were meant to be together. That's when Elise started living. That's when Michael opened up and let her see the little boy inside, the one who wanted to please but was afraid he wasn't good enough. That's when the artist in him opened up and he began creating wooden bowls and boxes that were even more beautiful than the ones he'd made before. They were perfect, just like Elise and Michael were when they were together.

But that was gone, destroyed by a single visit from the town whore and the accusations spilling from those too-red lips that had done a lot more than talk with too many men in town. The woman spent less than ten minutes at the Pentanis, but when she left, she took Elise's hope for a future with her, leaving pain and betrayal as a gift on what should have been Elise's wedding day. Of course, Michael had denied the woman's words with disbelief and later, anger. But the anger wasn't targeted at Cynthia Collichetti and her "supposed" lie; no, it was aimed at Elise and her refusal to trust and believe in him.

He had acted so righteous. Michael Androvich? The man who had spent the better part of his almost thirty-seven years rebelling against everyone, denying responsibility for anything, even his family and children? Yes, he'd been different since he and Elise got together; yes, he'd opened up to her, told her he loved her, even admitted a few of his fears, but what if he'd reverted back to the "old" Michael? What if the past several months of devoted father and committed fiancé were simply too difficult to maintain when temptation got in the way?

She'd been a fool to believe him and now her world was ruined and she had no idea how to get back to safe and risk-free. And what of Michael's children? She loved Kevin and Sara as if they were her own, but how could she continue in a relationship with them, knowing she would have to see their father in order to do it? Knowing also that despite her pain and anger, he was burned into her soul and if she weren't careful, she might just want to believe his declaration of innocence.

On the third day after the wedding that didn't happen, Elise went to work. Bad enough she had to show herself to all of Restalline as the silly woman who believed she could reform Michael Androvich, but now she had to face his brother and who knew what Nick would say about the situation? He'd called her twice, told her to take as much time as she needed. There'd been an odd tone to his voice, but she'd not had the strength or desire to ask about it. What could he possibly say to make the nightmare go away? She didn't need to leave her house to know the whole town would be talking about the wedding that didn't happen, and they'd supply their own reasons, true or not. *Poor Elise Pentani, whatever made her think she could tame a wildcat like Michael Androvich?* Or, *Such a nice girl, but so naive.* And of course, *Mark my words, she'll end up a spinster, living in that house, taking care of her father like she did her mother. So sad…she's such a good girl, she deserves a family of her own…but it wasn't meant to be…*

Maybe she should not have been such a good girl, thinking of everyone but herself, worrying about their needs, anticipating their wants. Maybe she should have done everything that flitted through her brain the second it landed there and to hell with the rest of the world. She could have spent the past ten years visiting different places; even

California would have been an adventure for a girl who had never been farther west than Ohio. And she should have dyed her hair, worn push-up bras and low-cut shirts, tight, tight jeans and stilettos. She'd look good in stilettos, and lacy underwear, lots of lace. Black. And a tattoo, maybe *Wild Thing* stamped on the back of her hip, so when she reached for a can of tomatoes in the grocery store, Mr. Mallory, the store manager, would follow the line of her low-slung jeans and he'd see it, and then he'd nudge the stock boy, and he'd see it, too. And then maybe they would start to wonder about her, wonder if there wasn't more to the "good girl" than the nurse who took their temperature and blood pressure in Dr. Androvich's exam room. They'd guess at the underwear she wore beneath her uniform and that would make their temperature *and* their blood pressure spike.

Of course, "Good Girl Elise" would never do that. Just like she'd never sleep around, or sleep naked, or have sex in Michael Androvich's truck, no matter how bad she wanted to do it. It wasn't in her DNA. Or maybe it was, but it was buried so deep, with so many rules and under so many prayers, she didn't recognize it. Maybe she was afraid of it and that's what sent her to confession every month. Or maybe that's what made her ex-fiancé cheat on her and get the town whore pregnant.

Elise spotted Nick's SUV when she pulled into the parking lot. No sense delaying the conversation that needed to happen a second longer than necessary. She hadn't been able to eat her oatmeal or piece of rye toast, the breakfast she ate every morning with the exception of Sundays when she had eggs and pancakes. Michael used to laugh as he watched her measure the oatmeal, cut in a few walnuts or bits of apple for the breakfast regime. He once asked what would happen if she ate waffles on Monday and cereal on Tuesday.

Would she explode? Oh, he'd liked to tease her about her rituals and routines, said she needed to try something different, something daring…like fresh blueberries.

But maybe what he'd really meant was she wasn't exciting enough for him; her need for the familiar and the routine was boring. Maybe what he really meant was *she* was boring. And that's why he'd cheated on her.

"Nick. Got a second?"

Nick looked up from the chart on his desk and smiled. Not a full-blown, glad-to-see-you smile, but a damn-but-this-is-pitiful smile. "Elise. Good morning." His voice held a hint of reservation and sympathy in it. He'd always been the mediator in the Androvich family, the brother who carried the load on his shoulders, did the right thing, protected the rest of the family. Even now, would he try to protect Michael, knowing his brother's wild-streaked past? Probably. The Androviches were a clannish sort, with blood that ran deep and loyalty that never ended, no matter what.

She would have preferred to stand so she could have her say and make a quick exit, but good manners and "Good Girl Elise" forced her to sit and say, "I thought the next time I saw you, I'd call you brother-in-law." The half laugh that accompanied those words spilled out like a deflating blood pressure cuff.

Nick fiddled with his pen, twirled it between his fingers. "Yeah, well." He tossed the pen aside, met her gaze. "I'm really sorry about all of this, Elise. I know it looks bad, but don't give up on Michael."

Yup, he was going to defend his brother. "Don't give up on him? You mean let him cheat on me and get another woman pregnant and keep my mouth shut?" Would the rest of the Androviches tell her the same thing? Would blood trump right? Nick shook his dark head and she wished she'd never fallen in love with Michael Androvich, wished she still thought herself in love with Nick. There was safety in daydreams that had nothing to do with reality.

"Of course not. I don't believe Michael cheated on you," he said in a quiet voice.

"Hah! We're talking about the man who gave reckless its name. Why I thought I would ever be enough for him is beyond ridiculous. Fifty women wouldn't be enough for that man, not once he got bored and needed excitement. Or grew tired of ordinary. It was just too darn much to expect him to be faithful, wasn't it?" She swiped at her eyes, blinked hard. "I didn't want to see what was right in front of me the whole time. But Cynthia Collichetti? That's just disgusting. I'll need to get tested for STDs. Did you know I had him do that before we..." She cleared her throat and went on, "Can we do that today? I'll prepare the lab requisitions and—"

"Elise. Stop. Listen to me. Michael and I haven't always agreed on things, and he's spent too many years carrying a boulder of pity on his shoulder, but you changed him. You made him better, made him want to be better." His dark eyes pierced her. "He loves you and he hasn't been with anyone since you, no matter what Cynthia says."

She stared at him, wishing she could store his words for the lonely nights ahead, when the memories of how things had been stole her sleep and suffocated her with sadness. "He loved me as much as he was able to; I do know that." And she did, but love, or her ex-fiancé's definition of it, wasn't enough to carry them through even the first minutes of marriage. Better she learned the truth now, before they slept side by side every night, had a child or two, raised Kevin and Sara together as though she really were their mother. *That* would have been too painful to survive. The last several months had merely been preparation for the real thing, a practice of sorts for what would come. Only the real thing had evaporated with Cynthia Collichetti's words, as though it had never existed.

"Don't you find it interesting that she waited until the morning of your wedding to seek you out?" Nick rubbed his jaw and once again she almost wished she still believed herself in love with him. Nicholas Androvich was the kind brother, the dependable one who cared for the sick and the elderly, who loved his wife and would never cheat on her. "Elise?"

"What? Oh." He wanted to know why Cynthia Collichetti had waited to drop the pregnancy bomb on her. Didn't he know that "surprise" was that woman's specialty? She didn't care whom she slept with or what families she destroyed. Elise had thought that evil woman was part of her ex-fiancé's past, not his present. "I think she likes to destroy people and is very good at it." She crossed her arms over her small chest. It was at least three sizes smaller than Cynthia's, whose dimensions Michael had probably enjoyed. A lot.

"Yeah, I think Cynthia's a very unhappy woman who thinks the only way she can get a man is to sleep with him, even if he isn't available."

"No kidding?" Sometimes her boss was more naive than she was.

"Michael was an angry guy bent on destroying himself, and that's why he hooked up with her. Once you came along, the jerk behavior stopped and he turned into a human being again. He would not risk losing that."

She wanted to believe him, but sadly, she didn't. Or maybe she couldn't. Somewhere deep inside, maybe she'd always known he would cheat and destroy their chance together. And now it had happened. "I think he would risk it, and I think he did. I asked him to take a paternity test, but—typical Michael—he got all indignant and angry, and then I knew he'd cheated. Oh, he said he'd take one, even wanted to know what I'd have to say when the test showed he wasn't the father." She blew out a disgusted sigh. "But we both know he's not going to take any test."

Nick's gaze grew intense, burned into her with something awfully close to disappointment. Well, she was disappointed, too, but the truth could do that to a person.

"You don't think he might have been upset because you didn't trust him? He needed you to have faith in him, but you believed a woman with an ulterior motive instead, one who might not even be pregnant at all."

"Why are you talking like Michael's an angel? He slept with her, Nick. You know that."

"Past tense. Not since he's been with you." When she rolled her eyes, his gaze narrowed. "I'll bet my practice on it."

That was a powerful statement. "Did you talk to him?"

"He's my brother. Of course, I did."

"And?"

"And what?" Nick sighed and ran a hand through his hair. "He's hurt." He paused. "Really hurt. You left him at the altar, Elise. Do you know what that does to a proud man like my brother? He was worried something had happened to you or your father, but not once did he think you were going to no-show on him." He shook his head. "He couldn't think of anything but getting to you, and you made a fool of him."

Elise stared at the picture on the credenza behind him. It was a picture of Nick and Michael walking out of the woods, side by side, Androvich Lumber ball caps on their heads. The brim of Michael's hat was pulled low over his forehead and his hair curled about his neck and around his ears. He was broader than Nick, more muscular. But he had the softest lips. And his touch...

"He did ask me to swab him and make sure you got the results."

She stared at him. "He agreed to a paternity test?"

"It was his idea." Nick shrugged. "Waste of money if you ask me, though I'm in the minority. Guess it doesn't help when your fiancée thinks you did it."

Elise ignored that last comment. "Did Cynthia agree?"

"Not yet, but I haven't asked. I'll have her come in for a blood test, but if my hunch is correct, she's not even pregnant."

That's what Michael had said. "You really don't think she's pregnant?"

"No, but what I think doesn't matter, does it? It doesn't even matter what you think now." He paused and his voice dipped. "It only mattered before you had proof, when Michael needed you to believe him."

She had no words for that. "I don't know what to say."

"There's nothing to say, Elise. Michael left town yesterday and I don't expect him back for a while."

"Left town? Where did he go?" When Nick just shook his head, Elise gripped the edge of the desk and said, "Damn him, he ran away and left me to deal with the fallout."

"I wouldn't call it that." Nick cleared his throat, met her gaze. "He's hurting right now; he'll need time."

"I'm hurting, too. Where did he go?" And then, "Did he take Kevin and Sara, too?" She loved them, loved spending time with them. They were supposed to be a family. They'd talked about seeing the Grand Canyon this summer…

"They're with Mom, and I'm sorry, but I gave my word I wouldn't divulge his whereabouts."

"Huh. That is so typical of that man." She stood, squared her shoulders, and said, "Fine. He wants to play hide and seek, let him, because I don't care. Do you hear me, Nick?" She swiped at a tear, then another. "I don't care where your brother is."

***

Elise had just finished the supper dishes when her father

placed a hand on her shoulder and said, "Time for talk."

"Sure, Papa. Give me a second." She folded the dishtowel, set it on the counter, and took a seat at the kitchen table. Her father was not one for "talks" but preferred to work around issues, tackle them sideways instead of head-on like his wife used to do. She'd been gone six years, and now, if something needed saying, Elise brought it up, along with a solution. If Dominic were initiating a conversation that didn't have to do with baking or deliveries, then something was up, as in a problem. "What is it, Papa?"

He toyed with the end of his fine mustache a second or two before zeroing in on Elise. At sixty-eight, he was full of energy, small-built and olive skinned, his salt-and-pepper hair clipped close, his smile wide, his gaze intense. The Women's Guild at church thought he was years younger and when he brought them fresh-baked cinnamon buns, well, they practically swooned. The widows in the group had their eye on him, especially Mrs. Viola Ricci, and Elise wondered if her father didn't have his eye on Mrs. Ricci, too.

"What you gonna do now that you no get married?"

"Papa!" It had only been six days since she no-showed at her own wedding. How was she supposed to know what she was going to do when she'd barely had time to accept her uncoupled state? She and Michael would have been on their honeymoon now in that quaint little town in upstate New York. *Magdalena.* Instead, her ex-fiancé had disappeared to an undisclosed location to do who knew what, and she was left to ponder the next few decades of her life. And the last few, too. Not a welcome or joy-filled prospect.

"You no think about it?" Those dark eyes softened and his thin lips turned into a frown. "Viola says you are afraid to trust Michael Androvich because you no trust anyone but yourself." He scratched his head and the frown deepened. "Viola says you too busy making everybody happy, do what everybody wants you to do, that you no know what makes *you* happy."

How dare that woman talk about her as if she were a project! "Papa, why are you discussing my situation with Mrs. Ricci?"

A faint pink crept up her father's neck, settled on his cheeks. He cleared his throat and said, "We talk." He shrugged his bony shoulders. "Everybody needs to talk."

What did that mean? Elise narrowed her gaze on her father. "Talk? Just talk? She's not the one who's been getting the leftover lasagna and stuffed shells, is she? Or the quart of wedding soup I swore was in the fridge yesterday?" She had her answer when his cheeks turned crimson, but she pressed on. "And when you came home two nights ago at 10:35 p.m., were you with her?"

His gaze skittered across the room, inched back to settle on her face. "Viola is my friend."

"Your friend." The words sounded dry and tasteless on her tongue. Her father had a friend, a woman he brought food to, which in Dominic Pentani's mind could represent a mating ritual, or at the very least, a "relationship." Was Mrs. Ricci his *girlfriend*? What exactly did that mean? Elise did not think she wanted to know. Actually, she was certain she didn't want to know. "I see," was all she could manage.

He patted her hand, gave it a squeeze. "I miss your mama every day. She filled my heart with much joy, much love. But she is gone and God is not ready for me to go with her." He paused and his eyes filled with tears. "The days are long. Viola makes the days shorter."

"Why are you telling me this?" Part of her didn't want to know about the woman who made her father's days *shorter*, but another part wanted every single detail.

"You a good girl, Elise. You make a father proud. But you no happy and I want for you to be happy." He cleared his throat, said in a low voice, "You no worry about me; you worry about Elise. Take a trip, go far away, see what you see." A tear trickled down his wrinkled cheek. "And bring back happiness."

"Papa, I can't just leave you." Where would she go? What would she do? And why?

"Viola is here. Days are shorter." He smiled. "Maybe nights will be, too."

Chapter 3

It was early afternoon when Michael drove into Magdalena. Several inches of snow and gusts of wind had followed him from Pennsylvania and deep into New York. The town was pretty much how he'd pictured it: lots of trees and land, a main street with non-chain names, and a feel about it that reminded him a helluva lot of his hometown. That was a good thing and a bad thing. The good thing was the small size of the town probably meant close-knit friends and families. The bad thing was the small size of it probably meant those close-knit friends and families were most likely busybodies. They had their fair share of them in Restalline, as he'd recently had the unlucky occasion to experience. Let someone have a bad string of luck and the whole damn town's got to come visiting, bringing food and a condolence or two, even if a person's not interested in either.

His mother was a true ringleader, but there was no stopping Stella Androvich. She was one tough woman with a prayer group on one shoulder and a baking crew on the other. Throw in the bits of wisdom that she tossed out, solicited or not, and, according to Stella Androvich, you could eat your way out of any heartache, no doubt about it.

Only that wasn't always true, and it especially wasn't true in his case, though she'd tried. Damn if she didn't try to pray over him, feed him, even offer advice pulled from the Androvich archives. Hadn't worked. Michael was heading out of town like a wounded dog and he was taking his battered heart with him. Nick had called yesterday to tell him about the test results. Yeah, big surprise there. He'd danced around the issue of *her*, and Michael knew his brother was itching to get a conversation going, but he'd promised he'd leave it alone. It must have killed him not to add his own thoughts on the whole situation, like Michael couldn't figure it out himself. What was there to figure out? Elise Pentani had dumped him. He'd done everything he didn't want to do but knew he needed to in order to have a shot with her. He'd opened up, trusted her with his damnable insecurities, shared his dreams. Hell, he'd loved her like she was his oxygen, and what had she gone and done? Buried him alive in front of God and all of Restalline because of a rumor that wasn't true. But really, because she just didn't trust him enough, didn't love him enough.

And that was the real story and he'd figured it out all by himself. It had taken him a few days to let the sad truth solidify in his puppy-sick brain, but driving helped sort things out, and walking among the trees in West Virginia, Pennsylvania, and finally New York, helped clarify the whole sad situation. Breathing winter air, standing in the woods, head thrown back, staring at patches of sky through the trees brought him peace. Calm. That was his prayer and his salvation, and while he might have once believed a woman with black hair and a healing touch would save him, he'd learned the truth. She didn't trust him, not enough.

It would be good to work on this project with one of his father's old friends. Michael had been excited when Gracie asked him to speak with Rex MacGregor of MacGregor's Cabinets. There'd been talk of the friendship Nick Androvich Senior and Rex MacGregor had shared, how they'd dreamed of working on projects together but life, children, and Nick Senior's fatal heart attack had ended all of that. But now, all these years later it was Rex who had the bad heart and wanted to get out of the business before he ended up like his friend. He planned to turn the company over to his daughter, but before he left, he had one more big plan, colossal actually, and he wanted an Androvich's advice and expertise. Depending on Michael's answer, the two companies could finally end up working together. Rex

MacGregor wouldn't say much more than that, preferring a "sitdown" instead.

The only downside to this whole deal was the fact that Michael had planned to spend his honeymoon here. He'd even mentioned it to Rex and had booked the honeymoon suite at the Heart Sent. His ex-fiancée had been in love with the whole rose-petals-on-the-bed idea, and fool that he was, he'd asked for pink ones, her favorite color. What an idiot! All that concern about the friggin' color of a rose petal, and she'd stiffed him at the altar. Nice. Wonder what she'd do with the ring. Not that he wanted it back, because hell, he did *not* want it, or any reminder of it, but he was curious. Would she have the guts to sell it? He cursed and shoved her to the far corner of his brain. No sense saying she was out of his brain because the damn woman had set up camp there from the day she'd cussed him out. Her territory kept expanding, like she thought it was friggin' squatter's rights, but maybe if he stopped fighting it so much, she'd eventually fade out. A beer or two might help.

Michael spotted the bed and breakfast and pulled into the driveway. If the snow kept up, somebody would need to get the driveway cleared. Maybe he'd offer, seeing as he had nothing to do for the rest of the day but make an excuse to the manager about why he no-showed for the honeymoon suite and why he was here now and not interested in the aforementioned suite or the rose petals. That would be tricky as he'd spoken with the owner, a Mimi Pendergrass, several times about those damn pink rose petals. Talk about a fool *and* an idiot. He parked the truck, made his way to the passenger side, and yanked out his duffel bags. He was really not looking forward to this, but the sooner Mimi Pendergrass saw he was "flying solo," the sooner she'd leave him alone. He hoped. *Dear God, please do not let this town be full of busybodies like the ones at home.*

He trudged up the steps of the big front porch, stomped his boots to get the snow off, and rang the doorbell. A minute passed and he was getting ready to ring again, when the door opened and a middle-aged woman dressed in a lime-green sweatshirt, jeans, and red loafers thrust out a hand and said, "You must be Michael."

He took off his hat and shook her hand. "Yes, ma'am. Michael Androvich."

"You can stop right there with the ma'am business. I'm much too young for that." She laughed and the little green and silver balls dangling from her ears twirled around. "Mimi Pendergrass is the name. Call me Mimi and come on in before you freeze to death."

He should tell her he'd been working outside since he was twelve and would rather work in frigid temperatures than a heat wave. But if he did, she might want to know more about him and the vacant honeymoon suite. "Thank you, ma'am—I mean, Mimi." Michael stepped inside and set his duffel bags on the carpet beside him.

"My, aren't you a fine-looking young man." She nodded her salt-and-pepper head and crossed her arms over her chest as if assessing his qualities. "Rex told me all about you, said he was good friends with your father." Her expression turned grim, her mouth pulling into a frown. "I am so sorry you lost him at such a young age. Rex said he was a good man."

Damn, what else had Rex MacGregor said? "Thank you."

"Are you tired? Hungry? I've got a pot of vegetable soup on the stove and I just took some homemade rolls out of the oven. How about a nice big bowl of soup?"

He'd stopped for a chili dog a few hours ago and a basket of cheese fries. They tasted damn good, too, especially with nobody to nag him about cholesterol, fats, or clogged arteries. Hell no, no voice yakking in his ear about genetic tendencies and risk factors. That was all gone, and so was she. Next time, he'd order *two* chili dogs. "I am a little hungry. Thank you." He hoped Mimi Pendergrass had real butter, not the fake spray stuff. Or worse, nothing at all. Once he got home and settled again, he planned to replace all the low-fat, no-fat crap in his house with real food. Real butter. Real bacon. Real cheese. Damn straight, that was exactly what he planned to do and nobody would be there to stop him, no one at all, especially not a feisty little Italian with a penchant for healthy eating and cooking everything with olive oil. He ignored the ache in his chest. Stress is what would do him in, stress caused by *her*.

"Do you want to freshen up first or are you ready to dig right in?" She stood with her hands on her hips, giving the impression she was used to being in charge, and something told him she was in charge of this town, or a lot of it.

"I'm all set. I can take my bags to my room later."

"Ah, yes." She motioned him to follow her into the dining room and gestured to the oak table with the cream-lace tablecloth and eight matching chairs. "Give me your jacket and have a seat." Michael shrugged out of his jacket and handed it to her along with his Androvich Lumber cap. "Michael." She paused, tilted her cropped head to the side, and studied him.

He knew what was coming, held his breath as he waited for it.

"About the other room you reserved." Another pause. "The honeymoon suite."

And there it was. He shoved his hands in his pockets and stared at her. If she wanted answers, then damn it, she was going to have to ask him, because he wasn't offering anything. "Right," was all he said.

"You won't be needing it?"

There were fifty questions stuffed in that one. "Nope."

"I see."

Doubtful.

"I'm sorry, Michael. I wish the woman you took such great pains to get those pink rose petals for could see them." She paused and her gaze met his head on, burrowed into his secrets, tore them open. "And for whatever reason she won't see them, I'm sorry for that, too."

"Thanks." Now his chest burned like frostbitten fingers. And then, because he had to change the subject before his heart burst, he said, "How about I grab a quick bite to eat and then clear off your driveway?"

***

There was no putting off visiting Stella Androvich any longer. Michael's mother hadn't contacted her, because according to Nick, she wanted to give Elise time and space. That didn't mean the time or space would go on and on, only that the limit hadn't expired. Yet. Elise could read between Nick's words: "Visit my mother and get this situation out in the open."

By now, most of the town probably knew the reason behind Elise's no-show at her own wedding. It wasn't that Nick or any of the other Androviches would have said a word, but the town had eyes and ears and was excellent at deciphering puzzles. If the Pentanis' next-door busybody, Geraldine Stouffer, just so happened to see Cynthia Collichetti enter the Pentani household the morning of the wedding and did *not* see Elise leave, that could be an important detail. Couple it with the groom's past—ahem—relationship with Cynthia, and a body didn't need to overexert brain power to figure that one out.

Even if Geraldine Stouffer didn't happen to see the comings and goings at the Pentani home, there would be Cynthia's so-called friends, who knew how to blend fact and fiction and might have detected a bit too much fiction in their friend's story to get catalogued as truth.

None of that would have mattered if the results had come back confirming Cynthia's accusations and while Elise might have been labeled naive, she would have garnered sympathy and more than one kind look from the town. But the results that landed on Nick's desk yesterday told a different tale. Michael wasn't the baby's father. In fact, there wasn't a baby at all. That truth might have taken longer to unearth if Nick hadn't paid a visit to Cynthia Collichetti and gotten her to agree to a pregnancy test and while she was at it, an acknowledgment of her obsession with Michael.

Hadn't Michael told Elise it was all a lie? Hadn't he sworn he'd never been unfaithful to her? And hadn't she called him a liar? Now what? She'd crumbled the second Nick told her the results, the tears falling so hard she'd not been able to stop them, even when he pulled her into his arms and tried to soothe her. *What had she done?* And how could she ever make it right?

Those questions plagued her a day later as she stood on Stella Androvich's front porch and rang the doorbell. She'd come to apologize for the shame she'd brought to the Androvich family, and the pain she'd caused them. When the door opened, Stella stood before her, wearing a sauce-splattered apron and a look that said she was not surprised to find Elise on her doorstep. "Hello, dear. You're just in time. The banana bread came out of the oven five minutes ago."

Elise hesitated, biting her lower lip as she tried to work up the nerve to say what needed to be said. Stella didn't give her an opportunity to speak as she opened her arms and pulled her into a warm embrace. "Oh, Stella, what have I done?"

"I know, dear, I know." She smoothed Elise's hair and held her close. "I'm sure you're hurting right now as much as my son is."

"I am so sorry." Elise eased away and forced herself to meet Stella's gaze. "So sorry."

Michael's mother nodded, her lips curving into a gentle smile. "Come inside before we get the whole town speculating more than they already are. I'll make you a cup of tea to go with that banana bread."

Stella Androvich believed that all manner of heartache could be solved and remedied with food. While her older son healed people's bodies, Stella healed hearts with spaghetti and meatballs, wedding soup, stuffed cabbage, pumpkin rolls, apple pies. The dish didn't matter as long as it was homemade and touched with love. Elise shrugged out of her jacket and sat at the old kitchen table in the spot Stella once told her had been Michael's. She pictured the Androvich siblings at this table, as toddlers, teens, and young adults, sharing meals, conversations, even arguments, in ways Elise had not known. "Nick told you about the results of the test."

"Yes." Stella placed a slice of banana bread on a plate and handed it to her. "He told me."

Elise stared at a gouge in the table near the plate, deep and scuffed out from years ago. Had that been Michael's handiwork? Was it an accident or had it been intentional, yet one more sign of the reckless person he'd once been? "I really thought Michael cheated on me, even when he swore he hadn't." She stared at the gouge in the table until it blurred. "Why couldn't I believe him?"

"I think you were afraid. I think you love him but you don't trust him, not one hundred percent, and the first time that trust was tested—" she paused and swiped at her eyes "—well, it failed miserably. But trust is a hard thing to build, and love and a promise to be honest isn't enough. You've got to trust yourself, too, and I'm not sure you do."

"What do you mean?" She had a feeling she knew exactly what Stella meant, but what surprised her was how the woman could see what Elise had only realized a few days ago.

Stella Androvich's voice turned soft, gentle when she spoke. "You're afraid to really open up and let yourself trust him, for fear he'll hurt you. Oh, I do understand that, and Michael might be my son, but he would not be an easy man to love or trust." Her lips pulled into a faint smile. "Nick, he's the kind one who's easy to love and, easier still, to like. Not Michael. He is so much like his father: ornery, strong-headed, hot-tempered, quick to judge. And the grudges Nick Senior used to carry? I do not even want to get into that." She sighed and shook her head. "That man was something else, but there was a soft spot about him that he didn't show many people. Why, he didn't even show me for the first three years of our marriage. But then it started to slip out and once, when Nick spiked a high fever and we worried we might lose him, well, then I saw the real Nicholas Androvich, the one who was afraid, the one who loved so much and needed so much to be loved." Her voice dipped, spilled out in a whisper. "When he stopped trying to hide that fear and started to really trust me, that's when the magic between us really started."

Elise wished she'd had this conversation with Stella months ago, but would she have understood it then? Probably not, when she hadn't acknowledged her own trust issues until after the failed wedding attempt.

"So, I'll bet you're wondering where this leaves you and Michael." Stella poured their tea and set Elise's mug in front of her.

"Actually, I'm pretty sure I know." An image of Michael in his wedding suit standing at her bedroom door seconds before he left flitted through her brain. He'd looked so handsome, so hurt, so unapproachable.

Stella lifted her mug, took a sip. "And what would that

be?"

"Whatever he has in mind for his future, I'm not part of it." There. She'd put sound to the words that had lived in her brain since the second she began to doubt Cynthia Collichetti's story.

"Don't be so sure. I've never seen Michael more devastated, not even when he had to marry Betsy, and let me tell you, that was painful for him. No, you leaving him at the altar took a chunk out of his soul, and it's going to take time to heal."

Those last words snuffed the air from the room. "You know Michael; why would he ever let me close enough to hurt him again?"

"Why indeed?" Stella reached out, clasped her hand. "Because you gave him hope, made him feel alive, made him believe in himself. Once he settles down, he's going to want that again, and there won't be a choice but to open up to you." She squeezed Elise's fingers and said, "But if you don't deal with your own trust issues, whether it's trusting him or yourself, or whatever it is you want from life, you're bound to continue down this road until you destroy any chance of a life together."

Elise nodded. If only she could talk to Michael, tell him how sorry she was, how she misjudged him…if only he would give them another chance… "You know where he is, don't you?"

"I do."

"And you aren't going to tell me, are you?"

Stella shook her head. "A mother's promise should not be broken." She paused and smiled. "But that doesn't mean you can't look for him, or maybe look for yourself." The smile spread. "Nick said he told you to take some time off. Why not do it, Elise? Go somewhere, clear your head, open your heart. Don't live your whole life in fear, living by someone else's rules and expectations. Live *your* life, do what *you* want to do. And start now." Her eyes filled with tears. "Who knows? Maybe you can even visit that bed and breakfast you were going to stay at for your honeymoon and see what a bed covered in rose petals feels like. Why not? Why on earth not? You talked about it for weeks, why should anything stop you?"

Chapter 4

Rex MacGregor was big and burly, with a thick head of reddish-white hair and a beard to match. His laugh was loud, his voice louder, and in the twenty minutes since Michael shook his stump-sized hand, the man told him two tales that ended with a laugh and a slap on the back. Rex MacGregor did not seem a likely friend for Nick Androvich Senior. But when the man closed the door to his office, his demeanor switched from rambunctious to thoughtful, and once he started talking about wood and the grain that ran through it, Michael understood why the two men had become friends.

"Your father knew how to spot black cherry, oak, anything you threw at him, and he could tell you how many boards you'd get out of it, too." He shook his head and folded his hands over his large belly. "I never saw anything like it. Used to test him to see how close he'd get. Loser bought a bottle of whiskey." He laughed and said, "Only good thing about losing was your old man didn't like to drink alone. I hear you got the same gift of spotting wood as your father."

Michael shrugged, uncomfortable with the compliment. He'd been working in the woods for so many years it was all natural to him now, no different than his mother knowing how to tell oregano from parsley. There was the feel, the smell, the look, same with a tree. "Do anything long enough and you figure it out."

"A humble man." Rex MacGregor's fleshy lips pulled into a wide smile. "There should be more of you." He frowned and muttered, "Not overbearing idiots like that good-for-nothing son-in-law of mine."

Michael cleared his throat and pretended he didn't hear the part about the son-in-law. "My sister said you're interested in some of our black cherry for your high-end cabinets. Do you know how much you'll need and when you'll want it?" He had enough problems of his own without getting dragged into someone else's, especially when it had to do with family or in-laws. It was one thing for him to get pissed at his siblings, but let an outsider voice an opinion about one of them, and that person was in for trouble. Blood was blood, and family was family, no matter what.

Rex mumbled something else that sounded like another complaint against the son-in-law and said, "How about we get started as soon as we can work out the details?"

"Sure. Let's see what you need and then we'll talk numbers and timeframe." Nick had met Rex MacGregor a few years back when he visited the old man's shop and he'd been impressed with the operation and with Rex. Nick said any man who was a friend of their father was someone they should get to know. Michael knew what he meant even though he didn't say it. Nick Senior had been dead a long time; hell, they'd been kids when he keeled over in the woods from a heart attack, and the memories weren't as sharp as they once were. Michael remembered heading into the woods with his father, pointing out trees, touching bark, tracing leaves—learning the texture, the smell, the names, all of it. Nick hadn't been in love with the woods like Michael was, or maybe it had been the opportunity to have his father all to himself that created the excitement and the interest. It didn't matter because even now, when Michael headed into the woods, his father was with him. Of course, he'd never talked about that with anyone but Elise because he didn't want his family to think he was a whacko or too sentimental; both were equally bad. But he hadn't minded telling Elise. In fact, he'd wanted to share it with her so she could know something more about his father, know something more about *him*, too. She'd cried when he told her.

He pushed the memory away and frowned. *Yeah, he*

should have kept his mouth shut.

"I told your sister the black cherry wasn't the only reason I wanted you to come." He unfolded his arms, placed two monster hands on the desk, and leaned forward, close enough for Michael to make out flecks of gold in those washed-out amber eyes. "I got a confidential matter, kind of a business and family issue that needs settling and the fewer people who know about it, the better."

"Okay." Sounded like the Androviches weren't the only family that had an overlapping of personal and business issues. There'd been a time not that long ago when Nick and Michael faced a stalemate, with Nick trying to force him to run the business and Michael fighting it hard. Then their sister stepped in and took over as though she'd been born to do it. Gracie running the company, diaper bag and all! The old man would be proud of her. Michael would like to think his father would be proud of him, too, for his skill and expertise in the woods as well as his craftsmanship making bowls and specialty boxes.

As for Nick, everybody was proud of the older Androvich son. That just went without saying.

"Your old man convinced me the future was in owning land. How the hell he knew that, I'll never know. We planned to go in together and buy up land right here, but he couldn't scrape up the cash, not with building his own business and three babies." He shook his head and his eyes misted. "I wanted to give him a loan to go in on it, seeing as it was his idea, but your father wouldn't have it; said if he couldn't pay his own way, he wasn't taking a handout. Damn, but he kept after me to buy the land, so I did. But we made a deal; when it came time to harvest the wood on that property, Androvich Lumber would do the work." Rex sighed, dragged a beefy hand over his face. "I always thought when that day came, your old man would be the one heading up the operation, but, if he can't be the one, why not his son?"

"Did my mother know about this, or Nick?" The possibility that the old man could have thought about more than heading into the woods every day and keeping his family fed was hard to picture.

"Doubt it. Your father wasn't much on sharing dreams; said they didn't fill bellies. But I saw the way he looked at the land. We might have worked out a deal for him to own a piece of it." He paused, blew out a breath. "I had a scare a few months back. Doc did a bunch of tests, put me on one of those 'heart-healthy' diets where everything tastes like cardboard or ground pulp. You know the kind. Anyway, I promised the wife I'd step aside and let go of the business." His expression turned grim. "I was all set to do it, too, had plans to turn the business over to my son-in-law, but hell, that damn fool Brody started making plans to sell that land for a resort." He cursed, blew out another deep breath. "What the hell was that boy thinking? Magdalena isn't a place for luxury resorts, and nobody in this town but Harry Blacksworth has a swimming pool, and he's the exception. Oh, Brody tried to deny it, said he was only considering the options but I saw the lie on his face plain as if he'd written it on his forehead. That's when I knew I couldn't leave that boy in charge of changing the toilet paper rolls in this place." He paused, met Michael's gaze. "So, I brought in my daughter. Bree's never been involved in the business, what with raising her family, but she's learning, and with your help, she'll learn even more."

"What?" What in the hell was he talking about? Michael didn't "train" people; he was a loner, a doer, the one who figured things out. He did not "teach" and he sure as hell did not want to get involved in the middle of a family situation with this Brody guy and Rex's daughter.

"Don't you worry. Bree's as sweet as a banana cream pie and a quick learner, too."

"I don't know, Rex. I'm not a—"

"Hold on." He held up a hand to silence Michael. "Just listen to the deal before you start shooting holes in it. You come in, get a feel for the land, and make sure there's enough usable wood to begin a harvesting program where you'll clear out so many acres at a time. You'll replant a certain amount, too, like you do at Androvich Lumber. And you'll keep the wood you harvest and pay me a percentage. If I buy some for MacGregor's Cabinets, that's factored into my cut."

The offer intrigued Michael. Acres of wood, all just waiting for him. That meant hours of work that would keep him busy and distracted from life's problems, especially those brought about by his ex-fiancée. Michael rubbed his jaw and said, "Any idea what kind of trees you got in the woods?"

Rex shrugged. "It would be a guess. I know there's sugar maple and beech, but there's just too much land to tell for sure." He opened a desk drawer and pulled out a packet of photos. "Here's some aerial views." He spread several 8x10 photographs across the desk and pointed to different ones. "Streams...hills...and this looks like a big ravine. There's dirt roads to get in there and drive around. Miles and miles of it." He grinned and spread his arms wide. "The wife used to pack me a lunch and I'd load up the chain saw and the dog and head into the woods with my pickup. If I ran into a tree blocking the road or some other mess that kept me from getting through, I'd pull over and clear the way. Those woods gave me a lot of peace. Nothing like being alone with your best friend and your thoughts, don't you think?" His voice dipped, gentled. "The dog and the truck died within a week of each other; just plain wore out. But they were good buddies, loyal to the end." His mouth turned down. "I still miss them."

Michael nodded. "There's nothing like a loyal animal or a truck. You can always count on them, even when they've only got three breaths left." *Damn straight on that one*. He cleared his throat and returned to the photos spread across Rex's desk. Anything to avoid an emotion tied to death and loss, even if it had to do with a dog and a truck.

"Right. So...back to the land. I was counting on you telling me what we had and how we should go about getting it out. You can get a truck in there as long as the snow's not too deep. I've got some damn good work vehicles that will do the job and a saw, too, in case you need to unblock the roads."

Michael studied the aerial views, noted the clusters of trees, the narrow roads, the hilly terrain. A job like this was best done in stages, carefully planned out and executed depending on resources, time, and the elements. "I'd have to get in there and poke around."

"Sure." And then, "When?"

Michael looked up, his gaze narrowed on Rex. "A few random pictures don't tell me anything. I have no idea what's involved here and I won't until I get down there and walk around. I'll need whatever information you have on the property: anything to help determine what's there aside from trees."

The old man nodded. "Then you're interested?"

Michael didn't miss the note of desperation in Rex MacGregor's voice. What the hell? A project like this might just make him forget things he didn't want to remember, like an ex-fiancée who'd dumped him. "I'm interested."

"Good. Very good."

"You're sure in a hurry to get this done."

Rex shrugged and his cheeks turned pink. "The wife's

not happy I'm still here. You know how they can get. They think you're doing it to spite them, but what you're really trying to do is see the job through, right?" He didn't wait for Michael to respond, but continued. "We fight about it once a week, sometimes twice, but Kathleen doesn't see that's what raises my blood pressure." He sighed and said, "This damn situation with my son-in-law is what really has me wound up. The sooner I get things in place and Bree trained, the sooner I can relax."

"Right." Michael did not look forward to working with a family member who had limited training and probably thought a tree was just a tree. Working with Rex's daughter was going to be a royal pain in the ass, and just because his sister had proven qualified to take over the family business did not mean every family member was. "So, if you leave and your daughter's in charge, what's to say the husband doesn't convince her to sell the land and make it a rich person's playground?" Damn, but this sounded like what almost happened in Restalline when Alex hit town pretending to be a researcher gathering information for a documentary instead of a scout for her uncle's development company.

The chair squeaked with Rex MacGregor's weight as he leaned forward. "That's where you come in. We sign a deal for you to harvest the trees and give us a percentage, which will provide an income stream for my daughter and my grandchildren for years to come." His full lips pulled into a wide grin. "And here's where we protect ourselves from money grubbers who can't see more than the almighty dollar. The deal with Androvich Lumber will last fifty years."

Fifty years of income for Androvich Lumber, too. If the proposal worked, that would be one helluva deal and protection for all of them, including his kids, Gracie's kids, and Nick's. But first, Michael had to make sure that what Rex thought was in those woods—viable timber—was really there. "Okay, how about we knock out the black cherry situation and then you get me the specs on the acreage?"

Rex stood and motioned toward the door. "Sure. I want you to check out the setup in the shop first and then you can meet my daughter. Bree is one of a kind, oh yes she is."

***

Michael Androvich might be the son of her daddy's friend, and he might be the one her daddy had in mind to take over the company, but goodness, the man was certainly lacking in the social etiquette department. Bree huffed and slid a glance his way. Did the man never speak? Truly, could he not engage in casual conversation for the pure politeness of it? *So, have you lived here all of your life?* Or, *do you like working for your father?* Even, *what does a person do around here for entertainment?* And when he did decide to grace her with a word or two, could he really not take the extra breath and brainpower to string the words into a sentence? With a smile? A softening of the voice would do, anything but the I-could-care-less aura that swirled around him like a clogged-up toilet. Since her daddy introduced them forty-five minutes ago, the man had done nothing but…well, glance through piles of papers, jot down notes, and study photographs. And why Michael Androvich had to set up camp in *her* office at the extra desk her daddy had talked her into because he thought she could use some help was past annoying. Well, help did not come in the form of someone bent on taking over her job.

Her daddy had been all hush-hush about the man's arrival and his reason for being here, but he didn't fool Bree. She knew people, knew when something was off, like a relationship turned sour or one that just plain fizzled and fell apart. Hadn't she been the first to pick out the problems between Stanley and Arleen Ketrowski? One look at the way Stanley was paying no attention to his wife during Sunday sermons for the past six weeks, and every attention to the new choir director, and it was obvious the man had a lot more in common with her than a shared hymn. Oh yes indeed! Something was up with Daddy. He'd been all skittish, his coloring redder than usual, those little beads of sweat on his forehead popping like they did when he was in a situation he did not want to be in. Uh-huh. She slid another glance at the man seated a few feet away. She'd bet this week's diaper allowance he was at the front and center of her daddy's uneasiness. Rex MacGregor had chosen his replacement, and now he had to find a way to tell his only child she wasn't the one.

Oh, but if she'd been a boy, well, that would have been a different story. She'd already be running MacGregor's Cabinets and her parents would be traveling the country in one of those fancy RVs her daddy talked about buying when he retired. It was just not fair that in her daddy's world, a daughter might spit out babies and bake a good pie, but she was not operating a company. He'd picked Brody for the job a while back, had even given him a big office and started to teach him about financial reports, sales analysis, and customer relations. But Brody didn't have the inclination for the "big picture" or all those numbers, and he didn't understand diddly about sales even though he was the sales manager for the company. He *did* like seeing how much money came in, and every night he'd come home with a list of what they'd get once *his* name was on the company letterhead. Fancy cars. A boat. Maybe a motorcycle. Even a second home.

It might have been talk of the second home that made Daddy rethink Brody as his successor; Bree was never quite sure. She'd been having a tough time of her own, with the miscarriage and Brody's obsession for a boy, and a life that was far from happily-ever-after, even if she couldn't admit it. So when Daddy offered her an opportunity to learn the company business and maybe run it one day, well, that was like saying he believed in her. And it did not get any better than that, even if Brody made a few snippy comments every once in a while about how he was perfectly capable of running the damn company and no way was Bree ever going to be *his* boss.

If her hunch was right, Brody might not have to worry about that because the outsider next to her was taking over. She stole a glance his way, zeroed in on the strong jaw, the nose with the slight crook, the full lips, the brown hair curling about his thick neck…

"Like what you see?"

Bree gasped. Michael Androvich's lips twitched but he kept his eyes trained on the papers in front of him. How had he seen her watching him?

"I wanted to make sure you hadn't fallen asleep. You haven't moved since you sat down." There, let him think about that.

"Nope. Wide awake." He held a photo up, studied it. "Do you know you've been talking to yourself for the past ten minutes?"

"I have not!"

"And humming. Bon Jovi's 'It's My Life.'"

"I did not." Darn, *had* she been talking and humming? That song was her very favorite, so maybe…

"Don't worry about it." He set down the photo and turned to her. "It's a good song. I've been known to hum it a time or two myself."

His full lips curved into a smile and goodness, those dark eyes softened like the middle of a chocolate lava cake. Bree fanned herself and fought the heat creeping up her neck.

Maybe there was more to Michael Androvich than she first thought. There was no harm digging around a little, was there? She smiled back. No harm at all.

"So your daddy and mine were friends."

He swiveled his chair to face her, crossed one booted foot over his thigh. "Yeah, they were."

Goodness, but the way those jeans pulled over his thigh muscles made a girl wonder what he looked like underneath. Muscles and tanned skin, she'd bet on that. Brody was a heap of muscle and tan, too, but his was all lumped together like a sticky bun. Michael Androvich was more of a sweet roll, all smooth and covered in frosting. And there was no way some girl hadn't latched onto that sweet roll. No way at all. So where was she and why did she let her man come here without her? She and Brody had never spent more than a night apart, not since the afternoon they stood at the altar of St. Gertrude's and promised their hearts to one another. That was babies and dreams ago...

The man cleared his throat. "Are you okay?"

"Hmm?" She stared at him, pushing aside the disappointments and sadness that had come with that promise. Life was not built on illusions, no matter how much a person wanted to believe in them. "Oh, yes, I'm fine." And then, because she could not quite stifle her curiosity, she asked, "Are you married?" The answer would tell her so much about the man. A *yes* would lend itself to more questions. Children? How many? Ages? A *no* and the manner in which he said it would tell her even more.

But no answer—what did *that* mean?

Michael Androvich's eyes narrowed and they no longer looked like the middle of a molten lava cake. No, they did not. Goodness gracious, they had taken on the look of charcoal, and the smile had flattened, too, become hard and unforgiving. From her spot several feet away, she could see the muscles in his neck bulging. "I'm sorry," she sputtered, darting a gaze to the clenched fist digging into his thigh. That fist bothered her more than the fierce glare. "I didn't mean to intrude." She glanced back at his face. The right side of his jaw twitched, then the left, but still he said nothing. "Okay then, I'm going to lunch. See you later." Bree grabbed her purse, scooted from the chair and out the door. Not until she reached the cafeteria did she realize she'd left her lunch bag in the desk drawer.

She'd just finished a sad imitation for a ham sandwich and a chocolate pudding from the vending machine when Brody slapped his lunch box on the table and sat down. He stared at the plastic container in her left hand and said, "Why are you eating that crap?"

Bree shrugged and plopped a mouthful of chocolate pudding in her mouth. She was not about to tell her husband the truth. *My mouth got me in a pickle again and I had to make a quick getaway.* "I like to try what's in the machine every once in a while. Maybe I'll see if Fred can switch out the ham sandwiches for turkey." Bree had gone to school with Fred Montgomery; Brody had, too, but he'd paid no mind to the curly-haired, underweight boy who wrote for the school newspaper. Fred used to say he was going to move to New York City, write for the *Times*, but his father died and his mother got sick and he never made it past Willowick. Bree set down her spoon, eyed her husband's pastrami and Swiss on rye. She fixed his lunch every morning at 5:15 a.m. because Brody claimed the bread got too soft if she made his sandwiches the night before, and he didn't like the way they stuck to the roof of his mouth.

"Wanna bite?" he asked around a mouthful. When she nodded, he held the sandwich to her lips, and she nibbled.

He laughed and shook his head. "You eat like a bird." He devoured the rest of the sandwich and chewed so hard she wondered how his jaw didn't ache. Her husband did nothing small-scale, and that's what had first drawn her to him in high school. That and his good looks and those eyes that had followed her from class to class, always watching, inching from her mouth to her neck, to her breasts, hands, belly, as if he wanted to devour her like a candy bar. As if he *would* devour her with those eyes right in Algebra 2 class, leaving nothing but an empty seat where Bree Lynn MacGregor had once sat. Two days of Brody Kinkaid in pursuit and by day three, when he walked up to her locker and smiled, his big frame towering over her, well, her heart still flip-flopped at the memory. Love burst through her, quick and fast, branding her his. He'd even written a poem he titled "The Promise," and while some might consider it trite, even silly, Bree had thought it the most beautiful profession of love ever.

"Remember the poem you wrote me when we started dating?" He'd handwritten it in his cramped style. She hadn't cared that he'd scratched out a word or two and misspelled *means*. It was the thoughts behind those words, like heartbeats, that counted.

His forehead wrinkled and he scratched his jaw. "Kinda."

Brody didn't like anyone to think him soft, not even his wife, but she knew he was mushier than a marshmallow at a campfire. "Does this sound familiar?" Before he could say anything, she recited, "'The promise I make this day. Means my love is here to stay. In all the months, even May. Nothing will stand in the way. Of the promise I make today.'"

"Shhh." Brody jerked his big body halfway across the table. "Stop it," he said in a loud whisper. "If the guys hear that, I'm done. They'll call me ten kinds of a sissy and I'll never live it down."

Bree sniffed and tried not to cry. "It's nothing to be

47

ashamed of; it's beautiful."

He sat down, the veins in his necks bulging, and blew out a long sigh. "I've got appearances to keep, Bree. If I'm gonna run this shop, I can't look like a sissy. The men won't respect me."

These last words snuffed out her hurt feelings. "Who said you're going to take over?"

"Huh? Not now, but once your dad leaves." His full lips pulled into a wide grin. "Brody Alan Kinkaid, President, MacGregor Cabinets. Kinda sounds nice, doesn't it?" He popped three potato chips in his mouth and fished in the bag for three more. Brody liked to eat his "sides" in threes. Three chips at a time, three cookies at a time, three pickles at a time. He called it a good luck habit that he'd been doing since he was in grade school.

But good luck had nothing to do with his taking over her father's business. Daddy might not have come right out and told Brody he wasn't going to be his successor, but moving Brody from the front office to the machine shop, not even letting him be sales manager again? And bringing in Bree to learn the business? Even the latest addition of Michael Androvich; all of those said Brody Kinkaid was not going to be president of anything Rex MacGregor owned, and it was clear to everyone except Brody.

"But what if Daddy doesn't pick you?" And then, because her daddy had told her straight up he wanted her to run the business if she proved qualified, she added, "What if he picks me?"

You would have thought she'd been talking about their dog. Brody threw back his head and laughed so hard, he sent himself into a coughing fit that lasted until Bree flew out of her chair and gave him three whacks between the shoulder blades.

"Damn!" Brody slurped his drink and cleared his throat.

"Don't do that to me again, Bree." He chuckled and swiped at his eyes. "Me, working for you? That's a good one. Brody Kinkaid doesn't work for his wife." His gaze dipped to her chest. "But I think you'd make a fine secretary. You could bring me my coffee, sit on my lap, and take notes." He rubbed his jaw and grinned. "I like the sound of that."

Well, she didn't like the sound of it, not one bit. "I don't think so." She gathered her trash and stood. "I'm learning about the business, Brody, and I don't mean funny business, which is all you seem to think I'm good for." She paused, added, "That and washing your stinky clothes and making you chili and chicken pot pie. Daddy sees possibilities for me, and if you can't handle that, then too darn bad."

Chapter 5

Elise pulled the afghan closer and snuggled into the cushions of the sofa. There was comfort in the familiar sofa that was only a few years younger than she was, and while the rose pattern had faded and the stitching frayed, it held memories of family, the Pentani family. Her mother had taken care of her on this very sofa as Elise recovered from all manner of ailments: bronchitis, fever, tonsillectomy, broken arm, bruised heart, tattered pride. Rosetta Pentani knew how to mend bodies and nurture souls with her kind words and soft touch, a gift she passed on to her daughter. Years later, Elise was the one who cared for her mother on the floral sofa, helping her sip broth, wiping her brow, reading to her. It was the reading that carried her mother through the long days and nights to a better time, a dream of how things might have been had her heart not given out. And Dominic Pentani might not have known what to say when his daughter didn't get asked to a dance, or how to put his wife's legs through "range of motion" exercises, but he knew how to put food in the bellies of his "two best girls": bread, rolls, cupcakes, cookies. Every bakery item came with a story and a smile.

When her mother died, Elise found comfort in eating and reading, two passive loves that added fifteen pounds to her five-foot-two-inch frame. The weight would have doubled and then some had her father not snatched an éclair from her hand one day and said, "What you do this for?" Those black eyes filled with sadness as he shook his head and whispered, "We must both end this. I feed you to stop tears, and you eat to stop tears. And both of us, so sad." He shook his head again. "It no bring your mama back." Her father's words stayed with her as she walked the weight off, starting at one end of town and ending at the other, her thoughts absorbed in the audiobooks that kept her company. The books and the mountains of daydreaming—those she could not give up even though they created a fictionalized world that could never measure up to her small and insignificant existence.

Elise sipped her hot chocolate and lost herself in *Pride and Prejudice*, a book she'd read countless times. She'd just reached the part where Mr. Darcy proposes to Elizabeth and is met with a scathing refusal. Oh, but if she didn't know the outcome, she would certainly believe there was no hope for this mismatched couple; indeed, they would live the rest of their lives apart despite the ache in their souls. But they *did* get their second chance; they *did* forgive each other, looking past the misunderstandings and lack of trust, to the real person, the one who was scared, uncertain, desperate for the other's love.

Why couldn't she be Elizabeth Bennet and Michael be Mr. Darcy? Why couldn't they have a second chance? Elise was so involved in the battle with her conscience over the right to a second chance that she didn't hear the doorbell until it rang in rapid staccato. She tossed the book aside, slid off the sofa, and tightened her bathrobe as she made her way toward the door. Who could it be? No one came to the house at night unless it was Mrs. Ricci, and she and Papa were having movie night at her house. They invited Elise for pot roast and to watch *Moonstruck* but joining your senior-citizen father and his "friend" because your own life was so lacking was just pathetic. She could have been married, building on a dream with the man who owned her heart. Instead, she was lounging on a sofa, dressed in flannel and peeking at someone else's happily-ever-after, and that someone else wasn't even real!

Elise opened the door and wished she weren't in a twelve-year-old bathrobe and fuzzy slippers with her hair pulled into a ponytail and her face scrubbed clean.

Alexandra "Alex" Androvich, Nick's wife, her "almost" sister-in-law, stood on the porch holding a red and pink gift bag, looking poised and beautiful...not that she had to do anything but breathe to look that way...

"I'm glad you're home. Got a minute?"

"Sure." Whatever Alex had to say was not going to take a minute. Elise could tell by the tone in the other woman's voice that she'd come to offer comfort, maybe even a bit of advice, none of which would only last a minute. Elise stood aside and Alex entered, her presence brightening up the dim living room. No wonder Nick had fallen head over heels the first time he spotted his wife at Uncle Frank's birthday party. She was tall and slender, with pale skin and white-blond hair and an air about her that spoke of breeding and manners. Definitely not from Restalline. Of course, none of them had known that the composure she showed was a cover for the loneliness in her heart. *That* had come out later, but not before she and Nick almost fell apart because of the lies...

"I didn't know if I should come, but I had to take a chance." Alex offered a quiet smile and when Elise gestured toward the sofa, she moved the afghan aside and sat. "*Pride and Prejudice*," she murmured. "One of my favorites, but who doesn't love Mr. Darcy?"

Elise plopped on the sofa, mindless of the afghan beneath her, and shrugged. "I'm guessing Nick might not be a fan. Actually, not sure how many men would think he was so great. I mean, women have swooned over him for ages; men would not be impressed."

Alex laughed. "You've got a point there." The laugh faded, shifted. "I am so sorry for what happened. All of it. In a way, it reminds me of what happened between Nick and me."

"Yeah, well, that might have been bad, but you didn't leave him at the altar."

Alex's eyes glistened with tears. "No, I didn't. I just lied to him and the whole town about who I was and why I was here."

"But you didn't—"

"I was going to sell all of you out; let's not forget that."

"But you didn't." And that's what mattered. Alex fell in love not only with Nick but with the town, and that gave her the strength to stand against her uncle in his plan to buy up Restalline and turn it into a resort.

Alex cleared her throat, said, "I hurt a lot of people." She touched Elise's hand, her lips curving into a soft smile. "Michael was the one who convinced Nick to talk to me, imagine that?"

No secret Michael hadn't liked Alex, had suspected her of coming to town for more than her supposed claim of research for a documentary. Despite the differences the two brothers had, blood was blood, and Michael Androvich was not about to let a woman—any woman—come between him and Nick again. "I know. He told me."

She squeezed Elise's hand, her eyes bright, her voice insistent. "We all want to help. You and Michael belong together, no matter how messed up things are right now. But Michael's an Androvich and they don't forgive easily and once a trust is broken—" she sighed and shook her head "—well, you've lived here long enough to know how stubborn they all are, especially the men."

And especially Michael. He was ten times less trusting than Nick, maybe twenty times, which meant Elise had a zero percent chance of working things out with him. "So, you came here to tell me I might as well give up on Michael? That wherever he's taken off to, when and if he comes back, it won't be for me?" Saying it out loud pinched her brain. It was one thing to acknowledge the futility of her chances to have a life with him, but to speak the words in front of someone else? That was pure pain.

Alex's expression turned fierce, then softened. "No, absolutely not. What I'm saying is that I know Michael loves you, but getting him to open up and admit it again? That's going to be a real challenge." Her lips pulled into a faint smile. "But not impossible. You know, you and I aren't that different. We're both afraid to trust other people, but we're especially afraid to trust ourselves. So, we do what we're supposed to do, pleasing those who are important to us, accomplishing feats that gain us applause and accolades, even if it's the last thing we want to do." When she saw the stunned expression on Elise's face, she stopped, then added, "How am I doing?"

"I'd say you pretty much nailed it."

Alex laughed and slid her a look. "It's so exhausting trying to be perfect all the time, isn't it?"

Elise fingered the belt on her old bathrobe and said, "Is that why I'm so tired?"

"Until I moved here, I ran from one goal to the next: college, degrees, awards, promotions. I even married a man who was completely wrong for me because I thought it was what I should do, and because my uncle approved of him. How sad is that? I never stopped to really think about what I was doing until I moved here and saw myself through the town's eyes." Her voice dipped, softened. "Nick once asked the name of the neighbor who lived next to me in Virginia. Do you know I couldn't tell him? I could, however, give him the name of the woman's dog. Pretty pitiful, huh?"

"Well, since we're confessing, I might as well admit I spent years telling myself I was in love with Nick and was not happy when you showed up." Elise laughed at the surprised expression on Alex's face. "I guess I thought that because I knew things about him you didn't, like he only eats the insides of éclairs and keeps a stash of caramel corn in his bottom left drawer behind the granola bars, I would be a better match for him. But one look at the two of you together, and even a lovesick girl like me could see the truth: you and Nick belonged together."

"I've never met anybody like him, and I almost threw it away. I think you've spent so many years doing what everyone expects you to that you have no idea what you really want." She lifted the gift bag from the floor and handed it to her. "I hope this will help."

Elise accepted the gift bag and eased the colored tissues aside. "Thank you," she said as she reached inside the bag. "But you didn't need to do this." She pulled out a blue and green hand-held mirror with glass jewels glued around it: red, green, blue, yellow.

"My father gave me a similar mirror for my eighth birthday." Alex paused, cleared her throat. "He told me to look in the mirror and I would see the true jewel." Her lips flattened, her brow furrowed. "He and my mother died a few days later, and that mirror traveled everywhere with me— college, Europe, my first job. But it would take years for me to understand what he meant. Maybe this will help you find your true path, not the one your father or the community wants for you, but the one *you* want."

The tears started then, big fat ones that rolled down Elise's cheeks to her chin, spilled onto her old bathrobe and snuffed her control. "But what if I have no idea what I want?" she croaked. "What if this is all there is? Me sitting here in my crappy old bathrobe, all alone, night after night, waiting for nothing? What then?"

"Shh." Alex pulled her into her arms, hugged her. "You can't give up. Do you hear me? You can't give up hope."

***

Elise packed her car and headed out of Restalline on a sunny day in late February, her heart filled with equal parts fear and excitement. She'd never taken a journey without mapping out the destination, but with two suitcases, a box of fruit, cheese, and bread from her father, and enough prayers to propel her forward, she headed into the unknown. There would be random stops in small towns where she could compare the hospitality to that of Restalline's, enjoy the food and the stories of those who lived there. Perhaps she'd visit two of three such places, chosen merely by her body's need to rest for the night. The very thought of such "randomness" snuffed the air from her lungs and made her jittery, but she fought it, pushing aside fears about bedbugs, undercooked and ill-prepared food, dirty restrooms. She sucked in a breath and glanced at the front passenger seat where the mirror Alex had given her rested. *Find your true path.* Right.

Of course, it wasn't exactly accurate to say she had no idea where she was going because she did have an eventual destination. The truth had landed in her subconscious days ago and worked its way to her brain yesterday when it had kept her up most of the night. She hadn't been willing to share this knowledge with anyone because they might think she was crazy, desperate, or just plain pathetic. Actually, they might think she was all three, and they might be right. But for once, she was going to ignore what others might think and follow her heart. Besides who would ever find out she'd traveled to the bed and breakfast where she and Michael had planned to spend their honeymoon? She wanted to sleep on a bed scattered with rose petals, and damn it, she was going to do it, with or without a groom. She sniffed and swiped her cheek. Pathetic? Absolutely. But that wasn't going to stop her.

***

"What the hell are you doing here?"

"Michael?" Elise's ex-fiancé stood in the doorway of the

honeymoon suite at the Heart Sent bed and breakfast, fists clenched, his dark gaze narrowed on her. She recognized that look on Michael Androvich; it spoke of anger. Red. Hot. Searing. She pulled the terry bathrobe tighter, wishing she had five layers of clothing on beneath the robe instead of nothing. When she could speak, she crossed her arms over her chest and said, "What are you doing here?"

He shook his head and let out a sound that might almost have been a laugh if not for the coldness of it. "Me? I'm working. Like I planned to do, when we—" he stalled, his expression turning darker than his Androvich Lumber ball cap. "Anyway, I've been working."

"Oh." He meant to say, like he'd planned to when they came here for their honeymoon, but he couldn't get the words out either, which meant he didn't want to think about it. Typical Michael; emotions were not welcome, but he'd come around when they'd gotten together, forced them out like frosting coming out of her father's cake decorating tools. Well, obviously those days were gone. She noticed the strain around his eyes, the tightness of his mouth. Had he been as miserable as she was? "I didn't know you'd be here."

He crossed his thick arms over his chest, leaned against the door. She remembered those arms, the way they pulled her to him and lifted her in the air as though she were as light as Kevin or Sara. And then he'd lay her on the bed and...

"Yeah, well, I am. Life goes on, so does work. But why are *you* here?" He glanced at the king-sized bed and scowled. "And why are you in *this* room?"

The tone in his voice implied she had no right to be here. He didn't have a hold on her, not an outright one anyway, and that made what she did or didn't do none of his business. "I wanted to see the place." She shrugged and settled her gaze on his neck. Bad idea, since that reminded her of the kisses she used to trail along his jaw, to his neck, his chest, his... "I had some time off, so I figured why not?" She dragged her gaze to his, forced out the words. "It's not like I'll have another opportunity to use it."

He didn't answer at first, just stared, but she didn't miss the way his jaw twitched, his shoulders tensed, his frown grew deeper. When he spoke, all he said was, "Right."

"This room is almost exactly as I'd pictured it. Quaint, old-fashioned." Her voice drifted. "When I opened the door, the room smelled like roses. There were pink petals on the bed, soft and velvety." *The only thing missing was you.*

"What do you really want?"

His words pierced her with their harshness. "I told you. I wanted to see this place."

He ignored her. "Did my mother tell you I was here?" He advanced into the room, closing the distance between them. Not a good idea. A too-close Michael Androvich was intimidating and made it difficult to formulate a thought.

"Of course not." That was one thing about the Androviches: they stuck by their blood, no matter what.

"Gracie then. She's a bleeding heart for a sad story. She put you up to this, didn't she? This sounds like my sister's kind of scheme. Throw the sorry-ass couple together and pray for a miracle." He shook his head. "She's writing some real fiction if she thinks that's going to happen." He paused, added, "More like fantasy."

The disgust in his voice stung, but it also made her want to lash back. "I get it, but isn't everyone allowed a little fantasy? You know, being with one person, but thinking about another?"

Oh, he didn't like that. "Is that what you were doing when we were together?" Those eyes narrowed to slits, the full lips flattened. "Pretending you were with someone else?

My brother maybe?"

Thinking herself in love with Nick had been a fanciful dream: safe, nonthreatening, nothing like real love, especially not with a man like Michael. She'd never felt so alive, so immersed in another human being. Michael Androvich had given her that, and her insecurities had taken it away.

"Well?" He crossed the room in three strides, stood close enough for her to see the gold flecks in his eyes. "Guilty, huh?"

She frowned. "Of course not, and you know that."

"Do I?" His voice fell over her, dripping with heat and sensuality.

Elise tried to ignore his closeness. "You *do* know. Nick wasn't real."

"And me? Was I real?" Those eyes held her, forced out the truth.

"You were real, but I didn't trust myself enough to see that." He wanted "real"; well, she'd give it to him. "I didn't trust *us* enough, so when the first obstacle came along in the form of Cynthia Collichetti—" she paused, took a deep breath and added "—my worst nightmare, I took it as a sign that we weren't meant to be together, that I had to back out before you destroyed me." She clasped her arms around her middle and finished with, "And I bailed."

He stared at her, his gaze moving from her eyes, to her mouth, her neck, back to her eyes. "So you were never all in, were you? Even when I was spilling my guts to you about feelings and crap that I'd rather puke out than say, you were just sitting back, holding on to your own issues. Wow." He rubbed a hand over his stubbled jaw. "Talk about being played."

"It wasn't like that. I didn't even realize what I was doing until the wedding."

"That was damn convenient, wasn't it?"

"I was scared." She willed him to understand. "And mixed up."

"*You* were scared? You think I make a habit of telling a woman I worship the friggin' air she breathes?" He didn't give her time to respond, but went on, his expression blank, his voice eerily soft. "I guess I deserved it though, didn't I? All those years never letting a woman get to my heart, and then along you came and carved out a nice chunk of it. Yeah, lucky me."

"Michael, it was never like that. I loved you." *I still love you.*

"Right. I guess I thought love was about showing who you really were, even the unlovable parts, and knowing the other person wasn't going to bail." His mouth flattened, pulled into a frown. "So, since we can't say that…."

"Stop it."

But of course he wasn't finished yet. He had to gouge her heart again and again. "Were my kids part of this play family you had going? Take them for pizza and have a movie night until it wasn't easy anymore? Damn you for involving them."

"I love them."

"Sure you do. You love everybody, don't you? Too bad you don't know what that word means." He leaned in, inches from her face, and said, "You've scarred enough people for ten lifetimes and if you're looking for absolution from me, you're not going to get it. I want you to pack up and go home, and I want you to leave me alone so I can pretend we never happened."

Chapter 6

"Mimi? Why didn't you tell me my ex-fiancée checked into the honeymoon suite?" Michael unscrewed the cap off his beer bottle and took a healthy swig. They were about to sit down to a pot roast dinner and he'd bet his chain saw that the biscuits in the oven would rival his mother's. He'd smelled the roast the second he walked in the door from an afternoon in the woods. He and Rex had taken a pickup and scouted the area. Nothing could settle him down like the beauty of the woods, and with the afternoon sun hitting the snow on the branches just right, it reminded him of home. Of course, home reminded him of *her*, and he'd had to work hard to erase that thought. All he'd wanted to do when he got back to Mimi's was take a quick shower and dig into that pot roast, but a sound from the honeymoon suite stopped him. It was a woman's humming of Bon Jovi's "It's My Life." He knew someone who used to hum that song. Michael eased his way to the half-opened door…

And there she'd been. Elise Pentani, ex-fiancée, inflicter of pain, bad memories, and torment.

"You mean Elise Pentani." Mimi gave him one of her how-should-I-know looks he was getting used to and shrugged. "You were already asleep when she arrived last night, but I did think it rather odd there was no Mr. Pentani with her."

"Mr. Pentani would be her father." She would have been Elise Androvich. He ignored the twinge in his gut and took another swig of beer.

"Well then, I'm glad there was no Mr. Pentani with her." Mimi smiled at him and motioned for him to take a seat. "I hope you're hungry." She dished out a healthy portion of pot roast and placed two biscuits on his plate. "My husband used to love pot roast, said it reminded him of winter and his grandmother. Food has a way of pulling memories out of you that you'd almost forgotten." Her voice drifted off in a way that told him the memories weren't always pleasant ones. "Anyway—" she forked a piece of potato and looked at him "—she's lovely." Michael stuffed half a biscuit in his mouth and chewed. This was not a conversation he wanted to have, now or ever. "She was in such a turmoil when she arrived," Mimi went on as though she thought he should know.

He waited for her to continue and when she didn't, he mumbled, "Hmm," and concentrated on buttering the other half of the biscuit. A turmoil? He'd been asleep a few doors down and hadn't heard a thing. Somehow knowing she'd been so close unsettled him. At least he'd told her to leave, and he meant it. By God, he did not want her around, a reminder of what a fool he'd been to believe in happily-ever-after. She'd been the only woman who had made him think it was possible, and look how that had turned out. The woman had screwed him up for good, and probably his kids, too.

Damn her.

"She was very apologetic for arriving so late," Mimi went on as though he were listening. "Said she got lost three times, but she said that was a plus for her, seeing as she had a horrible sense of direction."

Yeah, that was an understatement. He'd asked her to drive to the site one afternoon after she finished work. Far west side of town, he'd told her, but somehow that crazy woman had ended up on the north side and had the nerve to argue with him about the directions!

"…and when she saw the honeymoon suite and the pink petals on the bed, well, I had to turn away and give her a few minutes alone. Pure misery on that girl's face…so sad….tears in her eyes…"

She'd been the one to show him that a bed was for more than sex and sleep. It was also a place to share dreams, make plans, create a world where nothing could hurt you. A safe haven, that's what she'd called it, as he lay with his head on her belly, listening to her. Oh, that woman talked a great game, even got him to spit out his own stupid dreams, but it had all been bullshit. She hadn't told him about the fear in her gut that he'd leave her, that she wouldn't be good enough, that whatever crap she let swirl in her head could tear them apart. He could have helped her, could have reassured her. Somehow. And now it was too damn late. She'd destroyed them, destroyed a piece of him, and he wanted to despise her for that.

But he couldn't. That's why she had to leave the Heart Sent, leave this town and head back home, contained, out of reach, not down the hall within breathing distance. "She's leaving."

"Elise is leaving?" And then, "Michael?"

He glanced at his plate. Almost empty, except for a few carrots. But other than the first bites of biscuit, could he even say he remembered what the rest of the meal tasted like, or when he'd devoured it, or decided to leave his least favorite vegetable on the plate? No to all of the above. He cleared his throat and lifted his head. Mimi Pendergrass's gaze zeroed in on him, no doubt seeing way more than he wanted her to see. Pain was not an emotion he cared to share or acknowledge, never had been. "I talked to her. She's leaving."

Mimi set down her fork, placed her hands on either side of her plate and studied him. He did not want to be studied, dissected like a damnable frog in eighth-grade science class. "That wasn't the impression she gave me. Actually, she rented the suite indefinitely."

"Oh, hell, no." He tossed his napkin on the table and

stood. "Where is she? Did she tell you where she was going?"

"No, she didn't, but the tears might have clogged her speech. Sit down, Michael," she said in a tone that sounded a lot like the prelude to one of Stella Androvich's "Life Lessons" speech.

Damn, but he did not want a lecture from a stranger. He'd barely listened to his own family, but he could tell *them* to kiss off. This woman was a stranger and a senior citizen at that. He might be an asshole a lot of the time, but he did know how to be respectful toward his elders. Michael sank back into the chair, crossed his arms over his chest and waited. He wouldn't be disrespectful, but that didn't mean he had to listen to her either, or that he couldn't have his own say. "Listen, I know you're just trying to help, but I really don't want to talk about it."

"I don't blame you." She lifted her wine glass, took a sip. "You're hurt, feeling betrayed." The balls on her red earrings bounced when she nodded her head. "And so angry. Oh, yes, so damnably angry."

He let this one truth slip out. "Right."

"Part of you wants that person to simply disappear so you never have to see them again. No chance meetings, no orchestrated avoidance, nothing but them gone. For good." Her voice slipped, pulled away, dipped in what had to be remembering. "But what good would that do? They live in your heart, your brain, your past and future. There is no getting rid of them; they are burned in your soul. That is true torture, as surely as it had been true love." She paused, took a deep breath, and continued on as though he weren't there, as though she were speaking from a past filled with pain and knowing. "My husband disappeared two days after our wedding. He simply vanished, gone out to get gas and never made it home. I was devastated, certain something horrible had happened to him. The police found no traces for a hundred-mile radius. I drove around myself, ten miles one way, twenty miles the other, looking for a sign, anything. I prayed, I cried, I bargained with God to bring him home to me. On the tenth day, Roger walked in the door."

Michael had expected a more gruesome ending. Curiosity got him. "Where was he?"

Her lips curved into the faintest of smiles, and when she spoke, a bone-deep sadness covered her words. "He ran away. Imagine that? Said he got scared and had to sort things out in his head. Of course, he never thought I might be imagining him dead, or that the whole town was looking for him. Or that he'd humiliated me in ways he could not begin to realize. He simply told me he'd figured things out and was ready to commit to me for the rest of our lives. I hated him, wished him dead and told him so. I kicked him out of the house and he moved into Rusty's Bed and Breakfast, which even back then was dirtier than a barn. But he left flowers on my doorstep every single day and a note that said he loved me and wanted another chance. I ignored him, refused his phone calls. This went on for five months, and then one day, they stopped." She met his gaze, tears in her eyes. "Three days later the divorce papers came and with them a note that said he was setting me free, that he loved me, would always love me, but he realized I couldn't forgive him."

In a twisted way, Roger Pendergrass made his ex-fiancée seem not so bad. And that was bizarre. "Did you divorce him?"

She shook her head. "No. I tore up the papers, marched over to Rusty's, and told him to come home. We spent a lot of good years together, and some not so good. We lost our son, our daughter took off…those were some horrible years. Roger and I stood side by side, propped each other up as best we could, and got through it." She placed a hand over her heart, smiled. "He'll be here until I draw my last breath."

"I'm sorry."

"Thank you." Mimi cleared her throat and turned businesslike, as if she were conducting a meeting and not spilling her heart. "Why did I tell you this? Because those closest to us often hurt us the most."

She had that figured right. "I won't argue there."

"I could tell you stories about the people in this town who had their hearts trounced on, but they didn't give up." She nodded, "Made them stronger than before, just like me and Roger. But the difference now is that back then, nobody dared make a peep in public about a missing husband. It was all hush-hush: pretend he's sitting next to you in church or that he's too busy to take you dancing on Saturday night. Just pretend. Not now." She let out a laugh and her earrings jingled. "Relationship issues seem to be the town's specialty."

Michael sipped his beer, leaned back in his chair. "So, you're saying the whole town is a bunch of busybodies?" Great, just what he needed, another Restalline.

"No, gracious no." She laughed again, her blue eyes sparkling. "At least, that's not the way we see it. We believe in helping others find happiness and love, especially when that happiness and love are threatened. We've got a group called The Bleeding Hearts Society; we raise perennial flowers, beautify the town with color and flowers, but we also lend a hand or an ear when there's a heart that needs mending."

Mimi's definition sounded *worse* than a busybody. "So you butt into other people's problems and try to fix them."

She sat up straight, her lips pulling into a slow smile. "Exactly."

"Don't try that voodoo on me, Mimi. I don't need

anybody fixing anything." Damn straight. If he wanted help, his mother would have offered a notebook of ideas, and his sister would have been right behind her.

"Oh, I know. I wasn't referring to you, Michael." She pushed her plate aside, leaned forward on her elbows, and studied him. "I meant Elise. Once the town meets her, they'll fall in love with those sad eyes and that kind smile. There's a fragileness about her, as though her heart aches with each breath." She shook her head. "People will want to help, if she'll let them."

"She isn't going to let them because she's leaving town." Damn straight she was. And what did Mimi mean about his ex-fiancée being fragile? The woman didn't have a fragile bone in her five-foot-two body. And what would she "let" them do—try to convince Michael that he and Elise belonged together so the town could add them to their list of "achievements" like a patched-up relationship was an award? Well, that was a big "no thank-you".

Mimi shrugged, studied him with a shrewdness that said he had no clue what he was up against. "Whether she stays or goes is really not up to you, Michael. Haven't you realized by now that people will do what they'll do and there's not a darn thing you can do about it, no matter how much you try?"

***

Small towns had a feel about them that either pulled a stranger in with a handshake and a welcome, or pushed him out with a look and a "we don't want your kind". Restalline was the "pulling in" kind and if the rest of the town was half as hospitable as Mimi Pendergrass, Magdalena was that kind of place, too.

Elise couldn't get out of the Heart Sent fast enough after her encounter with Michael. She'd tossed on her clothes, grabbed her jacket and purse, and was gone. The where didn't matter, as long as she was not within striking distance of her ex-fiancé. *I want you to pack up and go home, and I want you to leave me alone, so I can pretend we never happened.* So he could pretend? What exactly did that mean? That he'd tried to forget her and hadn't been successful? Well, at least that was something. She wished the Androviches had told her Michael was in Magdalena; then she might have picked a different spot on the map to explore. But Michael was family, and blood forced them to honor his wishes that Elise not know where he'd gone. Of course, she hadn't confessed her need to visit her honeymoon suite in Magdalena, New York, either. The very idea sounded twisted, even to her, and it was her idea. Still, there'd been a pull to the place and she'd ignored so many of those in her life that she was not going to ignore this one.

She'd wanted to visit the Heart Sent and now, here she was. Unfortunately, the other half of the couple who should have been in the honeymoon suite was right down the hall. What a mess! Maybe Nick should not have insisted she take a leave from work because then she'd have a place she had to be. And maybe she should have blown through the money she'd been saving for years for her "future and security" because then she wouldn't have the cash to traipse around wherever she wanted for however long she wanted. And dang it all, maybe Michael Androvich was the one who should leave the Heart Sent because she'd rented out the honeymoon suite, and she wasn't budging until she'd had her fill. Maybe she'd stay in that room forever, like Miss Havisham in *Great Expectations*, broken-hearted and waiting for a groom who was not going to come.

The old Michael had returned; she'd witnessed that a short while ago: ornery, mean-spirited, hiding a world of hurt behind the looks and the words swirling about him. If only she didn't know what lay beneath it, it would be easy to dislike him. But she did know; she'd seen, touched, *loved*, and that wasn't going away.

Elise pulled onto Main Street and spotted small shops with names like Lina's Café, Miss Patty's Mentionables, Victor's Pharmacy, and Barbara's Boutique and Bakery, which reminded her of Restalline. She found a parking spot near the bakery and stepped into the cold late-afternoon air, anticipating the smell of fresh bread and baked sweets. There was something about creating these foods that relaxed her, transported her to another world where she didn't think about yesterday's regrets or tomorrow's worries. She thought of nothing but her creation and the care that went into making it. Of course, her father didn't like "experimentation" and insisted she stick with the recipe, but when she baked at home or at Michael's, she'd tried all sorts of variations and he and the kids had loved all of them. *These sugar cookies are better than my mother's, but don't tell her*, Michael had said. *You know I'm only marrying you because you're a great baker.* Even, *how about you make our wedding cake?*

The big front window of Barbara's Boutique and Bakery had been painted with sad representations of cupcakes, muffins, breads, brownies, and what looked like a biscotti but might have been an éclair stuck next to the "Help Wanted" sign. When Elise opened the door, the smell grabbed her. Burnt sugar was not something a person soon forgot, and this wasn't a drizzle of sugar, but more like a twenty-five-pound bag that had been scorched.

"Hi!" A young girl with a red ponytail and a big smile laid her hands on the showcase glass and asked, "Can I help you?"

"Umm—" Elise glanced at the fewer than twelve chocolate chip cookies, six brownies, and two éclairs in the case and said, "Guess I'm kind of late."

The girl followed Elise's gaze. "Oh, you mean because we're a little low? Well, I wish it was because it's almost closing time, but that's not it. Ramona was supposed to make the stuff but she got pneumonia and I tried to follow her recipe, but I'm sure you can tell by the smell that I hit a detour." She shook her head and the ponytail bounced back and forth. "You'd think this baking stuff wouldn't be so difficult, would you?"

"There's an art to it, like with anything."

"That's what Grandpa says." She rolled her eyes. "That man has a saying for everything, and I mean absolutely everything." She studied Elise a second before she said, "You're not from around here, are you, 'cause I haven't seen you before, and I would have noticed. Small towns make it really easy to notice when something's out of place, like a new person standing where there wasn't one yesterday." The girl grinned. "I got here a few months ago and if you're new, then that makes me the old person. Only as you can see, I'm not that old. So, *are* you new to town?"

Elise jumped in before the girl had a chance to keep talking. "I am. I'm visiting."

"Ah. Where you staying? Relative? Friend?" The grin spread. "Guy friend?"

"None of the above. I'm staying at the Heart Sent."

"Ohhh." The girl's blue eyes brightened and her voice softened. "That's where that guy's staying. Have you seen him? Kind of like a lumberjack; big, muscled, wavy brown hair, dark eyes. Older," she paused, added, "but still, a total hunk."

Michael. "Nope. Haven't seen him."

"You will; there's no missing that guy." She sighed. "I'm not after him or anything, but a girl would have to be blind not to notice him, and he's as nice as he is hot. He came in here a few days ago looking for sugar cookies, said he liked them real thin." The girl giggled. "With pink frosting and pink sprinkles. Can you imagine? Only a guy who looks like he does could get away with that one."

Yes, she could imagine. The first time she'd made him sugar cookies she'd decorated them with pink frosting and pink sprinkles. *Because real men do pink*, she'd told him. He'd unzipped her jeans, fingered her pink underwear, and said, *Indeed they do*. And then he'd proceeded to show her exactly what real men did...

"...and I was trying to make those darn cookies for him when I burned a batch. After the third try, I gave up. Maybe I'll see if Ramona will help me make them when she gets better and then I can call and tell him. He asked me to...do you know he gave me a ten-dollar tip and all he bought was a puny chocolate chip cookie?"

"What? Oh, how generous." Why would Michael ask for the cookies she always made him, especially *those* cookies, that served as a reminder of the afternoon they made love in his kitchen? She grew all hot and cold just remembering.

"His name is Michael," the girl said, her voice as sugary as the sprinkles on one of Michael's cookies.

"Michael," she murmured.

"Yeah, it fits him. He's not a Mike or a Mickey, just plain Michael."

Michael John. "Michael's a nice name," she said as if she were talking about a hunk of bread making a nice complement to beef soup. Matter-of-fact, conversational, detached...as if she hadn't tasted and touched every inch of the man and he hadn't done the same to her.

"I'm Lucy, by the way, Lucy Benito." The girl made her way around the counter and thrust out a hand. Elise took it, but her eyes were on the girl's belly.

"Yeah, I'm prego." She smiled and placed her hands on either side of her pumpkin-sized belly. "And this is so not a good place to work when you're pregnant." She shook her head. "I ate six chocolate chip cookies yesterday and an éclair. Ramona said I'm going to be sorry and Grandpa said I'm asking for heartburn and extra stretch marks, but Bree said not to pay attention to all of that. She said I'm going to be fine as long as I keep thinking positive thoughts." Her voice turned curious. "Do you have any kids?"

"No, no kids." Elise forced images of Michael's children from her brain. He'd made it clear he didn't want her having anything more to do with Kevin and Sara.

"Oh." And then, "I'm trying to stay away from all this baked stuff, but it's like they have their own voice that says, 'Lucy, Lucy, come over here.' And then I get bored and start sneaking." She blew out a long sigh. "I'm totally ridiculous, but I have zero willpower in the face of a good cookie."

That made Elise smile. "I know what you mean. My father owns a bakery and if I wasn't careful, I could eat a half dozen macaroons, but usually when I was upset. If I wasn't, then I only ate three or four."

Lucy Benito laughed. "See? That's it exactly. And when an hour goes by and nobody comes in, it's the worst. I do my homework or read a magazine…sometimes I draw pictures of what my baby will look like." Her face lit up. "I'm having a girl."

"Congratulations." Lucy had told her more about herself in ten minutes than some of Nick's patients told him in two years. Either this girl was really bored or didn't understand the concept of "too much information."

"Thanks. I haven't decided on a name yet, but Grandpa comes up with three new ones every day, all from the "old country," which is Italy, but I swear he's making them up. Alfonsia, Cosima, Vincenza?" She frowned. "Who ever heard of names like that?"

"Actually, I had an Aunt Cosima." She was her mother's

aunt, a broad woman with a long gray braid who hand-cut big sheets of pasta dough with gnarled fingers and a dull knife.

"Really? Huh." Lucy slid her a look, taking in Elise's dark hair and olive skin. "Well, this little girl is not a Cosima or a Vincenza. And not an Alfonsia either. Of course, Jeremy likes Rebecca and Sage, but I don't know…"

"Who's Jeremy?"

A faint pink crept up Lucy Benito's neck, landed on her cheeks in a perfect match to the frosting on Elise's sugar cookies. "He's just a guy friend." Pause. "The baby's father isn't in the picture." Another pause. "Jeremy and I aren't 'together.' That would be weird with me pregnant and all, but we hang out." The pink turned to crimson. "He cooks dinner for me and Grandpa twice a week; says that way he can try out new dishes on us. He's a chef at the new restaurant in town. It's called Harry's Folly and if you're into Italian, which I bet you are, you've got to try it. They make the best penne pasta with spinach and garbanzo beans. Yum."

"I will. Thank you." Elise would need a chart to keep all the people straight. This person cooked a mean lasagna, that one specialized in penne pasta with spinach and garbanzo beans. And this one had a saying for everything, while that one…

"So," Lucy paused and clasped her hands over her belly. "If you get bored while you're here and feel like getting involved in a goodwill-helping-the-community kind of thing, you could always come by here and try out the kitchen. I mean, if your dad owns a bakery, you probably already know about most of this stuff. At least you know way more than I do and I'm tired of this burnt smell."

"Where's the owner?" Lucy was friendly enough, but she wasn't a baker, not even close.

"Barbara? Oh, she's in Australia for three weeks. That's why Ramona's helping out or was until she came down with pneumonia. Mrs. Desantro pitched in and made enough stuff to last a few days, but as you can see, I'm almost out. She offered to come back, but it would be a lot more fun to have someone closer to my age to hang out with and maybe you could teach me how to make those sugar cookies Michael wants."

Elise ignored the comment about Michael and his sugar cookies and asked, "Who are Ramona and Mrs. Desantro?" Lucy threw around people's names as though Elise should know them.

"They're really great cooks, and Ramona is my dad's—" she paused, scratched her chin, and pursed her lips "—friend. I guess that's what she is. Anyway, she can really bake, and she makes the best lasagna and stuffed shells." Her voice slipped to a whisper and she leaned forward as though she didn't really want to put sound to her next words but couldn't resist. "I think her pizzelles are as good as my grandpa's, but I would never tell him that. It would destroy him."

"Pizzelles? They're my specialty." Her father insisted she fill the double-wire shelf at the shop with ten boxes of pizzelles every week. Half anise, half vanilla. And every week, they sold out. But three weeks ago, he informed her Mrs. Ricci would begin filling his pizzelle order. No doubt she would, but what else was that woman filling? Her father's need for companionship? Conversation? Sex? That last word slithered into her brain and she pushed it out with a loud cough.

"You make pizzelles? Wait until I tell Grandpa; he's going to want to meet you. People call him Pop or The Godfather of Magdalena because he knows everything that's going on." She laughed and nodded. "And he's going to want to know everything about an outsider who says pizzelles are her specialty."

Chapter 7

Rex MacGregor was not a man who took others into his confidence, preferring to rely on his own counsel, for good or bad. That's why the phone call Pop got yesterday surprised him. The man had sounded like he couldn't get enough breath in his lungs to spit out the words, and when he did, there wasn't much air in them. *I need to talk to you, Pop.* And after three more puffs, the word, *Trouble*, slipped out.

What in the heck could have happened to make a big old bruiser like Rex MacGregor get all twisted up? Made no sense, 'less it was about that dang son-in-law of his, Brody Kinkaid. Pop wished he could say different, but the boy didn't have enough sense or brains to figure his way out of an open door. That marriage was a train wreck waiting to happen unless the conductor got reschooled in the art of knowing where the track was and how to stay on it. Not that difficult if you practiced and didn't try to shortcut. Problem was, people got lazy and they favored shortcuts.

And that's most likely why Rex MacGregor, longstanding resident of Magdalena, past Rotary president, owner of MacGregor Cabinets, and fly-fishing champion of the region, was sitting in Pop's living room, a plate of pizzelles and two glasses of homemade red wine on the table between them.

"What's got you looking like you might not take your next breath and not certain you want to either?" Pop and Rex went way back, before there was a MacGregor Cabinets and Rex was the delivery boy at Cummings Lumber, hauling slab and timber all over the county. Young and single, a real whippersnapper, until that wife of his settled him down.

"It's about Kathleen."

Pop made a quick sign of the cross and glanced at the

portrait of Lucy hanging above the mantel. *This is how it started with us, isn't it, Lucy? These very same words, with your name attached, and oh, the pain and sorrow that followed. I hope Rex and Kathleen will be spared.* He inched his gaze back to Rex, scrubbed the emotion of his wife's past illness from his voice, and said, "Is she sick?"

"Huh?" The man scratched his forehead and ran a sausage-size hand over his face. "Sick? No, Kathleen's fit and better than ever since Doc put her on that heart-healthy diet. She thinks she's down a size because she's chasing after Bree's kids." He shrugged. "Could be some truth to that; those girls are real firecrackers, even the little one." A smile stretched from behind the beard, flipped into a frown. "Damn, Pop, what a mess, what a damn mess." He blew out a sigh and dug into his flannel shirt. "Here," he said, pulling out a folded piece of paper. "Read this."

Pop accepted the paper, unfolded it, and squinted at the typed print.

Hello, Mr. MacGregor:

My name is Gloria Blacksworth, from Chicago, mother of Christine Blacksworth Desantro. I'm quite certain you will know who I am, though we never actually met, and sadly, it is far too late for any formal introductions. I'm writing you "from the grave," shall we call it, because I have an intense desire to see justice done. Oh, I'm not a judge, certainly not. Far be it from me to condemn others for their sins. However, if the residents of Magdalena have cast their hate and dislike upon me, basing their assessments on my "alleged" deeds, or misdeeds, as it were, is it not also fair that I should reveal the misdeeds of others, so they may be cast in the same moral light as myself? I believe so, which is why I am contacting you.

I was highly distressed to learn that you, one of

Magdalena's most respected and influential business owners, were once days away from proposing to your wife's sister. For shame, Mr. MacGregor. That was not well done. My sources tell me you were keeping company with your wife's sister, Nadine, and had even picked out a ring. Goodness, that does not sound like a casual acquaintance now, does it? But what on earth happened to squelch the proposal? What on earth indeed?

Oh, but it was all hush-hush wasn't it? Nadine's sister, Kathleen, returns from secretarial school, sees a future in a man like you, throws you a smile and who knows what else (let's be honest, shall we?), and four months later, she becomes Mrs. Rex MacGregor. Seven months after the wedding, along comes your cherished daughter, Bree. Interesting timeline, don't you think? As for Nadine, your "sister-in-law," she condemns you and Kathleen to eternal damnation and vows to never speak to either of you again. I hear she's left the state.

I have a few questions for you, Mr. MacGregor. Do you think it ever bothers your wife that she wasn't your first choice? That maybe you really did love Nadine, and Kathleen stole your chance for true happiness? And your daughter, does she know the real story behind her parents' supposed "true love" match, or that she was conceived before marriage? So many questions, so many possibilities. So many secrets!

Don't worry about the answer to any of these questions, because soon enough you'll know; not only that, the whole town will know, too. Finally.

Good luck and Godspeed.

Gloria Blacksworth

Pop finished reading the letter, folded it carefully, and

handed it to Rex. "That's some downright vicious words from a mean woman." He rubbed a hand over his jaw, shook his head. Of course he remembered the story of Rex MacGregor and Kathleen Humphrey; anybody living here long enough knew how Kathleen pranced into town in those high heels and tight sweaters and stole that poor boy right from under her sister's pointy nose. Not that Nadine and Rex were a love match, but they were compatible, like butter on toast. Nice and easy. Pleasant without a disruption to the taste buds. But Rex and Kathleen? They were like a jalapeño pepper in your mouth, with the seeds left in. No way were those two not made for each other and no way was plain-and-simple Nadine going to entice Rex to take a trip down the altar once he spotted her sister. Still, it didn't sit well with the Ladies' Guild who avoided Kathleen like she was a hunk of cod left out in the sun. And Nadine's vow to curse her sister and Rex for the rest of her days did not help.

But Kathleen and Rex didn't budge on their commitment to each other and as the years passed, people didn't care so much about what had happened, especially when Rex MacGregor's business grew and he hired on their kin. And they sure liked it when Kathleen showed up in her pearls and high heels to hand out turkeys for Thanksgiving and ham for Christmas. Then there was the scholarship fund the MacGregors donated to every year for five high school seniors attending college. And though Pop could never get one hundred percent verification that this was true, some said the couple paid for the new organ at St. Gertrude's, the lights for the football field, and loaned a few of their employees money to help them out of a rough patch.

Now if Rex *had* married Nadine, she would have wrapped those purse strings so tight around her fingers, she'd cut off her circulation, and there wouldn't be any ham or turkeys for employees, no organ, no loans, no nothing.

Nadine would have scooped up her husband's good intentions and stuffed them in the laundry basket with his socks and underwear. Why did that Blacksworth woman have to unearth a past that was none of her business? Well, Pop was not going to sit by and watch that woman's words destroy innocent people. No sirree.

"What if Bree finds out? She's my baby girl. What will she think of us?"

Rex had gotten all pasty, like a lump of dough. Pop handed him a glass of wine and said, "Don't you worry, Rex; we'll set this straight. Just let me think on it a bit."

"What about Kathleen? She'll be mortified if our baby finds out that her mother was pregnant when we got married. We always said Bree was a preemie, and you know that child never goes looking for problems." He downed the wine in one gulp and shrugged. "She thinks every word out of a person's mouth is true."

"If those people are family, then you're right, she does. That's called a blessing and a curse, because in my time on this earth, I've seen families lie to each other more than strangers." Rex stared at him like he'd just said he saw the Good Lord last night. Pop adjusted his glasses and shrugged. "You haven't told Kathleen that skirt she wore last Sunday doesn't make her behind look big, even when you know you could set a table on it? And how about the apple pie she baked for your birthday, the one you told me was so sour you had to add a teaspoon of sugar on it when she wasn't looking? Did you tell her that? Heck no. You smiled, gave her a hug, and said it was the best dang apple pie you'd ever eaten."

Pop nodded when he spotted the guilt flash across Rex's face. "Yup, I know you did, because I would have done the same thing. Matter of fact, I *did*. Lucy took a fancy to decorating the whole house with flowers. Now I don't mind my flowers in the garden or even a vase in the kitchen or mantel, but look—" He pointed to the wallpaper, the chairs and sofa, the pillows, pictures, even the figurines on the mantel, all done in floral patterns. "You ever seen so many flowers in one place and not a one you can smell?"

Rex shook his head, his gaze intent on Pop. "Can't say that I have."

"Exactly. And here I am, despising the dang things, cursing the day my Lucy ever got it in her head to decorate in such a mish-mush way, but I'm hanging the wallpaper and the pictures and filling the vases with rose petals. When she looks at me, she's all excited like this room belongs in a magazine and then she asks me what I think." Pop's voice dipped with remembering. "And there was no way on this earth that I would say anything to my Lucy other than how beautiful it was."

"But we're not talking about a room, Pop; we're talking about my baby girl learning her parents lied to her."

Pop sighed. "Yup, we are. Wish it didn't have to be that way, but now you're in the middle of it, and you can't cover a lie with a lie. That's like covering manure with more manure. Either way, it still stinks. I say get home and tell Kathleen, then tell Bree." Oh, but this was going to be a mess. Poor Bree, she was in for a shocker. That girl hadn't been the same since she lost the baby, and he couldn't say if it was because her bonehead husband was after her for another one, or if Brody didn't like her learning her daddy's business. Or maybe the boy had issues with his wife using her brain. It was one of those, Pop would bet a dozen pizzelles on it, and Gloria Blacksworth's letter had come at a bad time. Did Christine know her mother was up to her old tricks again, even from the grave? Did Nate know? Only a matter of time before the truth blew the top off the kettle. Yup, only a matter of time.

***

Michael hopped in his truck and headed out of MacGregor Cabinets. He'd spent most of the day in meetings with Rex and the chief engineer. Something was off with Rex; he'd seemed distracted and less energetic, as though weighed down by a problem. Maybe his daughter was driving him nuts and he couldn't figure out a way to fire her. Bree Kinkaid talked more than anybody he'd ever met and when she wasn't talking, she made little sounds that expressed her state of mind: sighs, groans, grunts, gasps, laughter, giggles, even humming. It was downright ridiculous and a pain, and if she kept it up, he swore he'd call her on it.

People like Bree Kinkaid were why he worked in the woods. He didn't have the nonsensical chatter of a busybody who chipped away at his patience, asking questions that were none of her damn business. *How long will you be here? Doesn't your family miss you?* And then, even though he hadn't answered any of those questions with more than a frown, she'd had the gall to ask, *Do you have a family? Kids? A wife?* Damn, but the woman was a pain and the only reason he remained civil was because he wanted an opportunity to do a deal with Rex for his old man's sake.

Tomorrow he was heading back into the woods, alone. At least there he could find a little peace and he sure as hell needed it now. He'd been wired since he ran into Elise yesterday and his dinner conversation with Mimi Pendergrass only got him more juked up. Why did Mimi have to go all Stella Androvich on him and talk about hurting those you love, making mistakes, forgiveness, and all of that other crap he did not want to hear about? Elise Pentani had left him at the altar because she hadn't trusted their relationship enough. End of story. Sugarcoating a piece of crap still made it a piece of crap.

So, was she gone? Had she packed up while he was at work and headed north or south or wherever in the hell her brain told her to go? Or maybe she'd run home to Restalline. He'd lay his money on that one. Michael ignored the twinge in his gut when he thought about her, hours and miles away. She'd better damn well have gotten new tires because a woman traveling alone needed to be prepared with a trusted vehicle and a charged cell phone. Who knew if she'd gotten the tires or charged the phone? Damn that woman. Now he'd have to find a reason to call his mother tomorrow and work around the subject of "the woman he'd almost married" and find out if Elise's car had been spotted in Restalline. Or maybe he should just call Nick and ask him straight up. He'd catch grief from his brother, but Nick wouldn't try to pick apart the question like the insides of a stuffed shell, unlike Stella Androvich, who would attempt to determine the level of emotion and what it meant. *Michael, you're concerned about her, aren't you? I knew it! Does this mean you're thinking of a reconciliation? I have prayed every day and God has answered my prayers. Oh, Michael, I just knew you and Elise were meant to be together.*

He absolutely was not calling his mother. Nope. He'd call Nick. But what if she hadn't gone back home? What if she'd decided to drive around the country and check out other honeymoon suites or come up with some equally bizarre idea? What then? He should have taken care of the friggin' tires weeks ago and then she could drive to California and good riddance.

Michael had just rounded a bend leading into town when he noticed a woman walking along the side of the road. Why would someone be out here, trudging through the snow? Maybe she was headed into town. Maybe her car broke down or she didn't have a car. Maybe the woman's damned tires had worn out. The least he could do was offer her a lift.

He flipped on his blinker, pulled off the road, threw the truck in Park, and jumped out. "Need a ride?"

The woman pushed back the hood of her parka and said, "No thanks, I'm fine."

"Elise? What are you doing out here? Where's your car? Did you break down?" He forgot that he'd told her to leave town, forgot that he never wanted to see her again. He even forgot about the ache in his chest that would not go away.

"No." She looked at him like she thought that was a ridiculous question. "Why would you ask that?"

"Because you're walking on the side of a winding road on the outside of a town you don't know. Because a car could miss a curve and slam into you." Was it really necessary to have this conversation? Why couldn't she see she'd put herself at risk without him drawing her a diagram? "Because you could get killed." And then, because he was already getting pissed, he added, "I'll bet you didn't get those damned tires changed either, did you?"

Her lips twitched, twitched again like she was trying to hold in a smile, or maybe so she wouldn't start laughing. At him. "Michael, if I didn't know better, I'd think you might actually care if something happened to me."

He ignored the comment. "Tires? Yes or no."

She shook her head and that black hair he'd loved to touch spilled from her hood. "Yes," she said on a sigh. "I have four new tires, aligned and balanced."

Michael blew out his own sigh. Of relief? Frustration? Who the hell knew? "Good." And then, "Let's not stand out here like idiots. Come on, I'll take you back to Mimi's."

"Where's your jacket?"

"In the truck."

"Good place for it." She eyed him and for a split second it felt like the way things used to be between them: easy, relaxed, fun.

But nothing was the same and he'd better damn well not forget that. "Yeah, well, I didn't think we'd have to have a conversation about me giving you a ride. Seemed like a slam-dunk."

"Nothing is ever a slam-dunk with you, Michael." With that, she trudged past him and made her way to the passenger side of the truck. He hopped in and cranked up the heat. "Want your jacket?" She'd removed her gloves and clutched his jacket in her hands—kind of like she didn't want to give it up.

"Nah, I'm fine. Stay warm." He pulled onto the road, but he'd noticed her fingers relax on the fabric of his jacket. Was she stroking it? Hell, it sure looked like it. He started to comment, decided against it. "I see you're still in town."

"Yup." She leaned back against the headrest and closed her eyes.

Okay, he was not imagining things now; she *was* stroking his jacket…just like she used to stroke his…

"I'm not leaving, Michael." She sighed, kept her eyes closed, and spoke in that matter-of-fact voice she used when she wanted to tell him how things were going to be. *I'm not sharing you with another woman, so decide what you want and let me know.* As if he'd had to think about it. And, *You need to be around more for Kevin and Sara. You don't have to be perfect; you just have to be there for them.* He'd needed that kick in the butt and she'd delivered it. But the one that got him like a sucker punch was, *You live in my heart, Michael Androvich, right in the center, taking up so much space, I can hardly breathe.*

And now, here they were, sharing a ride like strangers, heading to separate rooms and separate lives. That's what he wanted. Wasn't it? "Elise—"

"So you might as well get used to the fact that I'm not leaving Magdalena until I'm ready." She opened her eyes, turned to him. "I've got a lot of things to figure out and this is as good a place as any to do it." Her voice rose, letting him know she wasn't as unaffected as she pretended. "This town is small, but there's no reason we have to run into each other."

"Right. How exactly would we achieve that? Maybe we should work out a schedule so we know when it's safe to eat dinner with Mimi. I'll take even days, you take odd. Unless we decide to eat at the diner; have you tried it out yet? I hear they have great chicken pot pie. There's a new Italian restaurant Mimi told me about, too. Harry's Folly, I think. Excellent pasta. You just let me know if you're heading to one of those spots and I'll do the same for you." He glanced at her. Yup, the narrowed eyes and pinched lips said *pissed*. Well, too bad. Did she really think they could coexist in the same town, breathe the same air, and pretend they hadn't planned a life together? Apparently she did and that pissed *him* off more than anything.

"Why do you have to deal in extremes when you're upset? Schedules?" She huffed and scowled. "Really, Michael."

"First, who said I'm upset? I'm annoyed; there's a difference. And second, I do not deal in extremes. I call it like I see it, and you knew that about me." He almost missed the turn into the Heart Sent but caught himself and pulled into the driveway. Another few inches of snow had fallen and it looked like Mimi had the snow blower out, even though he'd told her he'd take care of it after work.

"Oh, you call it like you see it, all right, but the problem is the *way* you see it."

He parked the truck, turned it off. "*I'm* the one who has an issue with how I see things?" Michael rubbed his jaw and rested his arm along the back of her seat. "I don't think so. I'm not the one who left you at the altar, am I?" Her eyes grew bright, but she held those tears. Strong, capable Elise would not let them fall. "And I didn't question the relationship or the trust and I sure as hell didn't listen to a person who had nothing to lose by lying." His voice shifted to a soft rumble. "I didn't give up on us or hide in my room. I stayed at that damnable church, so excited to see you, and when you didn't show, I knew something was wrong." He shook his head. "I thought you were in a ditch somewhere or your father had a relapse. Do you know I tore through that church and I don't even remember getting to your house because I was so worried about you? I prayed, Elise, and you know that's not me, but on this day I asked God to keep you safe, and your father, too…just let me get to you and I could help. But your car wasn't in a ditch and when your father opened the door, he was as spry as ever, even when he cursed me. And you? You were in your room and the only thing that was damaged was 'us.' We were gone, ruined."

"Don't."

He ignored her. "So, if you think I can see you, smell your scent, and pretend *nothing* happened between us, I can't. I'm not that good an actor." He sucked in a breath, pushed out the rest of his words. "That's why I want you gone. Because I can't pretend and I don't want to remember."

"The remembering or not remembering isn't always our choice," she said, clutching his jacket hard, her knuckles white. "Sometimes it just is."

"Yeah, and sometimes it's up to us to be smart enough not to get hurt again." Her eyes had glazed over like she wasn't really listening to what he said. She could ignore him if she wanted; it wasn't going to change what had happened between them or what could have been. That was on her.

"I'm only asking that we respect each other's space while we're in Magdalena. It's bad enough that people will find out our connection to each other, but we don't have to provide a show for them, too."

"A connection? Is that what we were? Like two pieces of wire?" Damn, but she could be cold. Why the hell did he care what she said? It shouldn't matter to him. Hell, it *didn't* matter to him, but he knew that wasn't true, and that made him even angrier.

She stared at him so long he didn't think she was going to answer, but then she said, "You know what we were to each other, Michael, even if you try to bury it with anger and denial. And if I came to you and begged you for a second chance, that wouldn't matter either because you're never going to trust me again, are you?"

Pain seared his chest, shot to his lungs, and shot out in the form of two words. "Probably not."

She blinked hard, opened the truck door, and was gone.

Chapter 8

Rex took his time getting home after he left Pop's and even considered stopping by Cody's for a quick drink and to fortify himself for what was to come. But what was the point of dragging on what needed saying? It wasn't going away, hell no, not when the sad tale had clung to the underside of Rex's conscience for too many years. Might as well blow it all out like an air compressor, once and for all. Kathleen would be beside herself. Hell, she might need a shot or two to work up the courage to tell their daughter, but Pop told him to do it quick, said the Blacksworth woman was devious, even in death, and couldn't be trusted not to send Bree her own letter.

Damn, why would a person be so cruel as to do that? He ran a hand over his face, pulled into his driveway, and glanced at the house. There were a lot of years of living in that house, some good, some not, but no matter, he and Kathleen had pushed through it side by side, had a daughter, three grandbabies, and plans to see the world once he retired. And now he had to tell his wife that their past had come back to punish them, and worse, it could erupt at any moment and spill into their daughter's life if they didn't do something—like tell her the truth.

Rex stepped out of the truck, his belly gurgling from the sausage sub he'd eaten before he received the letter. If Kathleen found out he was sneaking sausage subs, she'd throw a fit and then she'd take away his "cheat" day and good-bye Sunday éclair. Right now he wished he'd eaten the tuna on wheat she packed him along with those five puny almonds.

He climbed the back steps, wiped his feet, and opened the door. His wife didn't like him bringing any outside "contaminants," as she called them, into the house. That's why he kept his slippers by the back door and years ago, when he worked the lines cutting wood and such, she'd had him dump his dusty work clothes into the washing machine the second he opened the door, which kept her happy except for the time he didn't know she was having a church meeting in the parlor. Oh well. Not as if those ladies hadn't seen a man in his underwear before, not that they'd admit it.

"Rex? Are you all right? You look pale." Kathleen set the knife she'd been using to cut up more greens and rushed toward him. "What's wrong?"

"Oh, sweetheart." He clutched her hands, looked into her blue eyes, and fell back to the first time he saw her. The attraction had been instant, deep, and soul-shattering, and for a man who wasn't big on deep thinking and fancy words, that was a profound revelation. She'd felt the same way, and the only roadblock to their getting together was his "pending" engagement to her sister. Except that hadn't stopped them: not the fact that he'd been courting Kathleen's sister and all but made it known he planned to propose to her, not even Nadine's proprietary air and hints that she'd begun drawing up a wedding list. One look at Kathleen Humphrey, three words out of those red lips, and he was a goner. Nadine didn't want to hear that her soon-to-be-fiancé would not be extending an offer nor that her sister had moved into first positon as a potential Mrs. Rex MacGregor. Fights ensued, some of them as loud and mean as a catfight, with Nadine accusing Rex of going back on a promise to marry her, even though that was not anywhere near true. The woman's meanness toward her sister only increased Rex's desire to protect Kathleen, and it drew them closer than ever, some might say a bit too close, as seven short months after the quickie wedding two towns over, they welcomed Bree Lynn MacGregor into the world. Oh, Nadine had a thing or three to say about it, starting and ending with *whore* and *cheater* but by then the town had grown tired of her waspish tongue and constant accusations. They didn't much like how she badgered Rex or spoke ill of the baby. In fact, despite how Rex and Kathleen ended up together and no matter that Bree was conceived before the vows, it was Nadine who left a bad taste on their tongues when they talked about her. And not one person was sorry to see Nadine pack up and leave town—some said she left on a broom.

"Rex, come and sit down. I'll get you a glass of water and then you can tell me why you look all pasty." His wife led him into the kitchen and pulled out his chair.

"Just give me a sec." He thudded into the chair and heaved a sigh.

"Is it Brody again? I'll bet it is." She tsk-tsked as she handed him his water, her eyes bright, a flush on her face, as she prepared to launch into the many ways Brody Kinkaid was unfit for their daughter, beginning with his lack of brain capacity and ending with his mother's constant babying of her son. "What's he done now? Still trying to bully Bree into stepping down as your replacement? Or is he planning to file a formal complaint because he wants a longer lunch hour?"

"It's not Brody." Rex took a sip of water, wished it were a shot, and set the glass on the oak table. "Sit down, Kathleen. I need to talk to you. It's about Nadine."

The look on her face said she wished this were only about their knucklehead son-in-law. She slipped into a chair, clasped his hands, and said in a voice that didn't have much air in it, "What about Nadine?"

They hadn't spoken her name in years, not since Kathleen's mother passed and Nadine showed up for the funeral. Big to-do, but one sister came to the viewing the first day and one the second. Bree was off in her own little world and while she cried and missed her Granny, she didn't question her mother when Kathleen told her the pain was too deep for another day of viewing. Same thing with the funeral. Their daughter didn't ask about the skinny woman dressed in black who wore a big black hat and black sunglasses so nobody could see her face. That was the thing about Bree: she was too dang trusting, believing there was more good in people than bad, and worse, thinking some people had no bad in them at all. That was her biggest fault, no doubt about it. Well, she was about to learn that people didn't always tell the truth, not even her parents.

Rex spit out the details faster than a wood chipper on high speed. When he finished, Kathleen let out a moan that tore up his gut worse than the batch of hot peppers Pop Benito sent him last summer. "I knew it. I just knew this would come back to us one day." She sniffed and dabbed at her eyes in such a way so as not to streak a bit of that makeup she loved to wear. How Kathleen could think about her appearance at a time like this was way beyond Rex. Hell, he was ready to open a bottle of whisky and start chugging.

"Now don't go getting all hysterical. It's a situation we're going to handle by coming clean." He cleared his throat and slid his wife a quick glance before adding, "And that's why Bree is on her way over."

Kathleen gasped, her eyes wide and tear-rimmed. "No, Rex. I can't see her yet. What will she think? She doesn't even know she has an aunt and now we have to tell her why." She shook her strawberry-blond head, sniffed, and said, "How could anyone be so vicious? We don't even know this Blacksworth woman."

He pulled his wife into his arms, held her tight the way he used to when she needed comforting, especially during the month-after-month pain of no more babies once Bree came along. It was a sad and heartbreaking time, but they'd gotten through it together, and they would get through this, too, because they belonged together. That's who they were:

Rex and Kathleen MacGregor, husband and wife, life partners, and no rich bitch with a twisted sense of justice was going to threaten what they had. "To hell with Gloria Blacksworth. Any person who digs up the past for the pure sake of causing torment is evil. I say good for Charlie Blacksworth for finding a slice of happiness here." He paused, rubbed his jaw. "Maybe that's why she's gunning for us. We're a big part of this community, a place that accepted Charlie but would never let her in. Who knows, there might be more letters, with more secrets."

Kathleen drew back to look him in the eye. "The woman's dead, Rex. Why would she come after us?"

He shrugged. "Why not? She lost her husband and her daughter. What else does she have to lose? Good thing Miriam doesn't have any skeletons or that Blacksworth woman would have them dancing." He smiled at his wife, tucked a lock of strawberry-blond hair behind her ear. "It's going to be okay. Bree will understand."

Thirty-eight minutes later, Rex wondered why the hell he ever thought his only daughter would not only understand but accept the story behind her parents' marriage. He should have known better.

"You mean Mama stole you away from her sister, a woman I didn't even know existed?" Unlike her mother, Bree's face was tear-stained with smudges of mascara, blue eye shadow, and smears of black under her eyes like a baby raccoon. Damn, but the girl could give a good cry. At first, she thought the tale was a sick spoof because Rex and Brody had been known to engage in shenanigans that were not in the best taste, but when her father didn't crack a smile and her mother whimpered, well, their baby girl knew the truth was in those words.

"Your mama didn't steal anything." Rex clutched his wife's hand and said, "You can't steal something the other person doesn't own and your aunt didn't own me. I wasn't a table or a cabinet. I wasn't anything until your mama came along." His voice softened and he squeezed Kathleen's hand, offered her a smile. "She made me somebody."

"I do not want to hear this." Bree stood and paced the room, sniffling and swiping her hands over her face, her eyes on everything but her parents. "Why couldn't you have told me? Why wait until it's practically in the *Magdalena Press* to inform me of your clandestine relationship and that you were pregnant when you got married?" She whirled around, shoved her hands on her hips, and zeroed in on them with eyes like his. "All those righteous talks about clean living and how boys were only after one thing and I had to protect it like a quarterback protects the football. What about you, Daddy? Were you one of those kinds of boys after Mama?" She turned to her mother before Rex could stop her. "And you, Mama, were you one of *those* girls? Is that why you were so dang hell-bent on me saving myself?"

Kathleen flew out of the chair, hauled off, and slapped their baby girl across the face. The sound of that slap was plain frightening as it split the air. "That's enough. Your aunt was more interested in your daddy's paycheck than in him. I loved your daddy and I do not regret what happened. I have lived all these years worrying that one day you'd learn the truth. Well, now you know." Kathleen inched closer to Bree, nostrils flared, eyes narrowed. "But know this, too. *I would not change a thing.* Your daddy and I have raised you and loved you the best we knew how, and when God didn't see fit to give us more children, we believed it was His way of letting us love you more. But we love each other, too, and we respect each other." Her voice dipped. "Not every marriage can say that, and I will not apologize for having that opportunity."

Rex blinked hard. If that wasn't the dang best

proclamation of love and commitment he'd ever heard, then he didn't know what was. As for the last part, he didn't miss the way their baby girl bristled like a porcupine when her mama mentioned love and respecting one's partner: code for *Brody Kinkaid might be your husband and he might love you, but he sure does not show you the respect you deserve.*

Bree held a hand to the red mark her mama had left on her cheek and whimpered, "I'm hurt is all; real hurt and sad that you couldn't trust me enough to tell me the truth."

"Oh, baby girl." Kathleen pulled their daughter into her arms, held her close. "Your daddy and I just didn't know how." She smoothed Bree's hair, glanced at Rex, and offered a faint smile. "We'd do just about anything to protect you from an unpleasant situation." She tightened her hold on Bree, her voice turning fierce, her gaze determined, as she repeated, "Just about anything."

***

Bree headed to work the next day determined to put the news of her parents' past and the timeline of her birth behind her. She'd almost told Brody, but he'd been in a mood because the beer fridge he ordered hadn't arrived yet. As if he needed a separate refrigerator for his beer. Now she was glad she'd kept quiet. What good would telling him do when he'd probably only use the information to make snippy remarks about her daddy? She'd always thought Brody and her daddy were buddies: they'd gone fly-fishing, roasted a pig on a spit last fall, and built a treehouse for the girls in the backyard. But since this business with Brody getting the boot from the front office to the machine shop, her husband was a real sourpuss and he did not have one good thing to say about her daddy. Not that Brody even cared about the cabinet designs or learning how to run the place; he wanted the title and the money and he'd told her that, no bones about it either.

That little tidbit had given her a sick stomach for a good three days and Brody took it that she might be pregnant. The man would not give up on a baby, even though he said he wasn't going to push her. Brody Kinkaid wanted a Brody Junior. Well, he wasn't getting one from her, not now, probably not ever. There were only so many pieces to her, like a strawberry-rhubarb pie, and if everybody took a slice, what was left? She'd tried explaining this to Brody, but he couldn't get past the strawberry-rhubarb part, saying he preferred cherry. Goodness gracious, but the man could try her at times. It was a good thing her heart swelled every time she looked at him, or they would all be in trouble with a capital *T*.

Still, she wasn't seventeen anymore; she was a wife, a mother, a business person, with thoughts and ideas that were her own, not generated from her husband's brain. Brody would have to get used to her thinking for herself. He called a woman's independence the "ruination of the family" but that was just not true. Look at Christine and Nate; they'd figured out a way to make things work and Nate sure didn't seem to mind Christine having a business and using her head for more than how to stuff a turkey. Not that she could stuff a bird because Christine couldn't cook, but that didn't seem to bother Nate. The man cooked and baked, probably did dishes, too, and nobody would ever accuse Nate Desantro of not being a man's man. Brody divided the chores by inside and outside ones with childcare falling under the "inside" duties. His father had been the same way and his mother did nothing to change her son's thinking. Dang that woman; she had done Bree no favors on that account.

Their friends hadn't been able to get Brody to share the load either, even when the men set examples by helping with inside work, and again, nobody would ever say Cash Casherdon or Ben Reed were not real men. Oh, swoon on that one.

If it weren't for her mama pitching in to babysit and carpool, what would she and Brody do? It wasn't going to get any easier once Daddy retired and the demands grew, but dang it, she liked learning about the wood grains and the different finishes. And she especially liked chatting with the customers and the suppliers and had started a file with the names of their wives and children, even their animals. No reason a person couldn't add a splash of caring into a business arrangement. Besides, Bree really *was* interested in the new babies, the confirmations, the passed college entrance exams. Even the tonsillectomies and the knee replacements. Wedding anniversaries, too—one year, silver, golden. One day, she and Brody would celebrate their silver anniversary, and God willing, their gold, and having someone who wasn't a family member congratulate them was real special.

But there were a lot of years between now and those big anniversaries and a fence or two to climb in the meantime. Like how was she going to talk to Brody about her daddy's suggestion that she visit a few of their customers, especially the big one who was several hours away and would mean an overnight trip? That was not something Brody would want to hear. Maybe her mama could watch the girls and she and Brody could go together, kind of like a mini getaway.

She sighed and eased her car into the number two spot of the employee parking lot. Daddy said he was going to have a sign made with her name on it. *Bree Kinkaid, President*. She smiled; she did like the sound of that, and her husband was going to have to get used to it, just like he was going to have to get used to learning how to peel a potato or two and fry up a pork chop. Maybe his mama could give him a lesson or two.

Bree still had that sign for *Bree Kinkaid, President* in her head at lunchtime when she pulled out of the parking lot and headed for Barbara's Boutique and Bakery. Red with a touch of gold? Or would her name be better suited to silver? Maybe the sign should be red, white, and blue with a line of stars along the bottom. She cranked up the radio and sang "Born in the U.S.A." as loud as she could, wishing she could tell everyone the good news yet knowing she couldn't. Still, Daddy had set her mind at ease and she could just burst with happiness. Michael Androvich had *not* come to town as a potential president or even co-president of the company. All those fears she'd harbored were silly and untrue. The man was here to help Daddy with a massive project, top secret and all that, but Bree could be hush-hush, anything, as long as the one threat to her position was not a threat at all.

The project had something to do with the big tracts of wooded land Michael and Daddy had visited the past three days. Yesterday, Michael went by himself and when he returned in the afternoon, he was quieter than usual, his expression more serious, like he was thinking real deep.

What was he thinking about? Heck, what was he hiding behind those chocolate-colored eyes and that don't-bother-me-stare? She'd wondered this since the first time he walked in her office and refused to share any personal information. Nothing. Not even a picture of a dog. Or a child. And certainly no wife or girlfriend. She'd slid around that last question a few times, but he'd shut her down fast. So, fine. Bree didn't need Michael Androvich to say anything because she'd already figured out he had a woman problem by the way his jaw tensed and those broad shoulders squared when she asked him about a wife. All she needed was a little wiggle room and she could create all kinds of stories. Her mama said she should have been a writer because she had the most vivid imagination, like a kaleidoscope turning this way and that, bits and pieces bursting with color. Or a story.

But this story got legs once her daddy told her about the Heart Sent honeymoon suite that had been reserved by Michael Androvich and then canceled. Oh, oh, oh. Bree ached for that poor man whose heart must have been ripped apart. What on earth could have happened? Had the bride met a tragic ending? Or had she called the whole thing off before she walked down the aisle? There was no recovering from either of those pains, at least not for a good long while, and to have the courage to still come to the town and the bed and breakfast that should have been a memory maker? Well, that spoke of a kind of strength that was about a lot more than muscle.

She would find out, even if her daddy had told her to leave the man be. Daddy knew her better than that, knew too that it would give her something to think about besides the shocker her parents revealed yesterday. Bree parked in front of the bakery and stepped out. Everybody loved Barbara's cupcakes and what better peace offering to bring Michael than one of these? Or maybe two. Chocolate with chocolate peanut butter frosting; most men couldn't resist it any more than they could resist a peek at a woman's cleavage. Bree pegged Michael Androvich as a chocolate man, had spotted him eating chocolate chip cookies yesterday and brownies the day before that. The man had a sweet tooth and she bet Mimi had fixed him up but good in that department.

"Hey, Lucy." Bree smiled at Pop Benito's granddaughter. "How's Mama Bear and Baby Bear?"

"Great." Lucy patted her belly and grinned. "I'm starting my birthing classes in two weeks."

Was there ever anything as precious as a pregnant woman? They glowed, they glistened, gracious, they even sparkled. Bree had loved being pregnant, loved the thought of another human being growing in her body, dependent on her for its very life. "Are you excited? Who's going with you?" Brody had been so tender when they'd gone to their birthing sessions...

"Ramona Casherdon." The girl's cheeks turned the prettiest pink, almost the exact same shade as her T-shirt. "She and my dad are—" she hesitated, the pink turned crimson "—kind of friends."

"Well, isn't that nice?" Oh, but there was something as thick and juicy as a T-bone steak in that statement. Ramona Casherdon and Anthony Benito? Hmm. Thank goodness Tess was not going to the birthing classes with Lucy. Bad enough babies were popping out all around their friend like mushrooms in a forest, but to actually be involved in the birth, see it all and know you might never have one? That was the purest misery.

"I know she seems like an odd choice, but once you get to know her, she's pretty friendly. And talkative."

Now that was doubtful. Bree had known Ramona Casherdon a lot of years and the woman hadn't spoken five complete sentences to her in all that time, and she'd had plenty of opportunity. But if there was something going on between her and Anthony Benito, maybe Ramona had blossomed like a rose in the sun, and the goodness that had been inside for too many years had started to spill out. Bree liked that possibility, liked it very much. "Glad to hear it." She glanced at the case, couldn't help but lean in to get a better look. Five rows of the most perfect cupcakes filled the center case, swirls of frosting heaped on top and dusted with sprinkles. Brody brought her a half dozen of the strawberries 'n' cream for her birthday, their anniversary, and the birth of each girl, said they reminded him of her, all sweet and irresistible. That man had a way with words and when he delivered the sweets with a copy of his poem, "The Promise," well, it could not get much better than that. "I'll take a half dozen of the strawberries 'n' cream, three red velvet, three double chocolate, and three perfect whites." The strawberries 'n' cream would be a treat for her and Brody; maybe they'd take them to bed, feed each other, naked. He'd like that. Michael Androvich could dig into the others and once she'd lulled him into a sugar haze, she'd start poking around about the canceled honeymoon suite at Mimi's and the woman who had to be behind it.

"The cupcakes are so good." Lucy lowered her voice as if there were a roomful of health fanatics next to her and said, "I had two double chocolate ones."

Bree zeroed in on the girl's stomach and laughed. "You have the perfect excuse." She patted her own belly that, while relatively flat, did not look like it had pre-children. "I have no excuse but a dang sweet tooth and a hankering for strawberries 'n' cream."

Lucy started to box up the cupcakes, careful not to touch the frosting swirls. "There's a little extra something in these that makes them fluffy." She shrugged. "Elise said it's her father's secret."

"Who's Elise? I thought Ramona made these."

"Ramona got diagnosed with pneumonia; she can hardly make it out of bed. Elise is visiting and she's helping out for a few days." Lucy grinned and closed the lid on the cupcake box. "Her father owns a bakery. How perfect is that? Goodwill, karma, divine intervention, call it whatever you want; it walked in the door the other day with Elise, and I'm taking it."

"Good thing Barbara doesn't know you've got a stranger in her kitchen. She'd flip." Barbara Germaine was awfully persnickety about anybody taking so much as a peek in that precious kitchen of hers, too afraid they might spot the secret ingredients she used in her "award-winning" cupcakes, though Bree would like to know who offered the award other than Pop Benito on behalf of The Bleeding Hearts

Society at their annual bake sale. Goodness, some people were just so full of themselves. If it weren't for Barbara's sweetheart of a sister, Lottie, nobody would have offered to step in and help while Barbara traveled to Australia for her once-in-a-lifetime journey. Of course, the old coot had sent her sister to retrieve the "secret" ingredients before the temporary bakers were allowed in the kitchen. Huh. As if Ramona Casherdon needed Barbara Germaine's recipe to create a mouthwatering cupcake. But Ramona was out with pneumonia, which left a stranger in the kitchen.

"Elise?" Lucy poked her head in the kitchen and said, "There's somebody I want you to meet."

This could get interesting. Bree eyed the rest of the contents in the glass case. Éclairs, brownies, chocolate chip cookies… Busy little bees. They did look tasty. Maybe she'd pick up a couple of brownies, too.

"This is Elise. Elise, this is Bree."

Bree tore her gaze from the brownies that definitely had her name on them and looked up. A petite, dark-haired woman wearing a hair net and apron moved toward her, extended a hand over the side counter and said, "Elise Pentani, nice to meet you."

Talk about cute as a button, and fresh-faced, like a soap commercial. Bree returned the smile and shook the woman's hand. Elise Pentani's handshake was firm and said she knew what was what and nobody was going to tell her any different, especially a man. A quick glance at her left hand showed no signs of a wedding ring, but then most women wouldn't crust up a ring with dough, even if they were married. So, *was* she married? If Bree steered the conversation with her usual skill, she'd find out before she left the bakery. She started off with, "I hear the cupcakes are scrumptious. I can't wait to try one."

"Don't get just one." The woman's lips twitched.

"What's an extra calorie or two when you're talking strawberries 'n' cream?"

Obviously, Elise Pentani wasn't concerned about her weight, not that she needed to be, but it was a clue. Vote one for not married. Even Christine, who didn't look as if she carried an ounce of unnecessary flesh, pregnant or not, didn't make comments like that. Time to press a bit more. Bree pointed at the strawberries 'n' cream cupcakes and said, "I'll take two more of those and two, no, three brownies."

Lucy laughed and shook her head. "Once you take a bite, bet you'll be back for more before the end of the week."

"That sounds dangerous." Bree hefted her overlarge handbag on the counter, dug into her wallet, and fished out a credit card. "These aren't all for me. I'm bringing some to work." *And trying out the brownie as soon as I get to the car.* She handed Lucy the credit card and said, "A peace offering of sorts." That comment made her think of Michael Androvich and led her to her next question. "Elise, are you staying at the Heart Sent?"

The woman colored like an Easter egg dunked in red dye and nodded. "I am."

"You have got to check out the honeymoon suite while you're there. Ask Mimi to show you. Rose petals on the bed, so soft and velvety." Her voice dipped in remembering. "There is absolutely nothing like it. Ask her if you can lie on it and then close your eyes and just inhale that scent." Oh, but she missed that time in her life when she believed every night would be a honeymoon and every day would lead to nights like the ones she and Brody had shared at the Heart Sent. "I'm sure she'll let you do it. Mimi is a big romantic, thinks there's someone for everyone." She slid Elise a smile, prepared for her next question. Her friends would say it was none of her business, but Bree believed the essence of a person's life could be found in their relationship, or lack thereof, with a significant other. Look at Gina Reed and how she'd turned all lovey-dovey once she and Ben got together. And now they were having a baby. And Tess and Cash Casherdon had battled tragedy and found their way back to each other. And who would have ever thought a man who didn't smile or give a person the time of day unless it was his sister or mother would fall head over heels, crazy in love forever and ever with the last woman he should want? But there was no denying Nate and Christine Desantro were as perfect as the strawberry 'n' cream cupcakes sitting on the counter. "So, ask about the honeymoon suite; tell her Bree said you have to see it."

The woman nodded, but dang if her face hadn't gone all pasty like a cup of flour. Oh boy, there was something lurking behind those eyes and Bree would bet it had to do with the mention of honeymoon suite, which meant *man*, which meant there wasn't one. But had there been one? Hard to believe there hadn't been, but people were strange birds, and until you got closer and pecked around in their business a bit, you just didn't know. Still. "I know it's none of my business but my friends say I'm a silly romantic who wants to see everyone in love and together." Bree's smile spread, her voice turned soft, and she nosed around where she shouldn't. "Do you have a special someone?"

If flour could turn whiter than white, like fresh snow, then that's what Elise Pentani's face looked like right now. "No."

It was a puny word but the feeling behind it weighed more than Brody. That feeling said *I'm in pain…I loved and lost and now I am lost…* Oh, but that face and that one little word spoke of tragedy, so sharp it sucked the air from Bree's lungs. She knew what the look meant and what it felt like inside: empty, lost, desperate. When she miscarried, it had taken months and the concern of friends and family to help her through it. Maybe she could help; maybe Christine, Gina, and Tess could, too. Who had known more trials and heartache than the three of them? A wonderful idea burst into her brain, swirled and morphed into a thought so fast it made her dizzy. Michael Androvich might keep it hidden, but his heart had been bruised and battered, same as Elise; Bree would put money down on it. Maybe Michael and Elise could help each other heal that heartache. All Bree had to do was figure out a way to get them together and her friends could help with that. She offered Elise her brightest smile and said, "How about you meet me and a few of my friends for dinner tomorrow night? Harry's Folly, 6:30 p.m.?"

Chapter 9

Elise took one last look in the mirror, adjusted her scarf, and grabbed her jacket. Harry's Folly was on the other side of town, according to Bree Kinkaid, who had given her instructions and enough warm smiles and reassurances that Elise was going to have a great time to make her believe just the opposite. She didn't want to go, had thought of canceling six times since the woman extended the offer, but that would mean fabricating an excuse, and then there would be questions, too many of them. People were just trying to be nice, but even so, this was a town like Restalline, where inquisitiveness was second nature and one question led to twenty-five.

She'd only been here a few days, hadn't even visited all of the stores yet, but she did like what she'd seen, and Lucy Benito had turned out to be a true find, a young woman who wasn't afraid of her future even though she knew it would not be an easy one. Would Elise have accepted her fate with such calm and the resolve to find a way? It was hard to say, because Good Girl Elise would not have slept with a boy she didn't love, and if she did have a momentary lapse of judgment, she would have used six different forms of birth control. Even with Michael, she'd been careful; they'd wanted time alone before they thought of adding to a family that already included Kevin and Sara. And she'd been fine with that, more than fine.

Lucy had informed her that her grandfather wanted to meet Elise and had invited her to bake pizzelles with him soon. According to Lucy, pizzelle baking with Pop Benito was by invitation only, so she should consider his asking a privilege, though it felt more like a demand than an invitation. Still, she was a bit curious about a man who wore high-tops and sweats as his usual attire and was considered the Godfather of Magdalena. Something told her they would get along just fine, but something else told her he was going to poke and prod like Michael's sister, Gracie.

As she made her way to Harry's Folly, she decided to look at tonight as an offer of hospitality from a woman who thought she needed it. She'd seen the compassion on Bree Kinkaid's face when she made the offer; maybe the woman knew about sadness and loss, too. And maybe that's why she wanted to get Elise out and around women her own age. To share secrets. Great. Oh, please do not let it be that. Please, no. What would she say? *I left my fiancé at the altar, and guess what? He's in this town, working in some cabinet factory?* Hardly. At least Mimi Pendergrass hadn't poked around. She'd been kind, considerate, and very matter-of-fact about the presence of the two people who were supposed to be on their honeymoon, but were instead not married, sleeping in different beds, and doing their best to avoid one another. It must make for interesting conversation, though Mimi didn't appear the gossipy type.

The night air was crisp, the ground still crunchy with snow. Soon, it would melt and give way to spring and with it clusters of blossoms filled with fragrance and bursts of color. She'd helped the kids plant tulips and King Alfred daffodils along the side of Michael's log cabin, a surprise for him that wouldn't reveal itself until the bulbs pushed through the ground. Kevin and Sara had been so excited to hold onto the secret, certain it would bring yet another smile to their father's face. But Elise would bet the four new tires on her car that those flowers wouldn't bring anything close to a smile on Michael Androvich's face. In fact, she wouldn't be surprised if he didn't be-head all of them so he wouldn't have to look at yet another reminder of his ex-fiancée.

Just how long could a person carry anger and mistrust in

his soul? How long before he opened up his heart again? Years? Decades? Never? And did a person like Michael ever open up to the one who caused him the pain? Would a person like Michael give *anybody* a second chance? She pushed the thoughts away before they gave her a headache. Wasn't she supposed to be working on herself, figuring out what she wanted in life, accepting a world without Michael Androvich? So what if he was in Magdalena, sleeping a few doors away? So what if she still dreamed of him? So what if he lived inside her soul?

It didn't matter. It couldn't. She had to find her own way to a life that didn't include the man who owned her heart, and she had to accept that. Elise opened the door to Harry's Folly and stepped inside to the smell of fresh-baked bread, spaghetti sauce, and garlic. If she closed her eyes, she might think she was sitting in the Androvich kitchen with Stella at the stove, stirring a pot of sauce, fresh-baked loaves of bread resting on cooling racks. But the similarities ended there. The Androvich kitchen, with its tattered linoleum and dated table and chairs, spoke of comfort and tradition, while Harry's Folly had a classiness about it that started with the mini fountain in the foyer and the gold-framed paintings and continued to the leather booths, Tuscan lights, and the piano in the corner. This was the kind of place Elise imagined in upscale trendy spots with valets, market price, and waiters who stood behind you and scraped crumbs from the table with a butter knife.

Why hadn't Bree Kinkaid told her this restaurant was so much more than the "whatever's in your suitcase is fine, nothing fancy" when indeed it *was* fancy and nothing in her suitcase or her closet at home would be presentable? She shrugged out of her jacket, deciding it would be more obvious if she left it on, and handed it to the hostess.

"There you are!" Bree Kinkaid descended upon Elise in a

rush of smiles and a quick hug. "We're all waiting for you; come on, this way." She slung an arm through Elise's and pointed toward a large booth in the corner. "They're all anxious to meet you."

Elise glanced at Bree's black pants and red top. Only a woman with legs as long as hers could get away with those pants. But they weren't upscale designer clothes. Elise let out a small breath and said, "Great." But there was nothing great about meeting strangers and knowing you had a sorry tale to either hide or reveal.

"Ladies, this is Elise Pentani. Elise, this is Gina Reed, Christine Blacksworth, and Tess Casherdon."

Two of the women were pregnant: the dark-haired one named Gina and the black-haired one named Christine. All three offered what looked like genuine smiles and firm handshakes. And their clothing appeared normal, at least what she could see: V-necked tops and a turtleneck. Elise eased into the semi-circular booth next to the woman named Christine, pasted a smile on her face, and waited for the questions to begin. They would be innocent enough, but sadly there were no casual answers to explain her life right now. Train wreck? Self-imposed disaster? Spiral into spinsterhood? All adequate descriptions.

"I am so glad you could get out tonight," Bree said, scooting into the spot next to Elise. "These girls are like the sisters I never had." She flashed a smile at the women and added, "We've helped each other through a lot of storms, maybe a hurricane or two."

"And several tornadoes," the woman named Gina said, her voice dry, her eyebrows arched. "The kind that flattens entire towns."

"And there was that tsunami," blond-haired Tess added, shaking her head. "Disastrous."

Bree nodded, clucked her tongue. "But we dug our way

out and here we are." She turned to Elise and said, "Now let's get you a drink and you can tell us what you put in those cupcakes I bought because I have never tasted anything so scrumptious."

Talk of food and baking relaxed Elise and made her forget how nervous she'd been that Bree and her friends would try to unearth her past. The first mojito helped and so did the animated chatter and warm bread with real butter. By the end of the second mojito, Elise wondered why she'd thought these women might intimidate her. They talked about food, movies, babies, and husbands, and while Elise had no personal knowledge of the latter two, she nodded and pretended she did. When their entrees arrived, Elise dug into the restaurant's specialty, penne pasta with spinach and garbanzo beans. Christine told her this signature dish was created specifically for the owner, Harry Blacksworth—her uncle. What a small world, that got smaller when a young man stepped out of the kitchen and introduced himself as Lucy Benito's "friend." Anybody with a brain cell and a pair of eyes could see the lanky boy with the flattop was interested in more than friendship. Did Lucy know that? Was *she* interested? Elise had Lucy and the boy named Jeremy on her mind when she glanced up to find Gina Reed studying her in a way that made Elise feel like a slide under a microscope.

Gina fingered her glass and said in a casual voice, "You might as well know Bree's going to try and fix you up, so run while you can."

"Gina!" Bree stuck out her chin and huffed. "That is so not true."

"Sure it is. No sense springing it on Elise at the end of the night, like the idea just came to you." Gina Reed turned to Elise and said, "Bree's certain you've got a broken heart and she's determined to mend it. You know how some people fix patches in jeans? Bree makes it her mission to fix hearts."

"I do not." Bree set down her fork and snatched her drink. "I do not," she repeated, but this time there wasn't quite the conviction in her voice there'd been a second ago.

Elise tried to push back the spurts of panic inching up her gut. A fix-up? The last thing she needed was a do-gooder trying to heal her broken heart. "I don't want a fix-up. Please." She knew her voice came out as desperate, but she had to make certain Bree understood she didn't want or need anyone's help. "I'm fine. Really."

Tess tilted her blond head, studied her. "Bree means well, but she doesn't always go about it the best way."

"Will you stop talking about me as if I'm not here?" Bree gulped her mojito, her second, and finished it off. "I have enough people in my life who consider me less than competent; I do not need my best friends doing it, too."

Christine reached out and squeezed Bree's hand. "We wouldn't do that to you, Bree." She smiled, her blue eyes glistening. "We all value your opinion and we know you can't stand to see anyone unhappy." She met Elise's gaze and said in a gentle voice, "We've all had our share of heartache and I guess we recognize it when we see it. I think Bree spotted the pain on your face and had a solution." She shrugged, squeezed Bree's hand again. "That's all."

Bree sniffed and dabbed her napkin at both eyes. "That's right. I just learned the saddest tale the other day about a man at our shop and my heart is aching for him. When I met Elise, she had that same kind of pain on her face, like she'd eaten three jalapeño peppers, seeds and all. I couldn't ignore the look, not when I knew in my gut what it meant and might have a way to help." She worked up a smile, turned to Elise. "The girls and I have known our share of sadness and these three women almost lost the men they loved. I think I found somebody who could take your mind off your hurt, and I think you could help him, too."

Oh no, Elise did not want to hear a tragic love story when she had her own going on. "Bree, honest, I'm not—"

"Will you just let me tell you his story? Maybe you can be friends, and then see what happens? Lots of great relationships start as friends."

The other women looked at Elise with equal parts sympathy and resignation as if to say, "Let her go and get it over with because she's not going to quit." Oh, but Elise did not want to hear this.

Gina sighed. "Okay, Bree, go ahead and spill the tale."

Bree squared her shoulders and sat up straight as though she were giving a presentation to a boardroom and began in a soft voice. "This is the story about a man who's got a hole in his heart because the woman he loved gouged it out. It used to bleed, but now I believe it's scabbed over and one day it will just be numb." Gina rolled her eyes, but Bree ignored her and went on. "The first time I met him, I thought he was plain mean, with a streak of viciousness that was longer than the Hudson River, but he's not. He's hurt." She paused, her voice dipping lower. "Wounded, like an animal that's been shot in the gut and left to bleed out. Sometimes, when he doesn't think I'm watching, I sneak a peek and I see the sadness in those eyes, the slump to his muscled shoulders. It's like he wants to admit defeat to his heart, but he can't." Pause. "He won't."

"Bree, come on." Gina shook her head. "Are you making this up?"

"Of course not." Bree shot her a dark look.

But Gina wasn't as pulled in by the tale as the other two women, or maybe she was simply more practical. "So, the part about this guy wanting to admit defeat to his heart—you heard him say that?"

"No, but I didn't need to hear it. I saw it. All over his

face, in the way he sat in the chair and stared off as if he were reliving the whole tragic story."

"Do you know what happened?" Christine Desantro leaned forward and her expression grew serious, like she really wanted to know. Maybe there was a pain in her past that reminded her of this, or maybe she didn't want Bree to get worked up over Gina's comments.

"All's I know is the tidbits I've heard and the tiny bit he shared. Something about trust, but that's all he says. If I try to ask more, he clams right up, but his eyes get so sad, and sometimes I catch him staring at nothing, and that's when I know he's thinking about *her*." She took a sip of water, licked her bottom lip, and said, "I think he still loves her."

"What could have happened to pull them apart?" Tess Casherdon asked in tone that said she'd also known her share of grief.

Bree leaned forward, lowered her voice. "Daddy told me the man was supposed to get married and bring his wife here with him, but there's no wife at the Heart Sent."

Elise sucked in a breath as those last words stole the oxygen from the room. Was Bree talking about Michael? Was her father the man Michael was coming to see? *Do not let it be Michael...please, do not let the man with the sad eyes be Michael...* She clenched her hands in her lap, forced her expression to remain calm as the women speculated on why the man hadn't arrived in Magdalena as a newlywed.

"Maybe he got cold feet and couldn't go through with it," Gina said. "You know men aren't always the most rational creatures. They get skittish." She shrugged and forked a piece of chicken cacciatore. "I kept waiting for Ben to wake up and bail on me, but he didn't."

"Right, as if he would." Tess laughed and shook her head. "That man is so crazy in love with you, it's kind of sickening. I mean, does he really have to bring you flowers every week?"

"What's wrong with flowers? He's actually learned the difference between a Gerbera daisy and a Shasta daisy, tulips and lilies, and he even knows what a mum looks like." Her dark eyes sparkled. "Flowers are so much better than a bag of chocolate pretzels that I would devour in one sitting."

"She's got a point," Christine said. "Nate's been making me brownies every week and it has got to stop." She patted her belly and frowned. "I keep telling myself this is all baby, but I think there are a few trays of brownies in there, too."

"Well, I'm not pregnant, but Cash just has to hear me say I'm hungry for something, and next day, there it is: enough to feed ten people. Chili, veggie burgers, portobello wraps, stir-fry. No wonder we're always inviting my mom and Will for dinner."

"Huh." Bree tilted her head, tapped her chin. "I think you ladies need to give my husband a few cooking lessons."

Elise didn't miss the quick glances that darted among Gina, Tess, and Christine, seconds before Tess nodded and said, "Sure, Bree. Send him up. Anytime." But there was a hesitancy in her voice that told Elise Bree's husband wouldn't be taking cooking lessons from anybody.

"Sure." Bree's smile didn't reach her eyes but she kept it in place, motioning the waiter to the table so she could order two more mojitos. Elise tried to refuse but Bree wouldn't have it. "I am not going to drink alone and I seriously need another mojito so I can finish this sad story."

Was she referring to the sad story she'd been telling them or the one that had to do with her and her husband? The question was, did Bree know she'd been sending marriage distress signals? Not that Elise knew anything about marriage or how to make a long-term relationship work because obviously she didn't. But she did know what a relationship in trouble sounded like and Bree Kinkaid's had the makings of one.

"So what's the rest of the story, Bree? Do you know or are you guessing?" Gina asked.

Bree sipped her mojito and nodded for Elise to do the same. "All right then. I've pieced it together as best I could. I think whatever happened wasn't Michael's fault." She shook her head, took another sip. "I think he loved his fiancée more than any woman can imagine, and she took that love and crushed it." She balled her hand into a fist. "Then she ripped it into shreds until it was barely beating. And then—"

"I think you should slow down on those mojitos," Christine said, placing a hand on Bree's. "Taking care of three kids with a hangover doesn't sound like my idea of a fun Saturday."

Bree ignored her, turned to Elise. "Do you think she left him at the altar, you know, just walked off and that was it?"

"I…I…" *She didn't walk off; she never showed.*

Gina sighed. "Sure, that's exactly what happened. No doubt the whole congregation was waiting: the groom and the best man at the altar, the bridal party lined up and ready to go. Everything's in place for the ceremony to begin so the couple can start their happily-ever-after. But they can't start, and do you know why?" Her dark eyes widened and she looked at each of them, her voice turning soft. "No bride. She just no-shows." She leaned back against the leather upholstery and shrugged. "End of story."

"That is so cruel." Bree ran a hand through her strawberry-blond hair and scowled. "Michael is a wounded soul; it's so obvious to me now. We need to help him." She darted a glance at Elise, smiled. "And I have a plan."

"No." Tess spit out the word like it was vinegar. "No more of your plans."

"Oh, pooh." Bree rolled her eyes and heaved a gigantic

sigh. "What if we'd said that about you and Cash?" She pinned her gaze on Gina. "And you and Ben weren't exactly chummy. If it hadn't been for a little 'intervention,' who knows how long it would have taken you two to realize you belonged together?" Bree shook her head and zeroed in on Christine. "I'm not even going to get started on the many reasons you and Nate didn't belong together. That man makes Michael Androvich look like a puppy dog. But you got through it because somebody or several somebodies were on your side with a plan, and this is no different." Her voice dipped and her eyes glistened when she said, "Everybody deserves a second chance, and sometimes they just need a push in the right direction."

"I'd feel more comfortable if I knew the circumstances of the 'un-coupling,'" Christine said.

Gina jumped in. "Agreed. And you can't go tossing Elise into a ring she might not want to get tossed in."

Yes. Exactly. Elise tried to pretend nonchalance as though they weren't discussing the ins and outs of her personal life and the man they didn't know was her ex-fiancé. Did Bree think she was pathetic and needed help finding a man? Or could she read sad and lonely stamped on Elise's forehead? Or maybe she'd been pulled in by Michael's smile and those honey-brown eyes and could think of nothing but rescuing *him*. He did have a way about him...

"Elise?" Gina's voice sliced through her thoughts, pulled her back to the women in the booth. "Tell Bree to stop now before you end up sitting across from this Michael guy at dinner and wondering how you got there."

Elise turned to Bree, worked up a smile. She could do this; she could pretend she didn't even know this Michael guy. "Bree—"

"Just meet him," Bree said, holding up her index finger. "One meeting, that's all."

"But—" *If you only knew.*

"You're hurting; I spotted it the second I walked into the bakery." Bree leaned toward her, gentled her voice. "Every one of us sitting at this table has been there, and if it hadn't been for one another, we might not have made it out. Point is, we can help you get past that gouge in your heart if you let us." She inched closer, pinned her with those amber eyes, bright with tears, and said, "Let us help you. Meet Michael, talk to him. I think you'll have a lot in common, and if nothing else, you'll see that men hurt just as much as we do, and this one is hurting like our old dog, Raymond, who got quilled by a porcupine."

"Ouch on that visual," Gina said. "And here's something to consider. Elise might not want your help and if this Michael is like most guys, he would not be happy to know you were discussing his emotions and working on a plan to 'rescue' him. Men don't want to be rescued, whether they need to be or not."

Christine laughed. "They want to be the ones doing the rescuing."

"Right," Tess added. "And their version of a rescue is to barge in and try to fix things, even if we don't want them fixed."

Bree shrugged. "Okay, so no rescue attempt. I know that and I know how men have to think they're the saviors of our world." She scrunched her nose and said, "Why do you think I let Brody map out directions for me when I go to Renova? Daddy taught me to navigate when I was ten, but I let Brody do it, even if he always misses a step or two in the directions."

"Okay, then," Gina said. "You get what we're saying. Leave Elise and Michael alone."

"I can't do that in good conscience." Bree stared at Gina, slid her gaze to Tess, then Christine. "I have to try and help them get past this like you all helped me when I lost the baby. It worked. I got my life back."

The women gave her a look that said that was debatable, but none of them commented. Finally, Gina spoke, her voice carrying a gentleness to it that seemed uncharacteristic of the woman. "I'm trying to get you to see that it's none of our business, just like whatever reason Elise has for landing in Magdalena is none of our business." Gina's dark gaze softened on Bree. "If she wants us to know, she'll tell us, and we should accept that."

Elise snatched her drink and took a big gulp. Gina might just convince Bree to leave it alone. *Oh, please, let this conversation end.* But Bree wasn't about to keep quiet, not when she seemed to believe she could and should help.

"Will you tell us why you're so sad, Elise? Why you've come to Magdalena and why you looked like you were going to get sick when I mentioned your heart getting gouged?" Bree's eyes glistened. "Let us help you get your happily-ever-after. I know we can."

The emotion in the other woman's voice squeezed out Elise's calm. She didn't want to cry, didn't want to do anything but sit here with a smile pasted on her face, her expression blank. But they were all watching her, waiting for her to tell Bree to mind her own business and stop with the comments. Elise opened her mouth to do just that but, to her horror, something else slipped out, something that had no business connecting with sound, and less with formulating words. "I'm Michael Androvich's ex-fiancée."

The tears came then as the truth spilled out, beginning with how she'd scarred and humiliated the only man she ever loved, leaving him at the altar, accusing him of deceit and betrayal. Not believing enough in him or their love. But the other truths seeped through the tears, made Bree, Tess, Christine, even Gina cry. Elise would never get over

Michael Androvich, and she would never stop loving him. The telling got easier as the women shared their stories of the men they loved and almost lost. The mojitos and the hugs helped, too. When Elise admitted she was staying in the honeymoon suite at the Heart Sent, nobody acted like that was strange. In fact, the tears flowed harder, the hugs got stronger.

Tess Casherdon drove her back to the Heart Sent a little before midnight, walking her to the door so Elise didn't trip or follow the zigzag pattern the sidewalk made from one too many mojitos. Next time she'd try the melon mojito. She liked the sound of that. A melon m-o-j-i-t-o. Bree said there were all kinds of flavors: mango, apple, raspberry, orange, strawberry, even coconut. When was next time? Somebody had mentioned it, but darn if she could remember.

"You okay, Elise, or do you want me to take you to your room?"

Elise squinted up at her new friend, smiled. "I'm fine." She waved a hand in the air, let it land with a thump at her side. "Just fine and," she paused, considered the rest of the phrase, added, "dandy. Fine and dandy."

"Okay, well, take it slow. Call me if you need help picking up your car tomorrow or if you want to talk. I could meet you for coffee or you could come to the house. I don't have a baby to show off, but you could meet Henry, our rescue dog. He's a real character; hates it when people cry or get upset." Tess gave her a quick hug, her eyes bright. "We'll help you get through this."

Elise nodded and opened the door before she started blubbering all over Tess Casherdon's white parka. Maybe it was the mojitos that made her teary-eyed and close to bursting, but most likely it was the mention of her ex-fiancé and that whole sad tale. She sucked in a breath, scrubbed a hand over her face, and made her way to the stairs. When she reached the bottom step, Elise looked up, scrunched her nose. That was a lot of steps. Too many. And she was tired. Maybe she'd sit down and work up the energy to climb them. First one, then the next, and the one after that… Yup, that's what she'd do. Elise unzipped her jacket, plopped on the third step, and stretched out. A big yawn later and she fell fast asleep.

Chapter 10

Michael found Elise an hour later when he almost tripped over her coming down the stairs for a few of Mimi's chocolate chip cookies. "What the hell?" His ex-fiancée lay on her side on the steps, jacket still on, mouth open, head resting on a step. Michael leaned closer, inhaled the scent of roses and... Was that alcohol he smelled? Couldn't be, Elise didn't drink more than an occasional glass of white wine. He sniffed again. He knew alcohol, knew how it smelled when it oozed out of your pores, and Elise Pentani reeked of the stuff. He frowned. What had she been up to that she'd gone and gotten drunk, and who the hell had she been doing it with, that's what he wanted to know. And that's what he planned to find out.

"Elise." He placed a hand on her shoulder. "Elise, wake up." She mumbled something that made no sense and tried to snuggle her face against the carpeted step. What would she say if she knew her mouth was resting on a step? Carpeted or no, she'd flip. His ex-fiancée had some weird quirks and when she caught him on the sofa, booted feet on the cushioned arm, she'd gone into a long tirade that she called an educational blurb, about how the bottoms of shoes carried all manner of nastiness: dirt, spit, dog crap, animal guts, fertilizer...on and on she'd gone like a little warrior come to save the world from the gunk that collected on their shoes. Michael hadn't known whether to be pissed or laugh, but she'd been so serious he couldn't do either, so he pulled her onto his lap, kissed her, then headed to the kitchen where he unlaced his boots and kicked out of them. The smile she gave him told him she was pleased, and when he plopped back on the sofa, she snuggled on his lap and showed him just how pleased she was... *Damn*. He shoved those memories from his brain and dragged out the one of him waiting for her at St. Stanislaus church. That made looking at her and *not* wanting her possible.

He shook her shoulder, anxious to get her off the steps and into bed so he could continue another attempt at sleep with a stomach full of cookies. "Elise, wake up. Now." This time she opened her eyes, squinted against his closeness, or maybe it was from the drinks, and frowned. She stared at him so long that he started to worry the alcohol had caused more than a drunk. He'd read that people who drank too much, too fast could get a swelling of the brain and die. "Are you okay?" He leaned closer, checked her pupils, touched her forehead. Waited.

"Michael?"

Okay, so she recognized him. That was a good sign. "Yeah."

"Where am I?" She tried to sit up, let out a moan. "Oh, not good."

He would not lecture her tonight; he knew what it was like to have a person yammering in your ear when you'd had too much to drink and didn't want to think about anything but making the room stay still, not puking up your guts, and turning down the volume to zero decibels. Silence. Lots and lots of silence. That had never happened with the Androvich clan though because if it wasn't his mother scolding him with a look or a word, it was Nick, or hell, even Gracie. The whole "what could you have done differently" could wait for tomorrow. After the room stilled. After she puked. After the volume got turned down. Sure as hell, she was headed that way.

Michael gentled his voice. "If you can stand, I can get you upstairs."

She moaned, closed her eyes. "The room won't stop spinning." Another moan. "I feel wobbly."

Wobbly. He almost smiled. Elise used medical terms to

describe conditions, not words like *wobbly*. Michael eased his arms under hers. He had to get her upstairs because once the room started spinning, the stomach was next. "Elise, open your eyes." She inched them open, stared at him. "Look at me, don't take your eyes off my face, okay?" She nodded and he hefted her to her feet. "We've got one step down, there you go. Let's get you to the bottom."

"Michael…" Those dark eyes turned darker. "I feel sick."

He nodded. "I know, Baby, just keep your eyes on my face." He lifted her into his arms and made his way up the steps toward her room, his gaze locked with hers. For a few seconds he forgot why they could never be together, forgot the pain and misery of her betrayal, and remembered how they were together, remembered it all. Michael reached the honeymoon suite, opened the door, and led her to the bathroom. He eased her to her feet and removed her jacket. "You're going to throw up," he said, flipping on the bathroom light. "Do you want me to stay?" She'd taken care of him when he had the flu last year, same with Kevin and Sara. It wasn't a big deal, but Elise was private about that kind of stuff and she might think it was.

She moved her head an inch to indicate a *no*. "Just help me…" She pointed to the toilet.

"Sure." Michael took her arm, led her to the john, and helped her kneel. He spotted a small stack of hairbands on the cabinet next to her toiletries and pulled her hair into a ponytail. "I'll be right outside. Call me when you're done." He took one last look at her and closed the door. The heaving started three seconds later, gut-wrenching sounds that ate at him, made him wish he was in there instead of Elise. He was probably the reason she was in her current state anyway. Trying to forget, refusing to acknowledge the way things were, the way they could have been. Yeah, he'd bet a bottle of whiskey he was the reason she was hugging the toilet.

When the heaving stopped, Michael waited another five minutes and moved to the door. "Elise?" Nothing. He eased the door open, found her lying on the floor, curled up like a child, her eyes closed, face pale, lips parched. "Elise?" Michael knelt beside her, lifted her head onto his knee. She looked so helpless, so fragile.

Her eyes fluttered open and she whispered, "Michael."

He smoothed a few strands of hair from her face, tucked them behind her ear. "I'm here."

"Thank you." Those dark eyes grew bright, brighter still.

He touched her cheek, nodded. "Let's get you to bed. It really will be better in the morning." She clutched his hand, held tight as he helped her to her feet, held a glass of water while she rinsed out her mouth, then guided her to the gigantic bed they should have shared as husband and wife—honeymooners. He'd undressed her many times, but that was before, when he had a right to do so. Now, he had no right and that made his chest ache with a sadness he tried to ignore and couldn't. He pulled back the covers, removed her shoes, and helped her into bed. "I'll sit with you until you fall asleep," he said, tucking the covers under her chin.

She looked so small and pale in that big bed, so damn fragile. "Will you lie down with me? Please?"

Michael didn't answer at first, fought with common sense and logic. He should say "no" and take a seat across the room, away from the bed, away from the sound of her breathing. That's exactly what he should do. But he didn't. Instead, he kicked off his shoes and climbed into bed beside her. When she sighed and turned on her side, he flung an arm around her and tucked her against his chest. Within minutes, her breathing evened and she fell asleep. Michael kissed the top of her head, pulled her close, and drifted off to sleep.

***

Elise needed to stay busy so she wouldn't think of last night, not that she could remember much of it, but her brain hadn't been so saturated with mojitos that she didn't recall Michael carrying her up the stairs to her room, helping her to bed after she threw up...but what about the other parts? Had he stayed with her? She'd woken with her clothes on, which never happened when that man was near a bed, though last night had provided extenuating circumstances like drunkenness and emptying her stomach, but still, had he stayed? The pillow smelled like him, but that could be wishful thinking or an overactive imagination. And what about that wavy strand of chestnut hair on her shirt? Had that come from lying in bed with her, or when he carried her up the stairs? Oh, if only her head had been clear enough to catalog the events. There was only one way to find out what happened and that meant asking Michael, which at the moment made heaving into the toilet again a more welcome prospect.

She took a hot shower to help her pounding head, but just thinking about Michael Androvich and what might or might not have happened made her brain ache. The man had always been able to do that to her, even in the days when they were adversaries. Back then, he'd worked his way into her head, seen things she hadn't wanted him to see, like how she believed herself in love with his brother. But once he'd found a way to her heart, well, that changed everything; it made her world brighter, bolder, more alive than she could have imagined. That all changed when she stiffed him on their wedding day. The fact that he still lived in her heart made the brightness too bright, the boldness too bold. As for feeling alive, that had shriveled like a rose without water. People talked about love and being all in, and that was fine when it worked. Heck, it was better than fine; it was incredible. What they left to musicians, poets, and writers was what happened when it all fell apart, when the love that pulsed in their souls stopped beating. She tried not to think about her heart, her soul, or the person behind their misery as she threw on her clothes and made her way to Mimi Pendergrass's kitchen. Coffee might not solve her problems, but it sure helped.

"Hi, Mimi." Elise entered the kitchen and headed for the coffee pot. Mimi ordered coffee beans from some specialty shop in Montana and swore those beans had the richest, most fragrant aroma on the continent.

Mimi glanced up from the stove where she was stirring something in a stainless steel pot and smiled. "Coffee just finished brewing and there are pancakes warming in the oven. Canadian bacon, too."

"Thanks." Elise grabbed a mug, poured her coffee.

"Have a good sleep?"

Mimi kept her eyes on the contents in the pot, but there was something about the way she asked the question that made Elise wonder if she already knew the answer, knew too there was more to last night than sleep—like someone might have shared her bed, someone who had been a fiancé. Other than the night she arrived and a few random encounters, Elise hadn't spent much time with Mimi. Hard to do that when Michael was in the vicinity, and Mimi Pendergrass had pretty much "adopted" him, cooking beef stew, meatloaf, biscuits, even lasagna, all of his favorites. Maybe she had a son and Michael reminded her of him. Oh, that man knew how to turn on the charm if he wanted to, but he probably hadn't even needed to do that. Women spotted the sad eyes, the stingy smiles, the I-don't-care attitude and, darn it all, they wanted to help him, wanted to make him care.

"Elise? I swore I heard a bit of commotion last night. Did

you hear it?" Mimi asked again, glancing at her from the tops of her reading glasses.

Elise shrugged, stirred her coffee. Was Mimi tricking her or was she serious? Or had Michael told her about last night? There was one way to find out. "I did, and unfortunately I was the cause of it."

"You?"

She did act as if she didn't know, or at least not for certain. Mimi seemed like a woman who could draw a pretty accurate conclusion based on circumstances, life experiences, and intuition. "I had a few too many mojitos with Bree Kinkaid and her friends, and for someone who doesn't drink more than an occasional glass of wine, it wasn't good." She shook her head, wished she hadn't as pain surged to her temples. "I fell asleep on your steps. Thank goodness it wasn't the ones outside. Can you believe that?"

Mimi laughed, a rich sound that filled the air with remembering. "I can indeed. Back in my not so young but foolish days, I loved gin and tonic. My husband and I used to sit out back as the sun set, sip our drinks, and just talk about everything. Oh, but those drinks went down nice and smooth." Her voice dipped, softened. "We had such ideas, such plans...most were things we wanted to do together, not in some far-off place that took a three-day plane ride to get to, but in our own backyard." She nodded, laughed again. "Polka lessons, organic gardening, refinishing antiques, researching our ancestry, canning vegetables. Roger played Santa twelve years in a row until he fell ill. He loved children, always wanted a grandchild, but it wasn't meant to be." She sighed. "Some things are out of our control and that's a sour pickle to accept." She turned to Elise, her eyes bright. "I'm guessing Michael was behind the mojitos?"

"Maybe not the first one, but definitely the others."

How many had she had anyway? Great impression she

made on Bree's friends, especially when she broke down and admitted she was Michael's fiancée. They hadn't seemed to mind, had actually acted as if they liked her more because of it, like they understood how that kind of emotion could drive a person to act that way. Even Gina Reed, the most critical of the bunch, had been sympathetic. And hadn't they admitted to their own share of grief with their men?

"Michael still loves you. It's in the words he says but especially the ones he doesn't."

"Love without trust isn't enough."

Mimi set down her wooden spoon and turned to Elise. "No, it's not, but forgiveness and second chances are what gives us hope, even when we think none's left. I watch him when we're eating dinner, and he's always on alert, as if he's listening for you."

"Right, so he can blast me with his get-the-heck-out-of-here-you're-not-welcome speech."

"I don't think so. I'd say it's more like waiting, as if he's hoping he'll look up and there you'll be." She motioned for Elise to sit at the kitchen table while she removed the pancakes and Canadian bacon from the oven. "I know I haven't imagined the number of times he looks behind his shoulder toward the kitchen door when we're eating. So much so, I've almost offered to switch seats with him to save his neck muscles." She smiled and laid a plate of food in front of Elise. "I know love when I see it; I don't need the words spelled out." She eased into her chair, held her mug between both hands. "Michael's scared to trust his heart again, just like I was when my husband took off on me–two days after we married."

"He took off?"

"Oh, yes. At least you left *before* the wedding. Not my Roger. He waited until he had the ring on my finger and then he up and disappeared. I worried to death over that man for days, certain he'd come to a horrible end, but the worst thing that happened to him was a lapse of brain cells." Mimi relayed the rest of the tale, the eventual divorce petition, the epiphany, the reconciliation, and the many happy years that followed. "Of course, I told all of this to Michael." She nodded her salt-and-pepper head and her silver ball earrings bounced. "Wanted to give him something to think about."

Elise nibbled on a piece of bacon, thought about Mimi's story. "Did Michael say anything about last night?"

"Not a word, got all fidgety when I asked him if he heard a commotion, and when I mentioned that I'd ask you about it, that boy practically flew out of his chair." She winked and nodded. "That's when I knew whatever I'd heard last night, the two of you were involved in it."

Should she tell Mimi that if Michael didn't want to talk, he wouldn't, and it had nothing to do with like, dislike, or even hate. He clammed up, no matter who was doing the asking. She'd seen him pull this stunt with his whole family, his mother, too, though not very often. The running away wasn't a surprise either. That was typical "old" Michael Androvich. "Do you know when he'll be back?" The sooner she got this over with, the easier it would be to put the whole incident behind her.

Mimi tapped a finger against her chin. "I think he said tomorrow night. His brother is bringing his kids to a hotel a few hours away, said they're going to eat pizza and swim in the pool."

And he probably would let Kevin and Sara eat too much junk food and he'd forget to make sure they brushed their teeth, and they'd end up with cavities, or at least bellyaches. She wished she'd known he was meeting with the kids. The second the thought left her brain she realized the ridiculousness of it. It wasn't like Michael would have offered to let her tag along with *Let's play house, like we planned*, or *This is what it would have been like*. Still, that didn't stop her from missing the children or the way things could have been…*that* she missed the most.

"Don't be so hard on yourself." Mimi reached out to pat her hand. "It will all work out, you'll see. Once you and Michael figure out your problems, I have a feeling you'll end up like me and Roger, and that's a true gift." Her blue eyes misted, her voice dipped as she said, "A true gift indeed."

Elise thought about Mimi's words long after she'd helped her clean the kitchen and headed out for a brisk walk. Magdalena reminded her so much of Restalline that it did her heart good to take in the scenery, talk to the people, and breathe the mountain air. So Nick was taking Kevin and Sara to see their father. That was so like Nick, doing what was right for the people involved, especially children. Had Nick needed to remind his brother to see his kids, or had Michael been responsible all by himself? She guessed it depended on which Michael showed up: old Michael or new Michael.

The sun felt good on her face and while it was chilly, the fresh air cleared her head. Most of the snow was gone, offering hope for an eventual spring that would bring with it explosions of color and fragrance in the form of buds and flowers. She'd always loved spring, almost as much as fall. She made her way back to the Heart Sent and decided to call her father. He hadn't returned her calls and she hoped he wasn't working too hard at the bakery, even though Dominic Pentani did not consider what he did at the bakery work. Elise dialed his number and waited.

"Hello, this is Dominic."

"Papa, how are you?"

"Elise! I was just telling Viola I have not heard from my Elise in four days and I am wondering about her."

That was not exactly true. "Papa, I called you every night

and left a message on the answering machine. Did you not get any of my messages?"

Pause. "No, no messages."

"Papa, if you'd just let me get you a cellphone, you wouldn't have to worry about being home to miss a call."

"A cellphone. Bah. I have no need for such foolishness."

She sighed. "One of these days we're going to have a serious talk about it. So, what happened to the answering machine? Did you press the wrong buttons and delete everything?" He coughed, cleared his throat, and mumbled something Elise couldn't understand. "Papa? Are you okay?" He probably wasn't eating right, probably was sneaking candy bars and extra salami, plus a glass or two of red wine every night. She should have fixed him meals before she left, single servings he could pull from the freezer. Poor man, he sounded tired, and why wouldn't he be? He spent hours on his feet at the bakery and then more time fixing dinner, doing laundry, keeping the house straightened. "Why don't I come home for a few days? I could make you a pot of wedding soup and some sauce? Maybe a little minestrone?" She'd leave in the morning, get him situated, and then head back to Magdalena.

"Not necessary."

"I don't mind. Really." The more she thought about it, the more she realized her father needed her help.

"You want to come home already?"

He said it like he didn't want her home. "Just for a day or two to make you a few meals."

"Where are you?"

She hesitated, then offered a half truth. "A small town in New York that reminds me of home." He didn't need to know more than that or who else was there. "So, about those meals…"

"Viola made me wedding soup yesterday and tonight she

is making rigatoni and meatballs."

"Oh." And then, "Do you see her every night?"

Long pause. "Yes."

She opened her mouth to ask him if every night meant *all* night, but the words stuck in her throat, snuffed out by an image of her father and Mrs. Ricci naked in bed.

"I've been keeping company with Viola."

The words singed her brain, forcing unwanted visuals to bombard her. Goodness! "So, you and Mrs. Ricci are a couple?" She squeezed her eyes shut, waited for the inevitable that came seconds later.

"Yes."

How could one word convey so much? "And that's why you didn't get my messages, right? You've been staying at Mrs. Ricci's."

Long pause. "I have been staying at Viola's."

"Well then." Her father didn't need her food or her company, not when he had a sixty-something woman on the hunt for companionship at his side. Ugh. She could not think about that, not now.

"I am happy, Elise. Viola makes me laugh."

Sure she does. "Great. That's really great." At least he couldn't see her face through the phone because if he could, he'd see the shock and pain there. Or maybe he wouldn't; maybe her father was so caught up with Viola Ricci he could see nothing but that dyed red hair and those fake pearls she wore.

"We're going to a dinner theater in Sinclaire."

"That's two hours away." She clutched her phone, sucked in a breath, and asked, "Are you staying overnight?"

"We are."

He'd answered yes to every question she asked. What was next? *Are you going to marry Viola,* followed by a yes? Adult children should not be subjected to the dating and overnight trips of their senior-citizen parents. Obviously, her father wasn't pining for her, wishing she'd make a quick trip home to do a load of laundry or run the vacuum.

"Elise."

She recognized that tone in Dominic Pentani's voice. It said, *You are acting like a child*. Well, maybe she was, or maybe she wanted to protect her father from making a fool of himself. Since when did the man who made her pancakes in special shapes like hearts, flowers, and her initials start having sleepovers with the woman he sat beside at Mass? "I just don't want you to get hurt, Papa."

"You no worry about me. You worry about Elise."

Chapter 11

Michael and Nick sat on separate beds in the hotel room, legs stretched out, a six-pack between them. The kids were in the adjoining room, watching television and eating popcorn. He'd been careful about the sugary drinks, limiting them to one, and said a big no to the supersize candy bars they tried to con him into. Popcorn or nothing had been his offer, and no surprise, they'd taken the popcorn and a bottle of water. Michael turned to Nick and said, "Thanks again for meeting me. I know it was short notice, but I appreciate it."

"Sure, happy to do it." Nick took a swig of beer, rested the bottle on his thigh.

"Alex didn't mind?"

His brother sliced him a look that could mean anything and said, "She's making pasta with Mom and Gracie, and a batch of chocolate chip cookies, and who knows what else?"

"And that's a bad thing? I wouldn't mind if somebody made me pasta and cookies."

Nick scowled. "I'll bet you would if it came with an interrogation. You know Mom and Gracie will be nosing around, trying to pin down information on the subject they've become obsessed with and won't let go."

"Which is?" Actually, Michael would have thought he and Elise would be the big topic of conversation in the Androvich household, probably the whole town. What could trump getting stiffed at the altar?

"A baby." Nick blew out a disgusted sigh. "Mom started on me about a month ago; you know how she slips in those comments, not really a straight-out question, but more of an observation, like, 'There's nothing like a new baby in a family' or 'How old is Alex?' Of course, she knows exactly how old Alex is, but she wants me to know that my wife isn't getting any younger and if we don't get going, she'll hit 'advanced maternal age.' As if I'm not a doctor who deals with this kind of stuff."

Michael shook his head, took a long pull on his beer. "Better you than me, buddy."

"It's annoying, and Alex doesn't know how our family is. She grew up with an aunt and uncle who never showed any emotion and wouldn't recognize one if it sat in their lap. Walter's come around, but I don't exactly see him pouncing on her for baby details. No, that's *our* family's style."

"But we never pounce," Michael added, recalling the years his mother was after him about his drinking, his carousing, his recklessness. She'd been right but that didn't mean he wanted to hear it. "Our family lays the groundwork for the inquisition and then tag-teams to get information from the victim." He pointed his beer bottle at Nick, said, "You better warn your wife that Mom might look innocent, but she could sit on a judge's bench. Gracie's no better, especially when she thinks she's right."

"How do you tell your wife that your family's nosy and can extract information without you knowing it's being extracted?"

That made Michael laugh. "Tell her, welcome to a big family. Nothing's secret and nothing's sacred. Everybody has an opinion and they aren't afraid to give it, whether it's asked for or not." He rubbed his jaw, smiled. "I'm just glad you're on the hot seat for a change instead of me."

"Yeah, well, don't think they haven't been sniping about you. I had to hear how you're going to have to face what happened sooner or later, get over it, and find 'forgiveness in your heart' because Elise Pentani's the best thing that ever happened to your sorry ass." He paused, grinned. "I added the 'sorry ass' part."

"Thanks. I don't suppose you stuck up for me, did you?" His sister had cried ten buckets of tears when she realized he'd been stood up at his own wedding; even Stella's strong exterior cracked a bit. But neither had offered an opinion or comment. That was the Androvich way, let the truth settle in and *then* take a jab.

"I tried, but you know how Mom and Gracie are when they're working together. It's a no-win situation. Besides," he slid Michael a look that said he was about to take his own jab, "I think they might be right."

Damn. Nick had steered clear of the subject of Elise the entire night, and Michael had relaxed enough to think his brother wasn't going to bring her up, when *bam*, he did it. "We're not discussing her."

"I know. So, you probably don't want to know that she came to see Mom and spilled her heart and enough tears that Mom had to mop up the kitchen floor when she left."

"Right." He pictured Elise, eyes red, nose swollen, drenching the cracked linoleum in his mother's kitchen.

"Then I probably also shouldn't tell you that the next flood of tears came when Alex visited her, told her how you were the one who made me listen when she and I had our issues."

Interesting that Nick remembered the lies and betrayal behind his wife's presence in town as "issues." They were a helluva lot more than issues, but maybe that's what happened when you forgave someone: you let go of the harsh truth and softened it up with time and forgiveness. He wouldn't know about that. "I didn't ask anybody to get involved and if my ex-fiancée fell apart, well then, I guess she should have thought about that before she accused me of something I didn't do."

Nick threw him a disgusted look. "Don't be such an asshole. She's hurting, big time. I had to practically force her to take a leave of absence. She didn't want to, but she needs time to figure out what she's going to do with the rest of her life." He paused, added, "Especially if you're not in it."

"She'll figure it out; she's a resourceful woman." The words spilled out as though he didn't care, but his chest pinched when he thought of her in pain. Would he ever stop caring?

"Glad you're so concerned. Guess you don't care that she's left town."

Michael studied the label on his beer bottle, scrubbed the emotion from his voice, and said, "Where'd she go?" Nick didn't know Elise was in Magdalena.

"Dunno. She told Dominic she was going to visit a few small towns and take in the sights. Maybe head to New York State or Ohio. Or maybe Maine. Not sure." He scratched his head, frowned. "I haven't given it much thought, but that doesn't sound like a great plan when I say it out loud: a woman traveling alone, no destination, no one looking for her to be a certain place at a certain time. Maybe I should call her to make sure she's okay."

"I'm sure she's fine."

Nick stared at him, his jaw tense, his words measured. "She might not be part of your life anymore, but don't you care if something happens to her?" He ran a hand through his hair, sat up on the edge of the bed, and reached for his phone.

Michael snatched it from the nightstand and tossed it on his bed. "You don't need to call her."

"I know I don't, but I'm going to anyway." He stood, made his way to the other side of Michael's bed, and grabbed his phone. "I won't mention your name, okay? I just want to make sure she hasn't ended up in Utah or in somebody's trunk."

"Don't."

Nick sighed. "This isn't about you; it's about Elise."

"I know where she is." Damn, this would start a shit

storm of questions.

"What?"

When Nick's voice took on that edge, it was never a good sign. It spelled *pissed*. Michael shrugged, dreading his next words. "She's in Magdalena."

"Magdalena." Pause. "The same town as you."

"Right."

"Are you sharing the same room, too?"

Now it was Michael's turn to be pissed. "No. She's in the honeymoon suite. I tried to get her to leave when I found out she was there, but she refused to go, said she had every right to be there and I had to deal with it."

His brother tried to hide a smile. "I can picture it. Boy, do I wish I were privy to that conversation."

"No, you really don't. The woman wears me out and refuses to listen."

"Uh-huh." Nick crossed his arms over his chest. "Sounds about right."

"How is it that she's occupying so much of my brain and I'm not even with her anymore?" That was a question he'd been wondering since she showed up in Magdalena.

"You really don't know?"

Michael grabbed another beer, twisted off the cap, and took a long pull. "If I knew, I wouldn't have asked you." If he knew, he'd get a lot more sleep at night instead of the restlessness that invaded his brain every time he put his head on a pillow. Though, he hadn't had that problem the night Elise got tanked and he slept beside her. No, that night he'd drifted off in minutes, the sound of her breathing lulling him to sleep.

Nick shook his head as if what he was about to tell him was something Michael should have figured out by now. "The reason Elise is suffocating your brain is simple. You're not over her, dumbass." His dark eyes zeroed in on him, softened. "And you're never going to be."

***

It was dinnertime when Michael got back to Magdalena, but he wasn't ready to head back to the Heart Sent, not when his brain was still swirling with Nick's revelation. His brother had to be wrong—he just had to be. Worse, had been the pitiful expressions Kevin and Sara gave him when they asked if they were ever going to see Elise again. You'd have thought he was the one who'd done her wrong. What a mess. He'd avoided an answer, telling them instead that maybe soon he'd bring them to Magdalena for a visit. That had gotten them sidetracked and earned a scowl from his brother.

Sometimes a guy did what he had to do in order to keep things in line. Avoiding a direct answer regarding his ex-fiancée was understandable and made sense to him, even if it made no sense to anyone else. He'd gotten Nick to swear he wouldn't tell anyone that Elise was in Magdalena or that she was staying in the honeymoon suite. That would just stir up more crap than he could think about, starting with his mother and sister, and ending with half the town putting in their five cents. He was pretty sure Elise would not appreciate people knowing she was camped out in a honeymoon suite by herself. That was wrong on so many levels, and yet part of him understood why she'd done it. Hell, part of him almost wanted to camp out there, too...with her. But the other part, the still hurt and pissed part wanted to forget he'd ever asked about the Heart Sent and those stupid pink rose petals.

Michael parked in front of Lina's Café and headed inside for what Bree called the best homemade pies she'd ever tasted. Of course, she hadn't tasted Elise's banana cream pie. The place reminded him of an upscale version of Hot Ed's, minus the fried sausage and peppers smell.

"Howdy." An older woman with a bun snapped her gum and motioned for him to follow her. "New in town, aren't you?"

"I am." He smiled at her and slid into a booth.

"You that boy from Pennsylvania who's working with Rex MacGregor?" Her gaze narrowed on him like she'd already figured out he was.

"That's me." His smile spread. "Michael Androvich."

She nodded, her bun flopping back and forth. "I'm Phyllis. Rex told me about you. So did Bree." She paused, gave him the once-over. "That girl hit the nail on the head, she sure did."

Whatever that meant. "I hear I'm going to have to try out your pies." He tapped the menu on the Formica table and said, "But I could go for a burger."

"Sure. Burgers are great, with all the toppings to go with it, hand-cut fries, too. How about it?"

Of course he said *yes*. A place like this was bound to have good burgers, and who could resist a hand-cut French fry? His ex-fiancée had done her damnedest to retrain his taste buds, but there was no retraining the taste of a burger and fries. Or pizza. When Elise ordered pizza, she reworked the whole damn thing, switching thick crust for thin, tossing out the pepperoni, sausage, and extra cheese, and smothering the top with vegetables. No wonder the pizza tasted so good last night; it tasted like *pizza* instead of a vegetable garden. Michael glanced around the diner, taking in the glass case filled with desserts, the old-school stools and countertops.

He was comparing this place to Hot Ed's when Phyllis delivered a plate heaped with French fries and a hamburger. "Now save room for dessert. We make the best coconut cream pie this side of the Ohio state line. Strawberry-rhubarb, too, when it's in season. Take your time and think about it. I'll get you some extra napkins; you're going to need them."

Michael thanked her and bit into the burger. It was better

than Hot Ed's, juicier with a zest he couldn't identify. Of course, he would never admit this; Bernie at Hot Ed's had been cooking up burgers for as long as Michael could remember and it's what he did. Was the guy even married? Hard to remember more than his claim to fame, which was his sausage and pepper subs and his burgers and fries.

Michael was thinking about burgers when the door jingled open and a girl and a man entered. The girl looked to be about fifteen or sixteen with long, curly black hair and thick glasses. The man was about Michael's age, tall, broad-shouldered, dark-haired. The girl spoke first. "Can I get a piece of coconut cream pie for Uncle Harry? It's his favorite and I want to make sure it doesn't get sold out."

Something in her voice and facial expression made Michael glance at her again, zero in. It was then that he realized she had Down syndrome.

The man sighed and turned to her. "There will be more pie tomorrow, Lily. We don't have to buy it all up tonight."

"Christine said we have to bring her home coconut cream pie because that's what the baby wants." She giggled and rubbed her stomach. "And we have to keep the baby girl in her tummy happy."

Another sigh, followed by a smile, and a squeeze on the shoulder. "What will you do if it's a boy, Lily? Hmm?"

She grinned up at the man who had black hair like hers. "It won't be, Nate, you'll see. It's going to be a girl and we'll call her Joy. Joy Elizabeth Desantro."

He laughed, threw an arm around her, and pulled her close. "We'll see about that. Why don't we stick to the pies for now?"

"Okay." She wiggled out of his embrace and leaned close to the glass case. "I want the banana cream pie, Christine wants coconut cream pie, Uncle Harry wants coconut cream pie, and—" she turned, looked at the man she called Nate

"—what do you want? Raspberry?" She giggled. "Your unfavorite? Or your very favorite, blueberry?"

"Actually, I was thinking about an éclair."

She shook her head and her curly hair fluttered around her shoulders. "You can't, Nate. This is pie night. Besides, Pop said the new lady at the bakery makes the best éclairs he's ever tasted."

"What new lady?"

The girl shrugged. "Dunno, but you should get pie tonight and tomorrow we'll get éclairs!"

He laughed. "You're a tricky one, Lily."

"I know. Uncle Harry says I'm a trickster."

The man shook his head and turned toward the counter where Phyllis, the waitress, stood. "Hey, Nate. Hi, Lily. Looks like pie night, huh?"

Michael ate his burger and fries and took it all in, like he was watching a rerun of Restalline. He'd never believed in butting into other people's business because he didn't want people butting into his, but this guy, Nate, and Lily had him curious. It seemed that Nate was married to Christine, who was pregnant. Lily thought Christine was having a girl—Joy Elizabeth. And Pop? Who was he? And what about the éclairs? The bakery must be the one he'd visited looking for sugar cookies. A young, pregnant girl with red hair had waited on him and promised to call if the "real" baker made sugar cookies. So who was—

"Are you planning to have a piece of banana cream pie tonight?"

The girl named Lily stood next to his table, eyes wide behind her thick glasses, her expression serious. "I hadn't thought about it," Michael said, keeping his voice soft, his words gentle. "Why?"

She leaned toward him, whispered, "I took the last piece, but if you really want it, I'll get the cherry. It's good, too."

Michael rubbed his jaw, considered her offer. "Is banana cream your favorite?"

"Yup." She nodded, gave him a big smile. "Right next to pizzelles."

"I like pizzelles, too. And banana cream pie…and cherry pie…and blueberry pie… I don't think there's a pie I don't like." He paused, rubbed his jaw again. "Well, I don't like cabbage pie. Or onion pie."

Lily giggled. "Or broccoli pie!"

"Or asparagus pie."

"You're silly." She giggled again. "I'm Lily." She thrust out a hand. "That's my brother, Nate."

"Hello, Lily." Michael took her hand, smiled into the bluest eyes he'd ever seen. "I'm Michael."

***

She heard him walk up the stairs and open his door. If there were ten people outside, she'd recognize Michael Androvich's purposeful stride, the determination of step that said he knew where he was going and no one was getting in his way. Elise didn't need to check her watch to know it was after 8:00 p.m. She'd been sitting in the overstuffed chair in her room since 6:40 p.m. when she helped Mimi dry the last dish from the grilled chicken salad they'd had. Mimi hadn't questioned her when she said she was tired and planned to head to bed early. They both knew it was an excuse to sneak away before Michael returned from his trip, but what Mimi didn't know was that Elise planned to confront him about the other night as to what happened and, more specifically, whether he'd spent the night next to her.

One quick look in the mirror and she was out the door and down the hall. She knocked and waited. Having this discussion with her ex-fiancé was the last thing she wanted to do, especially in the room where he slept, but what were her choices? Talk in the doorway? Wait until she spotted him in Mimi's dining room? Or, maybe try to catch him around and about in Magdalena? The last was a definite absolutely not. That idea was worse than any of them.

"Elise?"

She blinked and there he was, strong, handsome, stripped down to a T-shirt and jeans, looking tired and vulnerable. He needed a shave and, from the circles under his eyes, a long nap. "Can I talk to you for a second?" He hesitated, glanced away, and rubbed his jaw. "Please, Michael, I need to talk to you."

He stepped aside and let her in but didn't close the door, as if he didn't trust what might happen if he did. Elise took in the duffel bag on the bed, the flannel shirt flung over the chair, the boots lying side by side. He'd never quite gotten the hang of putting his clothes away, preferring instead to "stack" them on his dresser for easier access. She'd almost gotten him to actually use the drawers when—

"You needed to talk to me?"

She nodded, clasped her hands together. "I want to apologize for the other night when I," she paused, cleared her throat, and forced out the rest, "when I wasn't myself."

His lips twitched, and this time it was his turn to clear his throat. "That's one way of putting it."

He was not going to let her off easy. She settled her gaze on the vicinity of his chin, a strong chin she'd kissed many times. That memory made her aim for his jaw but that also proved dangerous territory. As did his neck, and his shoulders, biceps, too…and those forearms…oh, and that flat stomach… Elise shook her head, tried to block out the memories of Michael Androvich's toned and tantalizing body and said, "You know I'm not used to drinking and I got carried away. I'm sorry you had to witness the results."

"No big deal. I always wondered what you'd look like drunk." She shot him a look that made him smile and goad her in earnest. "It's good to know you're human like the rest of us."

Elsie frowned and muttered, "Apparently I was a little *too* human."

That made him laugh. "It's really no big deal."

But what about the rest, was that a big deal? And what really happened? Did you sleep next to me, hold me tight like you used to as you drifted off to sleep, your cheek against my hair? "What happened?" Michael shoved his hands in his pockets and fidgeted. Oh, he did not want to answer that question. Would he, and if he did, would it be the truth, or a fabrication to avoid a situation he clearly wished to avoid?

He took so long to answer she didn't think he would, but then he dragged his gaze to hers and said, "I carried you upstairs, helped you to the bathroom, waited for you to be sick, and put you to bed."

There was something about how he said that last part that caught her attention. He was trying very hard to strip the emotion from his voice, but it sifted through, took hold of her chest and squeezed. "Did you stay with me?"

He shrugged. "For a while."

"In bed?"

His eyes turned dark, glittered in challenge. "Yeah."

She hadn't been dreaming when she smelled his scent on the pillow the next morning. He'd stayed with her, and she knew even if he didn't admit it, that he'd held her close, maybe even buried his face in her hair like he used to do. But why? Before she could consider the intelligence of the question, she blurted out, "Why would you stay with me, Michael?"

His full lips opened and out poured what might be the truest words he'd spoken in weeks. "Hell if I know."

That answer was so Michael. What had she expected—a

declaration of hope and promise and a let's-try-again? Michael didn't think in philosophical terms, and he hated when people overanalyzed what he said he knew in his gut. Instinct, he called it. She'd gotten him to agree that he knew things in his heart, too. But that last one was long gone, and if it weren't, he'd never admit it still existed, might claim it had never existed at all. Elise blinked hard, fought to keep the tears locked up until she made it back to her room. He could pretend she hadn't mattered to him, but that's all it was—pretending. "Thank you for helping me."

"No problem."

The nonchalance in his words hurt. "You know, whether you admit it or not, there was a moment or two when we were really happy, when we believed we'd be together forever." Her voice filled with sadness. "Maybe you don't want to remember those moments, but they did exist. Goodnight, Michael, thanks again." She crossed the threshold of his door, made it three steps down the hall.

"Elise." She turned, found him next to her, his expression a mix of confusion and uncertainty. "I remember every single minute with you." He clasped her face with his big hands, kissed her with such gentleness she almost cried. "And it's the remembering that's killing me," he murmured against her lips, seconds before he pulled her into his arms, held her so tight she felt his heart beating. Then he released her, stepped back as if he didn't know what had come over him. Seconds later he was back in his room, the door clicked shut behind him.

And Elise was once again alone.

Chapter 12

"Do you ever stop talking?"

"What?"

"Do you ever stop talking?"

What kind of question was that? "That's a silly question." Michael slid Bree a look that said he didn't think so. She huffed and decided to tackle Michael Androvich's lack of social skills. "That is not a polite question, in case you didn't know."

He stared at her. "I know."

She shook her head. Had his mama really not taught him manners? Everybody knew that if you wanted to make a point or correct another person's behavior, you did not tackle it head on. Instead, you slid into it, kind of rolled around like her dog did when she wanted to play, and then you got in position and said something like, *You sure are chatty today.* Or, *You're in a good mood, talking up a storm.* You didn't say, *Do you ever stop talking*, because that implied you talked too much, which she didn't, and it also implied annoyance on the speaker's part, which, of course, he was, because *"annoyed"* was Michael Androvich's middle name. Yup, Michael "Annoyed" Androvich. "For your information, there are a lot of times when I'm not talking." He raised a brow. "When I'm eating—"

"Uh-huh. You talk when you eat, too."

Bree ignored him, ignored what might be a twitch of his lips that said he was trying to get her riled up, or maybe he was making fun of her. Neither set well. "If you're going to laugh at my expense, then I'm not going to have this conversation." She folded her arms over her chest, waited.

"Okay." He turned back to his charts.

"Even though talking is what people do when they have questions or want to be civilized." The man didn't answer, didn't even look up. "It's called manners." She waited for a response, got none. "Fine then. If I have something to say to you, I'll write a note or send you an email. Fine, that's what I'll do and—"

"Bree?"

She glared at him. "What?"

"You're talking."

Dang that man! She swung around and pulled out the customer orders for the month. See if she'd say one word to him the rest of the day. Maybe she'd never talk to him again, see how he'd like that. No wonder he had relationship issues; the man had no idea how to *relate*.

The soft rumble of laughter jerked her from the many reasons the man in this room had relationship issues. Her gaze narrowed on the source of the laughter. Michael Androvich sat back in his chair, arms crossed over his chest, laughter spilling from those dang lips. Real laughter, too, not the polite fake kind some people use when they're only doing it to prove a point. This one came from his belly and his brain, maybe his heart, too. "Why are you laughing?" Even as she asked the silly question, she knew the answer. The man was laughing at *her*.

He shook his head. "You are so damn easy to torment." Another bubble of laughter, this one softer, less powerful. "Worse than my sister. She's a talker, too. Thank God she got married and now she shares the words with her husband." He ran a hand over his face, sighed. "It was damn exhausting to listen to her."

Bree knew she'd like his sister. This was the one her daddy said ran Androvich Lumber. Maybe when Bree took over the company she'd get to meet her. They probably had a lot in common, starting with their thoughts on Michael and his lack of social skills and ending with ways to make it in a male-dominated business. "I'd like to meet her someday."

"Bet you would. Two peas in a pod, and I'll lay odds Gracie can run circles around you with her words. But then, I've shut out half of whatever you said, so I haven't given your ability to challenge Gracie my full attention."

"Such kindness. You've just admitted you've been ignoring me. How do you know you haven't missed some very relevant information?"

"Like telling your mother to pick up diapers and dish detergent?"

Bree sniffed, shrugged. "That can be important. You might need to know which diapers to buy one day." The second those words slipped out, she regretted it. "Sorry. Really. I shouldn't have said that."

"It's fine." The dark eyes turned darker. "Let it go."

For once, Bree did just that, not because she wasn't going to circle around on that subject again at some point, but because she wanted to keep him talking right now. He was actually almost human when he talked—imagine that! "You know studies have been done that say a woman has so many words stored inside of her and she has to use them. That's why women talk so much, or most do, anyway. My friend Gina doesn't, and neither does Tess." She scratched her jaw, considered Christine. Nope. "Neither does Christine." She smiled, shrugged. "I don't know but I read it somewhere."

He didn't respond to that other than to shake his head again and study her like a butterfly pinned to a corkboard. When she started to fidget and opened her mouth to say something, *anything* to stop the stare, he tossed his pencil on the desk and said, "Grab your coat. We're going for a ride."

"Where?"

Michael stood and a slow smile stretched across his lips. "To a place your daddy showed me that's as close to heaven as you'll find. And I guarantee, even you will not have the words to describe it."

***

Of course, Bree Kinkaid yammered the entire trip to Rex's acreage; on and on she went about growing up in Magdalena, her kids, even how she'd eaten bags of blue Jordan almonds in hopes she'd have a boy. Talk about messed-up crazy. Michael didn't say anything, let the words suffocate the cab of the truck and seep out the vents. But when she mentioned her husband, her tone changed, grew hesitant, maybe sad was a better description and that put him on alert. He'd grown up with a sister and had spent enough time around women to know their moods. Happy, sad, pissed… Whether he wanted to acknowledge those moods that in his later years often had to do with him was another matter. Pretending ignorance was the safest bet: better yet if he grew testy with the women. That usually made them change their tune, but why would a woman put up with that crap? Why wouldn't she tell him to take his attitude and go take a hike? He'd only ever been with one woman who did that, and Elise Pentani had taken him straight to hell. Still, if he cut out the ending, it had been one helluva ride.

So what was up with Bree and "Husband of the Year"? It wasn't like he was about to ask because the little he knew about Bree Kinkaid told him she'd spit out way too much information. He danced around the subject of the husband and circled back to her kids, three girls, and from the sounds of it, a handful. She chatted on about dance class, soccer, and other nonsensical information, and the husband didn't come up again. That alone made him decide to meet this Brody character and size him up, make sure he wasn't the abusive type. There'd been a case of that in Restalline involving a supposedly mild-mannered science teacher. Goes to show, you just never knew.

They reached Rex's acreage and Michael pulled the truck onto the dirt road that led deep into the land the man claimed as his daughter's future. He stopped the truck a few miles in and hopped out. It was one thing to see the woods from a vehicle, but to stand among the trees, breathe in the scent of pine, bark, and damp earth? Hear the animals rustling in the brush, the birds and squirrels chirping, witness the magnificence of it all? Well, that was damn incredible.

When Bree stepped out of the truck, she stopped talking. Just like that. Maybe Michael had underestimated her ability to appreciate what he called heaven in the form of acres and acres of clean air, wood, and earth. While he'd hoped the raw beauty of the land would freeze her tongue and render her unable to jabber about anything, he had not expected the tears. Buckets of them. Uncontrollable. Shoulder shaking. Too damn many of them. Tears made him queasy, especially when they spouted from a woman. He'd only seen his mother cry a few times, the worst when they dragged his father from the woods. The sound stayed with him all these years later, marked with such pain he wanted to puke when he thought about it. Maybe that sound was one of the reasons he'd buried his feelings deep, covered them with enough resistance to ignore the occasional pecking that said, *Let the emotion out, just let it go.* But he couldn't, not until Elise, and then he'd dumped it all on her like Niagara Falls. Damn good that had done.

Bree's avalanche of tears began about twenty seconds after they stepped out of the truck. She lifted her face to the slivers of sky poking through the trees, closed her eyes, and drew in a breath. She didn't say a word. The shoulder shaking started first, like she was doing some weird exercises involving shoulder muscles, but then she got her head going, bobbing back and forth, eyes squeezed shut. Michael narrowed his gaze on her, worried she might heave all over his boots. Then came the tears that reminded him an awful lot of the time the pipe burst under the kitchen sink and they had water everywhere. Pain in the ass that was, but he'd take ten busted pipes if he didn't have to deal with one crying woman. He stood a few feet away, counting the seconds, fixing his gaze on the naked trees and snow…anywhere but on the woman and her distress. Didn't help and didn't stop the tears. Nothing did until he held out a hand and pulled her into his arms, patting her back like he did with the kids. That helped. Surprising what human touch and a drop of compassion could do. A few more sniffs and the tears shifted to whimpers, then stopped. Thank God.

He'd expected the talking to come next, reasons and excuses for the flood of tears and emotion, but they hadn't. Not one word. Bree had eased from his embrace, swiped her eyes, and asked that he take her back to the office, all the while avoiding his gaze as though she were the one who despised shows of emotion.

And now, he was back in his room at the Heart Sent and still wondered what the hell that was all about. Something was up with Bree Kinkaid and he'd bet a six-pack it had to do with her husband.

***

"Are you Brody Kinkaid?"

A big bruiser with monster biceps and a neck to match looked up from his beer and frowned. "Yeah, that's me." He scratched his jaw, squinted at Michael. "You're that guy from Pennsylvania Rex brought in."

Michael nodded, extended a hand. "Michael Androvich." Bree's husband shook his hand with the grip of an arm wrestler.

"Bree said you're doing some work for Rex." He sized Michael up as though he were deciding if he could take him in one punch or two. Silly ass probably didn't know that brawn was no match for brains. "I've seen you around, would have come up to say hello, but Rex gets his panties in a bunch if the shop people come into the office." He shook his head, muttered, "Damn bunch of prima donnas working up there."

Michael was about to ask if Brody considered *him* a prima donna, but he didn't, because the wrong answer might give the man an opportunity to try out his left hook, and it wasn't polite to start a brawl in another man's bar. O'Reilly's reminded him of Cody's in Restalline, a watering hole filled with drinks, laughter, and back-slapping—until the first punch. Then it was open season and the stranger in town always lost. He'd had his share of black eyes and bruised ribs from stupid drunken brawls, and he'd like to think he'd outgrown them, but the honest part of him knew he hadn't, which was why it was best to avoid them. "It's a busy place."

"Yeah, I guess." He slid a look at Michael and said, "So what do you think about my wife? Is she actually doing work or just making out the grocery list on that computer?" The laugh that followed said he didn't think her capable of real work.

"Oh, she's doing work all right. You should be proud of her. She's got the customers and reps eating out of her hand." He laughed and shook his head. "Even the ornery ones can't say no to Bree."

Brody Kinkaid crossed his arms over his massive chest and said, "What the hell does that mean? Are they coming on to her?" He didn't wait for an answer. "I swear if they did, I will tie them up so tight, they'll wish they'd never talked to her."

Tie them up so tight? What the hell was the guy talking about? "I'm sure they're not coming on to her. Bree would never allow that."

Brody puffed out his chest. "Damn straight she wouldn't."

"I just meant people like doing business with her. She's funny, intelligent—"

"Hey." Bree's husband took a step toward Michael, sliced him with a look. "Are *you* coming on to her?"

"What? Of course not." The guy didn't look convinced. In fact, he acted like he thought that's exactly what Michael was doing and the clenched fist said he knew what he was going to do about it. "Look, I'm not after your wife. All I was doing was paying her a compliment." Michael crossed his arms over his chest. He might not be as big as this oaf, but he could pack a good punch and when he unleashed his anger, there weren't many guys who could stand up to it.

"You sure? 'Cause I'm not having anybody looking at my wife that way."

"I'm sure; trust me on that." What was with this guy? Michael snatched his beer bottle off the bar, took a swig. He was tired of this conversation and really tired of this asshole. No wonder Bree had started bawling like her world was falling on top of her. Any woman who had to be subjected to a pinhead like Brody Kinkaid would suffocate.

"All right then." He finished his beer, swiped a hand across his mouth, and said, "We're good?"

Michael nodded, anxious to be rid of the guy. "We're good." Hell, he'd tell the guy anything to get away from him.

"One more thing." Brody pulled his lips into a wide smile. "Bree might think she's going to run the business when her old man retires, but I'll be the one steering that ship. Rex will realize she's not capable of operating in a man's world and then he'll turn it over to me." The smile spread, stretched to show gums. "And I'll be waiting. Oh, hell yes, I will be waiting."

***

There were times in Michael's life where he swore he

was on reality TV. He'd even looked for the cameras a time or two; that's how bizarre the situations had been. But no, there had never been a camera; the drama was just one more screwy chapter in his messed-up life. His ex-fiancée helped him out of the rut of expecting the worst, not looking for the good, but then she'd tossed him in a hole and stolen the bits of good he'd come to believe in.

So, tonight, after the headache conversation with Brody Kinkaid, Michael found a booth and decided on one more beer. He didn't see the woman in the tight shirt and painted-on jeans enter, didn't notice the three-inch-heel boots until he glanced at the bar. She was short, petite, with curves in the right places and an outfit that advertised those curves, along with an invitation to check them out. She wore a cowboy hat, pulled low, making it hard to see her face. He'd guess she was a looker by the men clustered around her, like bees to honey. One man rested a hand on her shoulder; another leaned in close, whispered something in her ear. A third handed her a drink, while a fourth tried to butt in. What struck Michael as odd was the woman's posture: stiff, unnatural, feet planted like she was prepared to nail somebody in the crotch if the need arose. Definitely not welcoming. He'd had enough of these kinds of women to recognize the step-by-step seduction beginning with the come-and-get-me clothes, the head-thrown-back laughter, the touchy-touchy hands on the men's bodies...but this one didn't really fit. Oh, she had the clothes down, that was for damn certain, but she wasn't laughing or touching. In fact, she looked downright uncomfortable.

He sipped his beer and watched. The man with his hand on her shoulder started massaging it, and when the woman tried to ease away, the hand followed. She removed the hand, stepped away. Good luck with that. The men inched closer, the hunter and the hunted, though sometimes it was difficult to tell which was which. Soon, one of the men would lay claim and the others would drift away. Back in the day, Michael had been the one laying claim more often than not. The sex was usually good but never worth the hassle that followed. *Call me* or *You said you'd call me* or *I thought you'd call me*. It was all such empty, ungratifying bullshit, and eventually, unless he was super horny or drunk, he passed.

Michael's attention turned back to the woman. The men had crowded out his vision, making it hard to see what was happening, though he didn't need a visual to know how this was going to play out. She and her chosen one would end up in a hot and heavy situation that would no doubt end in sex. The location could be any venue: an alley, a car, an apartment, hell, even O'Reilly's bathroom. Happened all the time.

When the woman's cowboy hat ended in one of the men's hands, he held it high, laughed as she tried to grab it. Not funny. What assholes. Michael stood to approach the group and get the hat back because his gut told him the woman did not want to be here. The man with the hat waved it back and forth as the other men drew back. It was then Michael saw the woman's face—*Elise?* He reached her in three strides, yanked the man with the hat by the arm, and snatched it from him. "Touch her again, and I'll break your jaw." Michael pushed him away, grabbed Elise's hand, and said, "Let's get out of here." She stared at him, eyes bright like she wanted to cry, and followed him from the bar. "You can get your car tomorrow," he said, once they were in the truck.

"Okay." She didn't look at him, just sat there with that ridiculous cowboy hat resting on her lap.

Michael blew out a breath, tried to calm his temper. And failed. "What the hell were you doing in there?" Of course she didn't answer. What could she say? *Seeing if I could get laid?* That thought really pissed him off. "Damn it, Elise, look at me."

"Can you just let it go?" Her voice cracked. "Please?"

Was she serious? "You want me to pretend I didn't see you in there wearing that second skin, with those guys trying to feel you up?"

She closed her eyes, rubbed her temples. "Yes."

"Well, sorry." He started the truck, pulled onto the road, his gaze darting over her. "I wish I could forget what I saw, but I'm pretty sure it will be embedded in my brain for a long while to come. You might as well tell me what happened and why, because I'm not going to let up until you do." He paused, added, "And you know how I am once I set my mind to something."

Big sigh. "Bree thought I looked like a schoolteacher; she said I needed a new look."

"Bree Kinkaid put you up to this?" Wait until he saw her; he'd tell her quick, fast, and in a hurry that she needed to mind her own business and butt out of Elise's life. His ex-fiancée did *not* look like a schoolteacher, and even if she did, what was wrong with schoolteachers? Would Bree rather she looked like a tramp?

"She meant well, and she was so excited, I couldn't disappoint her." Her voice dipped, turned soft. "Even though I knew I looked ridiculous, I couldn't say no to her." And then, "She's having a rough time right now."

Yeah, and he'd bet that rough time started and finished with Brody Kinkaid. Michael eased into the driveway of the Heart Sent. "I guess now would be when I should throw out the lecture about jumping off a bridge just because your friends do, but it never worked when my mother used it on me, so I'll save it and give you one of my own. Don't pull a ridiculous stunt like that again."

She pinched her lips together and didn't say another word as he parked the truck, followed her into the Heart Sent and up the stairs to their rooms, the cowboy hat dangling from her right hand as though she wanted to pretend it wasn't hers. Did she really think they were done talking about this? He paused at his door, debated the wisdom of forcing a conversation, tossed the debate in the trash, and went after her. She'd stepped inside the honeymoon suite, but he caught the door before she could close it. "Hey, we need to talk." There was real distress on her face, like she'd rather have a repeat of the post-mojito experience than hash out the reason behind the outfit. Too damn bad.

"Michael. Please. This is embarrassing enough; I see my mistake and it's not going to happen again."

Great. Now she was borrowing the line he used to tell his mother so she'd stop nagging him, even though he knew he was absolutely going to repeat what he'd done. Was Elise saying the words just to shut him up? He ran a hand through his hair, settled his gaze on the swell of cleavage pushing out of the skin-tight shirt. Elise had small breasts, perfect for his hand; there was no way she hadn't manufactured that look with a little help from a push-up or padded bra. But the average guy wouldn't know that; he'd think they were real, he'd dream about burying his face in the swell of that cleavage, imagine the nipples…

"Michael."

He adjusted his line of vision several inches, met her gaze. "What?" The frown she gave him said she knew what he'd been doing, didn't appreciate it either. "Sorry," he mumbled.

She grabbed a sweater, stuffed her arms in it, and held it closed with one hand. "I don't know what there is to talk about. I told you I realized my mistake and—"

"You don't need this crap." He pointed to her outfit.

"You'd be a looker in sweats and a T-shirt, and what I don't get is why you're listening to someone you don't really know about what you should wear." She bit her bottom lip, opened her mouth to speak, closed it. "What?" he asked. "Just say it."

"Bree said she thought you might like it, and she knew you were heading to O'Reilly's tonight."

He could not have heard her right. "You wore that to O'Reilly's for *me*?"

She looked away, shrugged. "You know I've always had issues with being daring and trying new things…"

"Not wanting to have sex in my truck outside of your house is not the same as wearing that outfit in public, especially in a bar." He took in the second-skin pants, the high-heeled boots, and rubbed his jaw. "If you'd wanted to prance around in that get-up at home, I would have been fine with that." Actually, more than fine as long as it was her idea and not someone else's.

A flush of crimson spread from her neck to her cheeks. "Wish I'd known."

"Wish you'd asked," he countered.

Her dark eyes glittered when she met his gaze, held it. "I wish I'd asked a lot of things."

Michael clenched his hands to keep from touching her. That was one thing about Elise: she could make him want her without realizing what she was doing. That innocence was a damn aphrodisiac he'd never been able to resist. Right now, he wanted to ease open her shirt, bury his face in her cleavage, and run his hands over that delicious body, second skin and all. Maybe she'd even wear the cowboy hat while she rode him… That thought made him hard, made him want to…

"Michael?"

Her voice spilled over him, soft and sweet as honey. He

blew out a breath, forced thoughts of sex with Elise from his brain. The other body part that was honing in on sex with Elise was not so easily distracted. "What?"

"Sometimes I wish I were more like your other women." Before he could tell her that was the most ridiculous thing he'd ever heard, right up there with second-skin clothing and cowboy hats, she continued. "I wish I could just have sex for fun and not care about the feelings that go with it." Her eyes grew bright, sparkled with emotion. "If I could, I'd have sex with you right here on this bed, all night, until we were so exhausted, we couldn't move. And tomorrow night, I'd do it again."

There was a half second when Michael couldn't think as desire consumed him, forced logic and common sense from his brain. *Sex with Elise, all night. Tomorrow, too. Sex with Elise, all night. Tomorrow, too.* Where did he sign up? He opened his mouth to tell her she would not regret it; he would please her until she couldn't think about anything but him and sex, but the tiny word *if* butted in, reworked his interpretation. She'd said, *If I could, I'd have sex with you right here on this bed…* Ah, shit. He should have known Elise was not going to have sex with him for the pure sake of sex. Why the hell not? He could do it, damn straight he could. But when he looked at her small hand holding her sweater closed, he remembered what it was like to be intimate with the woman he loved; the swelling in his chest, the pulse in his soul, the ache to become one. How the hell did he plan to have sex for the sake of sex when he'd experienced so much more with her? Simple. He couldn't. "I gotta go." Michael closed the space between them, clasped her face between his hands, and stared into her eyes. Then he planted a quick, hard kiss on her mouth and was gone.

Chapter 13

Pop had been waiting three days to meet Elise Pentani. Anyone who could bake a sugar cookie with just the right crispiness and a frosting that slid down your palate instead of leaching onto the roof of your mouth was someone he wanted to meet. He'd sampled the cupcakes and the chocolate chip cookies, too. The éclair wasn't bad either, filled with rich custard, just the way he liked them. But the real key would be the pizzelles. Could the woman pass muster? Only one way to tell, and he'd be doing the telling. He checked his watch. She ought to be here any minute.

When the doorbell rang at exactly 11:00 a.m., Pop smiled at the portrait of his Lucy and said, "She gets two gold stars for being on time. Let's check this girl out and see what's in her bag of tricks." Pop made his way to the front door, opened it, offered a smile to the petite woman with black hair like Lily's. "Elise Pentani, I presume?"

She smiled back, her face turning as bright as a seventy-five-watt light bulb. "Hello, Mr. Benito. Lucy's told me a lot about you."

"That girl's got more stories, just like her grandpa." He laughed and stepped aside so she could enter. She was a tiny thing, several inches shorter than Lucy—he shot a quick look at her belly—and several pounds lighter, too, he'd guess.

"She does keep me entertained." Elise shrugged out of her jacket, handed it to him. "I think she's told me about every person in Magdalena. I can't keep them all straight. One day she mentions Ramona, Lily, and Miriam, then Greta and Uncle Harry. And of course, Nate, Ben, Cash, all the guys she thinks are gorgeous." She smiled and shook her head. "But she always circles back to Jeremy Ross Dean, her 'friend.'"

"Hah." Pop hung her jacket and ushered her into the kitchen where he'd set out the eggs, flour, vanilla, and anise, all right beside his prized possession: his pizzelle maker. "That boy better not be sniffing around her or he'll answer to me. He's not fooling me with his yes-sir-no-sir routine. I can read between those lines faster than a Japanese beetle chomping on a hibiscus, and what I'm reading says, 'up to no good.'"

"I met him at Harry's Folly the other night. He was very polite." Her voice turned softer than whipped butter. "When he talked about Lucy, he turned redder than my father's homemade wine. Lucy said they're just friends, but I think maybe it will turn into something more."

"Well, it's not turning into anything until that boy passes the eight-point approval test." He slid her a look, lifted both hands, and began ticking off his list. "Loyalty, integrity, honesty, compassion, forgiveness, dedication, humility, and, a sense of humor. Until that boy shows me every last one of these and how they pertain to my granddaughter, I'm not giving him the thumbs-up." Elise Pentani tried to hide a smile but it poked through. "Now, enough about Lucy and that boy, I want to see about these pizzelles." He pointed to the pizzelle maker and said, "Show me what you got."

It didn't take the entire pizzelle baking session to figure out the girl knew how to bake, and given the opportunity and the exposure, she might edge Pop out of the numero uno position as the supreme pizzelle baker in town. He wasn't sure how he felt about that, but you couldn't be King of the Mountain forever, and this young lady needed a pick-me-up, so he could hand over the title of Supreme Pizzelle Baker if it came to that. What he'd rather do would be to help her get back with that Androvich boy. Oh, she'd spilled the whole sad tale before they finished baking the last pizzelle. What a mess. Staying in a honeymoon suite by yourself with the would-be groom down the hall? That would make a good tearjerker movie, but Pop had seen worse situations that ended in marriage and forever-afters. Look at Christine and Nate. And Gina and Ben. And Tess and Cash. He wouldn't go so far as to include Bree and Brody, because the jury was still out and the verdict looked cloudy.

"I'm getting hungry," Pop said when Elise laid the last pizzelle on wax paper. "How about you?"

"You mean all the pizzelles we ate weren't lunch?" She shook her head and grinned.

"'Course not. They were tests to make sure we didn't overcook or undercook them. Lunch is lunch, like a grilled peanut butter and jelly sandwich." He cocked his head to the side, studied her. "You ever had one of those? Homemade strawberry-rhubarb jelly?"

She scrunched up that little nose. "Grilled peanut butter and jelly?"

He nodded. "And homemade strawberry-rhubarb jelly. Nothing like it. Want one?"

"Um, sure."

"There's a trick to these, you know. If Lily were here, she'd make sure I did it right. Peanut butter on both sides, straight to the edges, and jelly heaped on top of one slice." He opened the fridge, pulled out the jelly, and set it on the counter. "Did you meet Lily Desantro yet?" When she shook her head, he said, "She'll be over later for a bag of pizzelles. That girl will keep you on your toes, yes, she will." Pop proceeded to make the sandwiches on wheat bread, though he would have preferred white, and explained that Lily was his checkers companion, and she was the only other person he knew who loved pizzelles as much as he did. "She makes a dang good pizzelle," he said, handing Elise their plates and motioning her to sit at the kitchen table. He poured two glasses of milk because he and Lily had decided nothing went better with grilled peanut butter and jelly sandwiches than a glass of cold milk, and sat down.

"It's gooey," Elise said, staring at the peanut butter oozing from the sides of the bread.

"Yup. Just use your spoon to scoop up whatever spills on the plate." He picked up his sandwich, took a bite. "Mmm." Elise nibbled her sandwich, still working on her first bite to Pop's third. "Well?"

She looked up, smiled. "It's good."

"Sure is. I used to make these for my Lucy when she got the cancer and nothing tasted good. She favored it cut in fours, ends trimmed, and only cherry jelly, nothing else."

"I'm sorry about your wife. You must miss her."

Pop nodded. "I do, but she's always with me." He laid a hand over his heart. "Right here. No matter what." He took a sip of milk, thought about his Lucy and all the years they'd spent together, the joy she'd given him. Could Elise and this Androvich boy find that kind of joy? Maybe he could help.

"Did you ever hear the story of the woman who put too much balsamic vinegar on her salad?"

"No." Pause. "Can't say I've heard that one."

"'Course not. Talk about leaving a sour taste in your mouth. She'd ruined the salad, but what was done was done. She could either fix it or throw the whole dang thing out. Now that was a lot of salad and it had taken her a long time to prepare. What a waste to dump romaine lettuce, red onion, cherry tomatoes, and cucumber in the garbage when maybe, with a little thought and work, it could be saved. How about adding more romaine lettuce, more olive oil, more tomatoes? More something. She decided to give it a try, because once she threw out the salad, it was gone." Pop let his words sink in a few seconds. "And guess what happened with that salad?"

Elise smiled. "She fixed her mistake and everyone loved

it."

"Hah!" He smacked the table with his hand, let out a laugh that filled the room. "Exactly. She fixed her mistake." Pop sat back, settled his hands on his belly, and nodded. "Yes, she did. So you know what I think, Elise Pentani? You're like the woman who poured too much balsamic vinegar on her salad, and I think you'll figure out a way to fix your mistake." He narrowed his gaze on hers. "And that Androvich boy will love you for it."

"I don't know, Pop. We're not talking about a salad."

Poor girl, she sounded so pathetic. "No, we're talking about mistakes and second chances. If I had to guess, I'd say that boy's hurting as much as you are. But he's scared and he's proud and a man doesn't do well when his woman shows the world she doesn't believe in him. You're gonna have to figure out a way to let him see that's not the case, that you *do* believe in him, and you'll stand beside him, no matter what."

She blinked, blinked again. "I don't know what else to do."

Pop reached across the table, patted her hand. "Don't you worry; relationships are Pop's specialty. We'll have you and that Androvich boy honeymooning for real at the Heart Sent soon enough, yes indeed we will." He squeezed her hand and said, "Now let's get Lily's pizzelles boxed up; she'll be here soon."

They had just enough time to clean up the kitchen and box up two dozen pizzelles when the doorbell rang. Dang, but Lily kept better time than a watch. Pop opened the door and there she was, looking fresh and spry with a yellow headband and matching scarf. He held out his arms and said, "How's my best girl?"

Lily stepped inside, gave him a quick hug and said, "I'm your third-best girl, Pop. First is Mrs. Benito, then Lucy, then me."

Pop laughed and nodded. "Right you are, Lily. Now why can't we have our checkers game today?"

"Mom and I have to babysit Anna while Nate and Christine go to some dinner thing." She squinted at him from beneath her thick glasses and said, "I think we're making pizza tonight." She grinned. "And I'm taking your pizzelles. Do I have to share?"

"Do you plan to eat twenty-four of them all by yourself, Miss Desantro?"

She giggled, replied, "Maybe."

"Uh-uh. Share." Pop nodded and turned toward the kitchen. "Lily, I want you to meet my new friend, Elise Pentani. She's visiting from Pennsylvania."

Lily moved toward Elise, her steps slow, cautious. "You're the lady from the bakery. Christine gave me one of your chocolate peanut butter cupcakes," she paused, added, "and an éclair. Yum, they were so good. Do you have more at the bakery?"

"I don't know if there are any left, but I can make more." Elise shook Lily's hand and said, "It's very nice to meet you, Lily."

The child nodded. "You, too. I think you should stay at the bakery and Barbara should retire."

Pop had heard more than one pleased customer share Lily's sentiment. If Barbara Germaine weren't such a stingy sourpuss, people might enjoy visiting her store. But that dang woman was so worried about giving away a crumb that most of the town preferred to buy the baked goods she sold to Lina's Café instead of visiting the bakery and risking Barbara's orneriness. "Elise is just visiting, Lily, but we're gonna enjoy her talents while she's here, aren't we?"

"Yup." Lily stepped closer to Elise, honed in on her hair. "You have hair like mine. Long. Black. Curly." She glanced at Elise. "Is your hair at least eight inches long?"

"I...I don't know. I never measure it, but maybe."

Lily turned to Pop, said in a matter-of-fact voice, "Do you have a ruler? I want to measure Elise's hair."

Oh, he knew where this one was going, had seen it coming the second Lily zeroed in on Elise Pentani's hair. This was going to be interesting, sure was. If Elise could wiggle her way out of what was coming down the pike, then she'd have no problem with the Androvich boy. Pop made his way to the kitchen, opened the "junk" drawer where he kept gizmos like twist-ties, rubber bands, paperclips, and the handy-dandy tape measure Nate had given him. He grabbed the tape measure and handed it to Lily. "Here you go. Now don't snap her head with it." He winked at Elise, who looked more confused than nervous. The nervousness would come once she heard Lily's plan. "I'll help you."

Finally, Elise spoke. "Can I ask why you're measuring my hair?"

"Paige Wright is sick and she lost all her hair. She's eleven." Lily eased the tape measure down Elise's back while Pop held the base in place. "She got a wig." She paused, scrunched her nose at the hash marks on the tape. "Paige's mom says there's lots of kids who need wigs and I have lots of hair...so do you." She squinted, read, "Fourteen inches. Wow, lots of hair."

Pop knew the second Elise figured out what Lily wanted her to do. Poor thing, she froze like an arctic blast had dumped on her. Not a word out of that mouth either. Lily's words probably froze her brain, too. Time for Pop to step in and thaw Elise a bit, give her an opportunity to see a way out of this dilemma. "Lily, I think what Mrs. Wright said was they were having a benefit so people could donate their hair if they wanted. She didn't say anything about *forcing* them to do it." He pinned his buddy with a look that said "enough" and took the tape measure, slipped it back in its case.

Lily frowned, stared at Elise. "Don't you want to help kids who lost all their hair? I don't want them to be bald; kids might make fun of them." She pulled her bottom lip through her teeth, said in a soft voice, "It's only hair. It'll grow back."

"I…" Elise looked at Pop like she'd been caught in a situation that was bad and worse than bad.

Lily shrugged and offered a smile. "It's okay, you don't have to. Lots of people are scared to cut their hair." She turned to Pop, signaling an end to the subject and said, "Can I have a pizzelle?"

***

"What the hell did you do to your hair?"

Michael stared at Elise's new haircut as though she'd shaved her head. Granted, she'd had twelve inches lopped off, but she still had enough for two heads and if Lily Desantro had the courage to donate her hair, then why couldn't Scaredy Cat Elise, do the same? She pasted a smile on her face and met Michael's hard stare. "I got it cut."

"Yeah, no kidding." He advanced on her, stopped when he was an arm's length away. "Why?"

Hair did not define a person and if Michael couldn't see that, then too bad. She shrugged, squared her shoulders. "Why not?"

His gaze narrowed on her hair, slid to her face. "Oh, I get it. Is this the new Elise Pentani, 'I don't give a damn, I'll do what I want'? What's next? A tattoo? Jumping out of a plane? Turning vegetarian? People do things for two reasons; to be like everybody else or because they're afraid they'll be like everybody else. So what's your reason?"

"What if I did it to be myself?"

"Yeah, whoever that is." He turned and started walking

away as if her presence disgusted him.

How dare he judge her! She rushed after him, talking to his back. "Why does it matter what I do or why? What business is it of yours?"

He swung around, glared at her. "I've got nothing against short hair or plane-jumping, or whatever else people in this world want to do. Live and let live. What I hate is how you're bouncing from one thing to another, hell bent on changing yourself into anything other than the person you are. You say you want to be yourself, well, *who the hell is that*? There might have been some things about the Elise Pentani I knew that needed work, but there was a helluva lot of good in that person, too." His voice dipped, his expression turned fierce. "But she's gone in hiding and I don't know if she's ever coming back. You see, the new Elise is trying to snuff her out, make her believe she wasn't worth anything to herself or anybody else, and that is just damn sad."

Elise opened her mouth to tell him he was wrong, that he had no idea what he was talking about, but the words wouldn't come out.

"Yeah, that's what I thought." Michael shook his head and walked away, and this time she didn't run after him.

***

"Why didn't you tell him the truth about your hair? It's for a noble cause, and throw Lily Desantro in and nobody's going to question your motives."

Elise stirred her hot chocolate and shrugged. Tess Casherdon knew about difficult men, had lived through some tragic, bitter times with Cash, but that was different. They'd found a way to get past the pain and make a future together. Michael wasn't interested in anything with Elise that involved moving forward. "Why can't I just let him go?" She set the spoon on a napkin, met Tess's gaze. "He doesn't want me; doesn't want *us*."

"I don't know about that. I'd say he's trying *not* to want you or what you lost, and I'd even venture to say he's losing that war, and that's why he's so grumpy."

"Grumpy?" Elise laughed. "That would be an improvement."

Tess shrugged, set her mug on the end table next to her. She'd told Elise that Nate Desantro had made it for them and Cash had done the finishing work. This log cabin had been Tess and Cash's dream home before the accident that tore them apart. Now, years later, they were married, sharing this home, building a future together. "Relationships and the men we share them with, aren't always easy."

"But look at the two of you." Elise tried to keep the envy from her voice. "You've got what you always wanted."

Tess looked away, blinked. "Not exactly." When she met Elise's gaze, there were tears in her eyes. "But I'm trying to be happy with what I have. Cash and I love each other, we love being together, even if it's just a walk in the woods with Henry. The only thing missing is a child."

Elise had assumed that either a baby wasn't in their plans or *was* in their plans, but not yet. "So, you want children?"

"Desperately." Tess swiped a hand across her face. "And everywhere I look, someone is pregnant, even little Lucy Benito, who has no significant other or solid means to support herself. But she's having a baby. And then there's Bree who used to pop kids out like a candy dispenser, and Christine who is having baby number two, even Gina, the friend we didn't think would ever date, let alone get married and pregnant. Do you know the first thing I did when I met you? I zeroed in on your belly. Sick, isn't it? I did though, like I could see right through your clothes and skin and into your reproductive system. Were you pregnant? Ovulating? Thinking about getting pregnant? Were your tubes in good shape?" A tear slipped down her cheek. "It's very destructive."

How sad. Elise leaned toward Tess, placed a hand on her arm. "I'm so sorry. Do you absolutely know you can't conceive?"

"Huh, well, there's a story about that, too." The truth behind her inability to get pregnant spilled out, from the unwanted pregnancy to the almost abortion and the subsequent miscarriage, none of which Cash had known about. "Cash doesn't blame me, and I try very hard not to blame myself, but there are days when I'm eaten with guilt."

"But the doctors didn't say you couldn't get pregnant, just that it would be more difficult. Are you seeing a specialist?"

Tess nodded. "We were, but it really ruins the romance in your life. It became so mechanical that we both started to dread making love." She shook her head and Elise wondered how the woman had kept such sadness from freezing her soul. "I try to keep busy so I don't think about it, but it's always right there in this tiny corner of my brain, and it doesn't take much to get it going." She sighed, toyed with the wedding ring on her left hand. "A commercial with a baby in it, a pregnant woman...a family, even a puppy. You know what the hardest part is? I see the way Cash is with Christine and Nate's little girl, and Bree and Brody's kids. He'd make a wonderful father and I feel like I robbed him of that." Her voice cracked, split open. "I'm responsible." The tears slipped down her cheeks, to her chin, then her neck.

"Don't say that." Elise moved toward her, pulled her into her arms and patted her back. "Just because life doesn't work out the way we've planned, doesn't mean it isn't going to work out. You'll get your baby, one way or another."

Tess sniffed. "Yeah, probably four-legged ones."

"Henry might want a companion," Elise said, thinking of the Lab mix rescue who had greeted her when she arrived.

"But you have other choices. Adoption, foster care, what about one of those?"

"Yes, we're absolutely open to anything." She paused, added, "But I'm not so sure about a companion for Henry. He's more of a people dog, not a dog's dog."

Elise laughed, glad Tess could make a joke out of a situation that was tearing her apart. "What about the youth camp you told me about? It's summer and holidays, right?" When Tess nodded, Elise said, "There might be a child or two who needs extra attention. You have no idea what impact you could make on their lives." She squeezed Tess's hand. "I've seen it. We had kids in our town who just needed to know somebody cared about them." She and Nick used to work at the free clinic once a month, back when she was certain she was in love with him, and when he spent time with the kids, their faces lit up like he'd given them a Christmas gift.

"I know you're right." Tess cleared her throat and rubbed her temples. "Why is it we can't be happy with what we have, that we feel we need that one more thing, and then everything will be perfect?"

Her words pinched Elise's heart. "Human nature, I guess. I always wanted to stop the world until I got everything in order, a perfect alignment if you will; a career, a relationship, marriage, kids. But guess what? There is no perfect, or stopping until you get things in order, because the second you think your life is set, something blows it up."

"I guess we only get slices of happiness, huh, never the whole pie?" Tess's voice turned soft, dipped in sadness. "Bits of joy, for a day, a year, and maybe that's it, no guarantee they'll be there tomorrow."

"It's hard to accept so much uncertainty though, isn't it?" She and Tess were a lot alike, letting life's disappointments steal their joy, fearing the unknown, trying to control every situation, even ones they couldn't possibly control, until they exhausted themselves and those around them.

Tess's lips pulled into a faint smile. "It's miserable."

"Let's both try to find our slices of happiness and bits of joy." Elise raised her mug, saluted her new friend. "Even if it's in a mug of hot chocolate."

That afternoon forged a friendship between the two women built on loss and hope. When Elise met Cash, she was taken in by his good looks and easy charm, but there was something raw and untamed beneath the smile that reminded her of Michael. She hoped Cash and Tess would be gifted a child to love, no matter how that child came to them, and she hoped Tess would find her joy, just as she prayed she would find hers.

Chapter 14

Brody burst into Bree's office, his face redder than a candied apple and a big grin on his face. Heavens, it was wonderful to see him like this. She tossed her pen aside and smiled back. "What's got you looking like you just won the lottery?" She glanced at the paper in his hand, wondered if he *had* won the lottery. Brody and a few of his buddies in the shop played the lottery every payday, ten bucks in, along with a wish and three prayers they'd hit it big. Of course, they'd never cashed out more than a few dollars and that went straight into buying the next round of tickets. But if it made her husband happy, it was cheap entertainment. "Did you win?"

He made a face like he did when she asked him to watch a chick flick with her, and said, "Hell no, this is better than the lottery." He tossed the crumpled paper onto her desk and said, "It's my ticket out of the shop."

Bree picked up the paper, smoothed the edges, and realized it was fancy stationery. The only people she knew who still used the stuff were her high school English teacher and her mother. But when she started to read the letter, she knew neither of them had written such horribleness. Partway through, Brody sat on the edge of her desk, swung his big leg back and forth and said, "So, your old man knocked up Kathleen." He let out a laugh, slapped his knee. "If that don't beat all."

"Brody!" How could he be so cruel? "Don't say that."

His gaze narrowed on her, a smirk on his face. "Don't say the truth? Don't let anyone know Mr. and Mrs. Holier than Thou were screwing before they got married and she got knocked up? Oh, I've been waiting for this—" he crossed his arms over his chest, nodded "—a long time. Your old man thinks he can treat me like crap, toss me back to the shop and I have to take it? I don't think so." He nodded toward the letter. "That's my insurance policy against the bullshit he might try to pull."

Was he serious? He was talking about her father. "You mean you're going to try to blackmail him?"

He shrugged. "Think of it like a friendly reminder. You know, one of those I-just-want-you-to-know-I-know kind of things. Should make the transition to the front office a helluva lot easier."

Bree clutched the letter in her hand. "Where did you get this?" And how many others were floating around Magdalena?

"Mom got it in the morning's mail." He rubbed his jaw, laughed. "She couldn't wait to bring it to me. So, where is the old stud?"

That was enough. "Brody Kinkaid, you will stop disrespecting my parents this second, and I mean it."

His voice dipped. "Or what? You gonna hit me with your high heel? Give me a tongue-lashing? Honey Bee, I been waiting to get back at your old man for the way he disrespected *me*, and now I found a way. It's plain and simple. All he has to do is put me in the president's spot, like next week, and I won't say a word about any of this."

"Since when does a husband make demands like this? We're a family, Brody, and that includes my parents."

"Your daddy made it personal."

"He made a business decision and you're mad because you got the boot. Have you not figured out why he did it?" She sucked in a breath, pushed out the words before she lost her nerve. "Daddy took you out of the president slot because I'm a better choice." There, she'd finally said it.

His eyes turned to slits, his nostrils flared, and he blew out a breath like a bull about to charge. "The only reason he's giving you the damn job is because you're his daughter.

That's all."

"That is just pure wrong." She pushed back her chair, stood. "And if you can't see it, then too bad."

"I'll tell everybody about him and your mother; see how uppity they are then."

"You do that and see what happens. You'll look like a fool. And just so you know, people knew about this long before your family moved to town, but they didn't go blabbing and judging like you and your mother." It was her turn to glare and blow out angry breaths. For the very first time in her entire life, she truly disliked her husband. "If you want this marriage to last, you better keep your mouth shut. Do you hear me, Brody Kinkaid? You just better keep your mouth shut." She didn't wait for his response but grabbed her purse and headed out the door.

She returned forty-five minutes later, cried out and carrying a box from Barbara's Boutique and Bakery. Michael was back from his jaunt in the woods and if he noticed her red eyes and swollen nose, he was kind enough not to say anything. But then most men detested tears, treated them like they were a case of the chicken pox and must be avoided, no matter what.

Bree set the box of baked goods on the edge of her desk. Today's goodies included peanut butter cookies, macaroons, and brownies. Lucy said Elise still hadn't gotten around to making those pink sugar cookies, which Bree considered quite telling. First, why would Michael insist the cookies be pink with pink sprinkles unless he'd had a positive experience with them? Memories of Elise? Second, were the aforementioned cookies baked by his ex-fiancée, hand-delivered, too? Possibly even hand-fed? Oh, indeed, the plot was getting thicker than her grandma's chicken gravy. But if Elise *were* the baker, and Bree believed she was, why hadn't she produced those pink sugar cookies? Were the memories too tragic, too painful, to consider?

Enough "maybes" and "what ifs" because Bree intended to find out. She took the box and made her way to Michael's desk. "For that sweet tooth of yours," she said, handing him the box.

"Thanks." He took the box, opened the lid, and peeked inside. "Peanut butter cookies. Macaroons. Brownies," he murmured as if he wanted to inhale every one of them. Michael grinned and said, "If you want any, you better get them now before they're all gone."

"Oh, no, I'm fine, but thank you." She was not about to tell him she'd eaten two macaroons in the car and had six cream puffs sitting in a box on the passenger seat, waiting for quitting time. He lifted two peanut butter cookies, bit into one. There was nothing like watching a man enjoy his food. She used to love to watch Brody devour a 16-ounce T-bone steak, his jaws working in such earnestness, like he might grind the bone to gristle. But she was not happy with that man right now, not one bit. Blackmail! She'd bet his mother put him up to it, probably told him he deserved to run his father-in-law's company and he most certainly deserved a home-cooked meal every night from a wife who stayed at home and was not flitting to an office. In the kitchen. Pregnant. Oh, but Georgia Kinkaid made her see purple. Who would have known when she said "I do" to Brody she was also saying "I do" to his mother? Ugh. Had she really told Brody to keep his mouth shut if he wanted their marriage to last? What a horrid thing to say! Of course she hadn't meant it, but he'd been equally horrid, and whether or not his ego was bruised like a soft peach was really not the issue. Compromise and acceptance were the issue. She sighed. And tonight they'd have a discussion about that.

"You okay?" Michael asked, chewing on the second

cookie. Something in the way he asked the question said he knew she wasn't. She must look really bad to make him ask that question because he was not a man to lay out emotions on the table and dissect them. Or even ask about them. "I'm fine. Thank you." She wasn't ready to talk about her husband with anyone, not yet.

He nodded, picked up a pencil, and fiddled with it. "I've got a question for you." He studied the pencil a second, slid his gaze to hers. Oh, but those eyes were on fire. "I hear you've been giving my ex-fiancée clothing advice. Maybe hair advice, too."

Yikes! He knew she'd figured out his connection with Elise. Goodness gracious, but those eyes were sparking like they were about to burn a hole right through her.

"Well?" His voice singed her. "No comment from the woman who has a comment about everything?"

She latched onto the easiest response first. "I had nothing to do with her haircut. It's cute, though, don't you think? Very stylish and it'll be a whole lot easier to care for and—"

"What about the outfit?"

Now *that* idea had her name written all over it. Bree clasped her hands together, inched back a step, and offered a smile that flopped like pancake. "That outfit was pretty sharp, wasn't it?" She tried for another smile; this one lasted two seconds before it shriveled under that look of his. "Didn't you think the cowboy hat was a nice touch? They had matching his and hers ones—" she glanced at the top of his dark head and pictured a Stetson on it instead of that infernal Androvich Lumber ball cap he seemed to love "— but I didn't want to rush things. She was a bit hesitant, but when she came out of the dressing room in that get-up, well, I knew that was her look."

His mouth opened a tiny bit and the words slipped out. "She looked ridiculous."

"She did not!" Oh, but he was furious and that's exactly what she'd hoped for when she'd convinced Elise to buy the outfit. Bree owned a similar one but Brody wouldn't let her out of the bedroom in it.

"Yes." He crossed his big arms over his chest, stared hard. "She did."

Bree shrugged, noted the way his jaw clenched and unclenched. "A matter of opinion, but I'll bet she got your attention, didn't she?"

"Yeah, she got my attention all right. Me and every other man in O'Reilly's, but I wasn't undressing her with my eyes or pretending I was interested in what she said so I could touch her."

No, you weren't, Mr. Androvich, because you've already undressed her and touched her lots of times, haven't you? And if you could open up your heart again and give her a smidge of trust and be honest about it, you'd admit you still loved her. And then you'd admit you still wanted to be with her, marry her, have children with her. Bree tried not to smile as his words flitted through her brain. She didn't have to be an interpreter to understand what they meant. Nobody who didn't care made comments like that with as much anger and frustration as this man did. Oh, he cared all right, but he was fighting it hard. "You didn't like the way those men were looking at her, did you?"

The glare said he did not, and the snarl said she was an idiot for asking the question. She might not have a degree in psychology, but she knew people, knew what made their hearts ache.

"Are there more outfits like that one?"

Bree pretended she had no idea what he was talking about. "Of course there are more outfits like that one. Hats, too. Goodness, you don't think the manufacturer only made one, do you? It's no different from Daddy's cabinets.

There's a factory that—"

His loud and very annoyed sigh cut her off. "I meant, does my ex-fiancée own any other outfits like that?"

"Oh." *Hah*, this was going much better than planned. Michael Androvich didn't like the idea of another man seeing so many curves and wishing he could see more— without the clothes. Oh, yes indeed, this man loved his ex-fiancée and if it took a second-skin outfit, high-heeled boots, and a cowboy hat to make him realize that, well, he wouldn't be the first man roped in by his emotions. "No, she didn't buy any more, if that's what you mean." She cut him a look, smiled. "But that doesn't mean she won't."

He uncrossed his arms, stood. "She won't, and you're not going to give her any ideas, are you?"

"Me?" Bree's lips twitched. The man was on fire, smoldering with feelings. "Of course not. And while we're on the subject, why didn't you just tell me about Elise instead of keeping it stuffed inside? Did you really think I wouldn't figure it out the second I met her? That girl is carrying a weight on her shoulders that's got her tipping the scale at two hundred pounds, and you're behind it." She shook her head, placed her hands on her hips. Men really did not understand how relationships worked. "What's the story on these sugar cookies with the pink frosting and pink sprinkles, the ones you apparently are desperate to taste again, and Elise is equally determined *not* to bake? Now why wouldn't she make a silly old sugar cookie?" She eyeballed him with a do-not-BS-me look and said, "Unless there might be some serious memories in those cookies. Hmm, how about that?"

He ignored her commentary and analysis, asking a question of his own. "What do you mean Elise doesn't want to bake them? How would she do that? In Mimi's kitchen?"

Oh, she had him now. He didn't know Elise was lending

a hand at the bakery. "Who do you thinks been baking what's in that box on your desk?"

He glanced at the box of sweets, then back at Bree, his expression a mix of confusion and disbelief. "Elise?"

"Y-e-s. Elise has been helping Lucy at the bakery because Ramona Casherdon has pneumonia, and the owner's in Australia, and—"

"Stop. You're hurting my head. Is Elise working at the bakery, yes or no?"

Bree smiled, let the truth slip out. "Yes."

***

Michael headed into the opening of Rex Macgregor's woods on foot, his boots sloshing against the melting snow and decayed leaves covering the road. He'd needed to get away after Bree laid that last bit about Elise working at the bakery on him and this was the best place to think. As long as he didn't fire up the chainsaw, like the last time he tried to sort out his feelings for Elise Pentani and ended up in the hospital with a slashed arm, he'd be fine. Hell, he'd be better than fine.

In another week, the sun would turn brighter, hang around longer, and then the buds would pop, the trees would come alive, and the scrub that looked like dead twigs and branches would sprout color. He needed to get back into the woods because office sitting was not his thing. How could a person sit at a desk every day, look out a three-foot-wide window into a parking lot, see the birds but not hear them, the trees, but not touch them? It was friggin' depressing. Give him brisk air or sweltering heat and at least he knew he was alive. Soon, he'd be back at it, the only question was where. He'd gone over the proposal he had in mind for Rex's property with Gracie last night and she'd been excited about the prospect, had a few ideas of her own he hadn't thought about. Who would have believed his little sister would run the company and be so damn good at it?

Would Bree Kinkaid have the same success with her father's company as Gracie did? It would be something to see those two together, sitting in the boardroom, hashing out details about lumber and sharing a recipe or two while they were at it. Gracie wouldn't appreciate that last thought, but he hadn't meant it as a put down. He was proud of her; she'd found a way to blend family and business, and not a lot of people could say that. Bree would have a harder time with a husband like Brody at her side. What had ever possessed her to marry the guy? Maybe she'd gotten pregnant. He knew all about getting a girl in trouble and having to do the right thing. *Damn*, did he know that one. As bad a screw-up as that had been, he got Kevin and Sara out of the deal, and that made it worth it. He picked up a stick, ran his fingers over the smooth bark. Sugar maple. He picked up another, did the same. This one was beech. Tomorrow, he'd meet with Rex and see if they could come to terms on the price and specifics of the deal.

But what about Elise? *What was he going to do about her?* This is why he'd avoided relationships with women who expected you to give them a piece of your heart—and sometimes your male parts. They put them in a jar and hung onto them like trophies, and forget getting them back. Ever. Elise Pentani had his heart *and* his male parts, too, because damn if he wanted any other woman but her. Did she know it? Hell, he wasn't going to tell her and Bree Kinkaid better keep her mouth shut, because that cat-ate-the-goldfish look she gave him said she had him figured out, and he was full of bluster and bullshit. That woman should mind her own business and spend her energies trying to reel in that husband of hers. Piece of work, that's what Brody Kinkaid was, or maybe he was just a piece of crap who didn't respect his wife.

Michael couldn't find his answers in the trees that usually gave him such peace, so he headed to the one place that might actually offer help and fill his belly, too. Barbara's Boutique and Bakery smelled like chocolate and powdered sugar, but he wasn't thinking about either when he entered the bakery. No, his thoughts were on the one woman who could mix up his emotions as though they were a batch of sugar cookies—pink frosting, pink sprinkles.

"Michael! How are you?"

He smiled at the young girl with the pregnant belly and wished he could tell her he was great, life was great, she and her baby would be great, but he couldn't. Sometimes life was a lot less than bearable; sometimes it was stifling. But he couldn't tell her that, so he softened his voice and said, "I'm fine, how are you?"

Her face lit up like the twenty-five-year old star on his mother's Christmas tree. "I'm great." She pointed at the glass case filled with all sorts of goodies. "What would you like today?"

Michael glanced toward the closed door behind the counter, wondered if Elise was there. "No sugar cookies yet?"

The girl's face fell like an underbaked cake. She shook her head and springs of red curls bounced around her shoulders. "No, sorry. I thought we'd have them by now, but," she paused, cleared her throat, "they're not on the schedule yet." She leaned forward, lowered her voice, her blue eyes wide and serious. "I tried to get those cookies pushed to priority, but the baker said she couldn't fit them in."

Couldn't fit them in, huh? And why would that be other than she didn't want to remember what she was trying to forget. He knew all about that, and he should save her the headache right now and tell her that whatever plans and ploys she had wouldn't work. "I see." Michael offered the girl a smile, the kind that hinted it was just for her, and said, "May I speak with the baker?"

She glanced toward the door, her brows pulled together, lips pinched, as though on the verge of a monumental decision. "Well, I guess so." And then, "Sure. Maybe if you ask her she'll move the cookies to the number one slot."

Doubtful. "Thanks, I'll do that."

"Hold on a sec." The girl opened the door behind her, popped her head in, and called, "Can you come out here?" Michael couldn't hear the response but a few seconds later, the girl was back, hands pressed on the counter, a bright smile on her face. "She'll be out in a minute."

He nodded. "Thanks." What was this girl's name? Lina? Lisa? Laura? Damn, but he thought it started with an *L*. He'd never paid much attention to names, or words for that matter, had relied instead on moods. You could tell a helluva lot about a person from the way they walked, sat, carried themselves, even the way they ate their sandwich. Michael pretended to study the contents of the glass case so he didn't have to carry on a conversation because right now, he just wanted to find out about those damn sugar cookies.

The door opened and with it came his ex-fiancée's voice. "Look at these sticky buns, fresh out of the—" She sucked in a breath like it was her last, her hands clutching the tray of sticky buns, and stared at him.

"Hello," he said as if her presence were a mere coincidence and he'd just stopped in to buy a few cookies.

"Elise, this is Michael," the girl piped in. "He's the one I told you about who's looking for the sugar cookies. Remember?" She smiled at Michael. "They have to be extra thin with pink frosting and a dusting of pink sprinkles. Right?"

"Right," he said, his gaze fixed on Elise. "Best sugar

cookies I ever tasted. So thin, the frosting sweet, but not too sweet. But I think the trick is in the sprinkles. What do you think?" Memories flooded his brain, pulled him back to the afternoon he'd stood behind her in his kitchen, worked his hands over her shirt, traced the lines of her bra. She'd been shaking pink sprinkles on the frosted sugar cookies, but when he started to unbutton her shirt and ease it off her shoulders, she stopped. When he unfastened her bra and took her breasts in his hands, she moaned and dropped the sprinkler on the floor. Memories of an afternoon filled with hot, all-consuming sex right there on the kitchen table next to a tray of pink sugar cookies, stole his thoughts, his breath, *his heart*. He remembered all of it, and he'd bet she did, too. "So, do you think the trick's in the sprinkles?"

"I think so," the girl said, tapping her chin. "Too many sprinkles make them taste gross. Too little and it feels stingy. But if you can hit the sweet spot, then you have a winner." Her smile landed on Michael, spread.

"I think you're right." He settled his gaze on Elise. "It's all about hitting that sweet spot."

Her face turned the color of a red maple. She looked away, cleared her throat, and began placing the sticky buns in a box.

"So can you make the cookies for him? I'll help, as long as you tell me exactly what to do."

Elise didn't respond right away, a sign that she must be thinking about that afternoon in the kitchen, too. But when she spoke, there was nothing soft or sweet in her voice. "Sure," she said, fixing her gaze on the top of a sticky bun. "Why not?"

Chapter 15

Michael Androvich wanted his damn sugar cookies? Well, she'd give them to him, all twenty-four, sprinkled in pink with matching frosting, super thin, just the way he liked them. Of course, they might end up on his head, or at his feet, but he'd get those cookies. He'd come to the bakery to torment her about an afternoon she couldn't forget, and then acted like he didn't know her, like she was nothing more than a baker with an order to fill. Was that so he didn't have to explain anything to Lucy, or was it an attempt to show Elise just how much he didn't care about her anymore? Who was he kidding? He might not want to marry her, but he wanted her; she'd seen it in his eyes, in the way they followed her, honed in on specific parts of her body—neck, shoulder, thigh—as if remembering how he'd touched her there, as if he wanted to do it again.

She let herself into her room, closed the door, and set the box of cookies on the chair by the dresser. Her gaze caught the edge of the jeweled mirror Alex had given her, the one that was supposed to help her find her true self. Elise picked it up, stared. Who was the woman with the short hair and sad face who stared back at her? Where had the one gone who smiled and sang off-key, who had plans for the rest of her life with the man she loved? *That* woman had disappeared, but not until she'd messed up everything, all because of fear. Elise stared harder, focused on her eyes, her nose, her mouth. *This* woman must accept her failings; she must learn to trust, learn to accept herself. She sniffed, placed the mirror on the dresser, her anger with Michael gone. If he thought she needed cookies to remind her of what they'd shared and how she'd thrown it away, then maybe he didn't understand how much she'd loved him, how love much she loved him still. The last was insignificant; Michael was who he was: proud, strong, determined, and unbending. There would be no second chance with him, only the remembering, and that would have to be enough. She picked up the mirror again, looked into it.

Tomorrow, she would say her good-byes and then she would leave Magdalena, maybe head to another small town for a week or two, soak in the scenery and the people, compare them to Restalline and Magdalena. She'd always wanted to head west, and why not? Nothing held her back— no husband, no children, no commitments. Nothing. This was her life now and she would accept it, eventually return to Restalline, but not as Nick's nurse. With her father planning trips and outings with Mrs. Ricci, he needed someone to bake his breads, make his cinnamon rolls, and run his shop. She could do that. She would be very good at it. And when Kevin married one day, and later Sara, she would make their wedding cakes. Why not? She swiped at a tear, cleared her throat. *Why not?*

"Elise?" Michael's voice reached her through the door, followed by a knock, softly at first and then louder. "Elise? I know you're in there. I need to talk to you."

She set the mirror on the dresser, made her way to the door, and opened it. "Hello, Michael." She stepped aside so he could enter and closed the door.

His dark gaze narrowed, zeroed in on her eyes. "Were you crying?"

The smile she gave him wobbled and fell flat, so she attempted humor. "When don't I cry about something? You know me; I'm a sucker for a sad story."

"Any story in particular?" he asked, his voice gentle, curious.

She shrugged. "Not really."

He opened his mouth as though he wanted to say something, closed it. Michael didn't really want to know why she was crying, even though he already knew. It was because of him, but that was too much to handle, so he'd pretend he believed her. That's what people did when they didn't want to face tough issues; they pretended.

Elise turned and lifted the box of cookies from the chair. "For you," she said, handing them to him. He took the box, opened the lid with great care, and peered inside. The smile that slipped across his face said he was pleased, more than pleased. He removed one, took a bite. "Just like I remembered," he murmured, his gaze fixed on her lips. "Perfect."

Elise looked away, cleared her throat, and said, "Lucy was very excited about getting you those. If I didn't know better, I'd say she has a crush on you."

"What?" His cheeks turned red. "The girl's going to pop out a kid any second. Why would she have a crush on me?"

He really didn't know how attractive he was with his rugged good looks and I-don't-give-a-damn attitude. "I'm only telling you what my woman's intuition says."

"Ah." He set the box of cookies on the chair, rubbed his jaw. "And what does your woman's intuition say about why I wanted those cookies?"

He was really going to ask her that? Fine, let him ask, and she'd deliver the truth. "You don't want me to forget what I did or what I gave up."

That seemed to surprise him. "What? That is so off-base." He moved closer, stared down at her, his brown eyes glittering. "Did you consider it was because I couldn't stop thinking about that afternoon in my kitchen when you made me cookies?" He tucked a wayward lock of hair behind her ear, traced her jaw. "That I wanted to eat those cookies again and relive that day?" His fingers trailed down her neck, hovered at the base. She should move, make him stop, but she couldn't. "That maybe I was tired of fighting it, maybe I needed to taste that sweetness again."

She couldn't breathe, couldn't think to make sense of his words... "Michael."

"All that sweetness, so damn intoxicating," he murmured seconds before he bent his head and kissed her, coaxing her lips open, delving inside to taste. Oh, but she had missed this, missed him. She placed her hands on his chest, eased her fingers to the cords of his neck. He deepened the kiss, his fingers working the buttons of her shirt, pushing it aside to cover her breast with his big hand. He broke the kiss, nuzzled his face against her breasts and said, "I've got to have a taste."

But the taste never came because he jerked back, his expression dark, his gaze on her opened shirt. "What the hell is this?"

"What?"

"This," he repeated, gesturing toward the lace bra. "Red? See-through? What the hell?"

He acted like he'd just seen his mother in one. Elise pulled the opening of her shirt closed and glared at him. "I didn't know you'd find it so offensive." Damn him. So much for listening to Bree's thoughts on what men liked. First the haircut and now the bra, and he hadn't even seen the matching underwear. Michael really didn't find her attractive, not anymore, not since he saw the messed-up, insecure girl beneath the woman who pretended to have it all together.

"It's not that." He shook his head, blew out a sigh that sounded an awful lot like frustration, and said, "But why?"

"Why what?"

His dark eyes burrowed into her, digging for a truth she didn't want him to see. "Why all of it? The haircut, the bra, the skin-tight shirts. Where's the Elise Pentani I knew? The one I—" he caught himself, cleared his throat and continued

"—the one I knew?"

What had he almost said? The red splashing his cheeks and the flustered speech meant something, but what? If she didn't have to look into those eyes, hear the softness in that voice, well then, she might be able to fake her way through an answer. But Michael Androvich had a way about him that made it hard to pretend. She shrugged, looked away. If she had to speak this truth, at least she didn't have to do it eye to eye. "I don't know." There was too much emotion in her words and she hoped he didn't hear it, but of course he did.

"Hey." He grasped her chin with his fingers. "Look at me."

She would not cry. *She could not cry*. Elise blinked twice. Three times. Darn, but the first tear slipped, then the second, and after that, it was a rainfall.

Michael pulled her into his arms, stroked her back, his face buried in her hair. "Shhh. Don't cry. It's okay."

Oh, how she had missed this closeness. *Missed him. Missed all of it*. "Stupid hormones," she said, easing away. If she didn't move now, she'd want to do something ridiculous, like lay her head on his chest and beg for another chance with him. She sniffed and forced a smile. "They make me half-crazy and way too emotional."

He stared at her, shoved his hands in his pockets, his jaw tight. "Yeah, sure."

She swiped both hands across her cheeks, offered another tight smile. So fake, so absolutely pretend. *I am dying without you, Michael, can't you see that? Can't you see all I want is another chance?* "Sorry, I got your shirt all wet."

He shrugged. "No problem." That gaze narrowed, the voice sharpened.

"Okay then." Elise started to fasten her shirt, fumbled with the buttons. Could she humiliate herself any further?

Michael reached out, took both of her hands in one of his.

So big, so strong. Her fingers stilled. "You don't need tight shirts and red underwear to make you sexy," he said, his voice spilling into her, sucking the air from her brain. "You're sexy all by yourself."

She could argue that on several counts, and opened her mouth to point out exactly how unsexy she was, but stopped when he shook his head and said, "Don't." And then, "For once, just don't." He ran a finger over her lips, traced the curve of each one. "Very sexy," he murmured, seconds before he leaned in and took her mouth with such tenderness her heart ached. "Let me in." Elise opened her mouth, welcomed the taste of him, hot and sweet, and oh so tempting.

"Michael," she murmured against his lips. Not a plea to stop, though it should be. Shouldn't it? He pulled away and when those dark eyes met hers, she knew he wanted her, knew he would have her too, if she didn't make him leave this minute.

"Tell me to go and I will."

Michael Androvich would give her a night, but would he give her a lifetime? He'd once promised his heart but she'd crushed it with her insecurities and ruined their chance for a happily-ever-after. And now he wasn't promising anything more than a few hours of hot pleasure. She wanted all of him, the commitment, the love, the promise. Taking anything less could destroy her. Elise opened her mouth to send him away and said, "Stay."

***

Michael rolled over and drew in a deep breath. *Roses.* The scent covered him, filling him with memories of last night with *Elise.* He inched his eyes open. She lay on her side, the white sheet riding low over her naked back, black hair spilling onto the pillow, breath falling in a slow, even rhythm. What the hell had happened last night? Having sex, no, making love with his ex-fiancée was the last thing he'd planned, hell, the last thing he needed to complicate his already screwed-up life. But he'd done it. One look into those dark eyes and he was a goner. There'd been few words, but the intensity of the joining was like she'd grabbed his heart bare-fisted and squeezed. Shit. Now what? *Now the hell what?* He tried to ignore the pinch in his gut, working through him like 150-proof grain alcohol. Getting involved with Elise in any way that involved a bed and nakedness was a very bad idea.

Who was he kidding? He didn't need a bed or nakedness to do the deed. A wall, a table, the floor, and a flick of a zipper could pretty much do the trick. And that was a problem because if he didn't shut things down right now, he wouldn't be able to. Hell, he'd already let his brain admit they'd made love instead of *had sex*. He couldn't even say how that knowledge had slipped through his defenses when he'd barricaded his head *and* his heart from everything associated with Elise. Problem was, there was no escaping the woman. She'd been the only one to ever touch him bone-deep in his soul, searing him like a soldering iron.

He raked a hand over his face and eased out of bed. Maybe he was a chicken shit but he was not ready to deal with his feelings or her questions. Even if she didn't voice the questions, they'd be there, all lined up in that dark-eyed look of hers that would want to know what had happened, what it meant, what it didn't mean, and would it happen again. Oh, there would be so many questions in that one look that his brain pinched just thinking about it. Damn it, no. Not now. Not yet. Not until he contained whatever threatened to explode inside him, things like uncertainty, need, and desire. Yeah, lots in the desire area. Michael stood beside the bed listening to her breathing, part of him, the weak part, thinking about crawling back into that bed and holding her close, repeating last night, but with words and promises this time.

But the other part, the part that relied on self-preservation through shutting down and shutting out, said, *Hell no. I will not be played for an idiot twice.* That was the part that burrowed into his brain, killing all thoughts of reconciliation and second chances. He yanked on his jeans, snatched the rest of his clothes, and got out while he still could.

***

Michael sat in Lina's Café reading the *Magdalena Press* and eating a ham and cheese omelet. The hash browns were almost as good as his mother's, the omelet was a tie, and the rye toast was the best he'd ever tasted. He wouldn't mention the rye toast to his mother when he returned to Restalline because she'd take it as a challenge to beat out Lina's rye. Funny thing about Stella Androvich was that she liked food prepared *her* way, the Androvich way, and didn't think other cooks quite measured up. Somehow, she'd conceded that Elise's sugar cookies were up to par with her own, same as her peanut butter cookies, and cupcakes. Not the chocolate chip cookies, though: too many walnuts, not enough chips, baked too long. Michael scooped another forkful of omelet into his mouth, chewed. His mother sure had an opinion about everything, especially food and women, but she'd liked Elise. As a matter of fact, Elise had been her choice for him long before Michael realized she *was* a choice.

"Hi, Michael!"

He glanced up from his plate, narrowed his gaze on the young girl standing next to his booth. She'd been in the diner a few nights ago picking out pies. Lily, that was her name. "Hi, Lily." Michael smiled at her, set down his fork.

She glanced at his plate and said, "They have really good 'dunky' eggs and the best pancakes. Buttermilk."

"Ah. I'll put them on my list to try next time."

Lily nodded, touched her hair. "I got my hair cut. Do you think it's too short?"

Michael studied the black curls that had swirled halfway down her back the first time he met her. Now they didn't reach much past her ears. "I like it," he said. "And that's a cool headband, too." He pointed to the pink and green elastic headband that kept everything in place. "Nice touch."

She grinned, patted the headband as if to make sure it was still in place, and said, "Thanks. I was kinda nervous, but then I thought about the kids who don't have any hair, and I wasn't so nervous anymore."

"Oh." And then, "So you donated your hair?" He'd heard of people donating their hair for cancer patients who needed wigs, but he'd never actually known anyone who did it.

"Yup." She touched her hair again, pulled on one of the curls. "Me and Elise."

"Elise?" *His* Elise? He grew very still, waited.

"Elise, my new friend." Lily grinned. "She has black hair like me, but hers was even longer. She donated twelve inches; I only had ten."

Elise had donated her hair for a *cause*, not because she was trying to follow some trend. So, why hadn't she told him? Why had she let him believe his accusations were correct? "When did you meet Elise?"

"She was at Pop's, making pizzelles with him." She pushed up her glasses, studied him. "Did you meet Pop Benito yet? He's my buddy; we play checkers and talk, and sometimes we make pizzelles, or sometimes he just gives me my own bag. Do you like pizzelles?"

Michael didn't answer. He was still thinking about Elise donating her hair and making pizzelles at some stranger's house. And then there was the bakery where she worked with the pregnant red-headed girl. In the short time she'd been here, Elise had fit right in, and if this kept up, she'd be more at home in Magdalena than she was in Restalline. Would she stay here?

"Michael?" Lily leaned closer, eyeballed him. "Do you like pizzelles?"

"Huh? Oh, yeah, yeah I like them." *Would* Elise stay in Magdalena?

"Okay, I'll put you on Pop's list. We're making some this Saturday."

The door to Lina's opened and the man she'd been with the other day poked his head in. "Lily? Are you ready?"

She held up a hand, said, "Hold on, Nate." Lily turned back to Michael and said, "I left you the banana cream pie this time, but you better hurry before someone else gets it." She flashed him a grin and said, "Bye." Then she was gone, hurrying toward the man she'd called Nate.

***

There was only one way to stop the nearsightedness going on, and Pop knew how to do it. He walked into Lina's Café, spotted his target, and made his way to the man's booth. "You Michael Androvich?"

The "target" looked up from the *Magdalena Press*, brown eyes narrowed, like he wanted to know who was asking the question before he gave up a crumb of information. Smart boy. And Pop gave him extra points for reading the local paper that had to do with resident information, like who took a trip to their grandparents', who planted a new maple tree, or even who had a baby. Lucy would get listed soon enough, and then Pop would see if Jeremy Ross Dean changed his tune and became more than a "friend" to his granddaughter. The boy didn't have to think he was going to jump in and play "daddy" or "husband" and have "sleepovers." No sir, not on Pop's watch. One step at a time, nice and steady.

Now the young man in front of him had taken a misstep

or two and that's why Pop was here: to get him back on track and headed toward Elise Pentani and their happily-ever-after. A man didn't order pink rose petals for his future wife for the heck of it. Most men didn't know a rose from a petunia, let alone have the foresight to pick a special color. That said a lot and Pop was a great interpreter of words, actions, *and* relationships. He could tell that a man like that had a soft spot in his soul that beat with love, and while that soft spot might have grown a callus or two, it was still there, still waiting. And Pop knew how to soften it up and get it beating again with just the right words.

"So, are you Michael Androvich or do I have the wrong person?"

"I'm Michael."

Those eyes could stare a person down, but not Pop. He'd been evil-eyed by bigger and meaner men than this one, and the Androvich boy was a big one, but not mean. At least not unless he was protecting something that was his; that's how Pop figured it and he'd bet he was right. Kind of like Nate Desantro protecting his family; nobody wanted to get in the middle of that one. "I'm Angelo Benito," Pop said, thrusting out a hand that was half the size of Michael Androvich's. "People call me Pop."

Michael Androvich relaxed when he heard that, and dang but the boy actually smiled, a real smile, too, not one of those half-fake ones that reminded Pop of a garage door that got stuck halfway open and was no good to anybody.

"I've heard about you." The smile spread. "Actually I've heard quite a lot about you."

Pop grinned. "Then you better have heard about my pizzelles, too." He winked. "They're my specialty."

"Why don't you have a seat and you can tell me about those pizzelles? My mother's pretty big into those, too, and if she were here, she'd want a taste test."

"I welcome the challenge." Pop slid into the booth opposite Michael Androvich. "I been making these since I was a boy, but every now and again, I get challenged, and there's been a time or two when I've been bested." He shrugged, glanced across the table. "It happens, and it's all in how you handle the defeat." Pop scratched his jaw, nodded. "Just the other day I got challenged and dang, but I come close to ending up on the short end of that recipe. The new girl in town showed me what's what with her tricks and the way she handles her ingredients like they were living and breathing. That's an art and I recognize it." Pop didn't miss the way Michael Androvich got all still and silent. "What? What did I say?" Of course, he knew exactly what he'd said; slipping in the bit about Elise Pentani without mentioning her name had been a good chess move.

"The new girl in town?" The boy's face burned like a bonfire. "Is her name Elise?"

Pop settled back in the booth, tapped his fingers on the table, and let the questions mix with the smell of coffee and fried bacon. He didn't answer until after Phyllis dropped off his coffee and a plate of pancakes with two sunny-side eggs. He'd been ordering the same thing since back in the day when he and Lucy came here after Sunday Mass. Now he and Harry Blacksworth met every Wednesday and the order was always the same. Some things shouldn't change and one of them was breakfast at Lina's. "Elise," he said as he drizzled maple syrup on the center of his pancakes. "Beautiful name." Pop glanced up, met the boy's gaze. "Yup, that was her name." Pause, let the boy think on that and what the comment could mean, and then ask, "Do you know her?"

Oh, but the red scorched his face. "Yes. I know her." That voice dipped, turned soft as taffy. "But I think you already know that, just like I think you know we were

197

supposed to be on our honeymoon, but instead we're staying in separate rooms at the Heart Sent." Michael nodded, the dark eyes turning darker. "I don't like games, Pop, and I don't like being gamed, so why don't you just tell me what you've come to say and spare us both."

The boy had spunk, kind of reminded Pop of himself back in the day when Lucy's father tried to give him a hard time about keeping company with his daughter. The old man had danced around ten issues that might start with a comment as mild as, *Weren't you just here two days ago?* and ended on a note that tasted like it had been sprinkled with red pepper. Pop had called him on it, and from that day until the old man drew his last breath, they'd respected one another, even considered themselves friends in a loose sort of way. And now Michael Androvich sat across the booth with the same expression Pop had used decades ago. "Fair enough." He forked a bite of pancake, popped it in his mouth and chewed. Michael and Elise would have beautiful babies, dark hair, dark eyes, with tempers to match. "I told her the story about the woman who put too much balsamic vinegar on her salad."

"Say that again?"

Hah, now he had the boy's interest. "I told her the story about the woman who put too much balsamic vinegar on her salad. She ruined the dang thing and that left her with two choices: fix it or throw it out. Now they were talking about a lot of salad and a lot of effort. What a waste to dump it all in the garbage when maybe with a little thought and work, it could be saved. How about adding more romaine lettuce, more olive oil, more tomatoes? She decided to give it a try, because once she threw out that salad, it was gone." Pop forked another bite of pancake, pointed it at Michael. "And guess what happened with that salad?"

Michael Androvich crossed his arms over his big chest

and sighed. "She fed it to her sister."

Pop laughed. "She got no sister. Guess again."

"No idea."

That boy sure could scowl. "Funny, because that fiancée of yours figured it out quick as lightning."

That perked him up. "What did she say?"

Pop set down his fork and placed his hands on the edge of the table. "She said the woman fixed the salad. You know what that means, don't you?"

Oh, but that boy's heart was aching with the not knowing what to do, what to say, how to fix things. Pop had to give him a nudge so he could figure it out. "She wanted to make things right with you, but you're not an easy one, are you?" Pop narrowed his gaze, leaned forward. "You want people who've done you wrong to pay, even if it hurts you as much as it hurts them. That's your choice, but you best know it comes with a price. Do you know Elise came to see me a little while ago? Said she's leaving town, no idea where she's going or how long she'll be gone." He checked his watch, frowned. "Huh. Wonder if she's already left."

Those words booted Michael Androvich out of that booth so fast Pop thought there might be a spring in the seat. The boy pulled out his wallet, flung down a twenty, and off he went out the door. Pop reached across the table, eased the *Magdalena Press* in front of him, and opened it. There was nothing like the threat of someone leaving to get a person to state his true feelings. He sipped his coffee, smiled. Nope, nothing like it.

Chapter 16

Michael headed toward the Heart Sent, ten miles over the speed limit. He needed to get to Elise before it was too late. It was one thing to say it was "over" and he wanted to pretend he'd never met her, but that was like saying he'd given up chocolate and wanted to pretend he had no idea what it tasted like. Who was he kidding? The woman was embedded in his brain, lived in the recesses of his soul, the beat of his heart. He would *never* be over Elise. Not ever. Last night brought back memories of how good things had been between them, how no woman had ever touched his soul the way this one did. He wanted her again, wanted to take her to bed and stay there for three days. But that wasn't all; he wanted to spend time with her, talk with her in and out of bed, share dreams, build a life together.

He loved Elise Pentani, would love her until he took his last breath. That was damn scary to admit, but it was scarier to keep lying to himself. He was tired of the pretending, tired of not being able to touch her, talk to her, share in her life. Magdalena was supposed to be their honeymoon destination, but it had turned into a battleground. Why couldn't it still be their honeymoon destination?

When he reached the bed and breakfast, he parked the truck, ran inside, and bounded up the steps to Elise's room. "Elise!" He banged on her door. "Elise!" What if he were too late? What if she'd already taken off to who knew where? With her sense of direction, she could start out for Montana and end up in Minnesota. "Elise!" Dear God, do not let him be too late.

The door opened and Elise Pentani, love of his life, stood before him, looking at him as if he were crazy, which at this very moment, he might be. "Michael?" Her expression turned grim, worried. "What's wrong?"

"Don't go," he blurted out, not caring if he sounded weak. This was the woman he loved and he was tired of pretending otherwise, especially to himself, and if that made him weak, too damn bad. "I can't stand thinking you'll drive away and I won't know where you are." He advanced into the room, clasped her shoulders, and met her gaze. He had to make her see that she couldn't leave and if she did, she wasn't going without him. "If you want to leave, I'll come with you, I don't care where—Arizona, Texas, even Utah. Kevin and Sara would love the adventure. I doubt I'd be cutting trees, but I suppose I could turn bowls and jewelry boxes…"

"I thought you said you'd never sell your work, that it could only be given as a gift."

There was an edge to her voice. Surprise? Disappointment? "I'd do it for you."

"No." She shook her head, touched his cheek. "I would never ask that of you, and besides, I don't want to move to any of those places." Her lips pulled into a faint smile. "I want to live in Restalline, in a log cabin surrounded by tulips and daffodils in the spring and roses and daylilies in the summer. *Your* home, Michael, with you and Kevin and Sara, and whatever other children God may give us." The smile spread to her eyes, made them sparkle. "That's all I've ever wanted."

Her words made his chest ache. How could he have thought he could live without her? "I love you, Elise Pentani, with every part of me." He stroked her cheek, placed her hand against his chest. "You're in my heart, and if I spend the rest of my life with you, it won't be long enough."

"Oh, Michael, do you know how much I love you?" Her voice cracked. "How many times I dreamed you'd say those words again?"

"I've been a fool and I guess everyone saw that but me."

Her lips twitched. "You do have your moments."

He laughed. "That I do." His laughter faded and he turned serious. "Marry me. As soon as possible."

She leaned on tiptoe, kissed him softly on the mouth. "Yes, I'll marry you, Michael Androvich." Elise trailed kisses along his jaw, his chin, his neck. "As soon as possible." She eased away and looked him in the eye when she said, "Wherever you want, I'll be there. I promise."

"I trust you." And he did trust her. They were being given a second chance and they weren't going to blow it. Trust was about more than believing in a person only if you could prove what they said was true. Trust was about believing them when you couldn't prove what they said was true, when all you had to go on, was their word.

"I've done a lot of thinking and I can finally say I trust myself to do what I want to do, not what everyone wants or expects me to do." She smiled up at him. "And it feels wonderful."

Michael tucked a lock of hair behind her ears. "Lily told me how you donated your hair for cancer. I'm sorry I acted like such a jerk. That was a really brave thing to do."

Her voice dipped, softened. "If you've met Lily, then you know she can make you feel like anything's possible. She takes difficult choices and reasons them out so they make sense."

"Yeah, I kind of got that impression. But she's a bit of a conniver, too." He smiled at Elise's expression. "Who else could convince me to buy a slice of banana cream pie after I'd stuffed myself with a ham and cheese omelet and four pieces of rye toast?" He shook his head, traced her lips with his fingers. "She and Pop make a good team. He's the one who gave me the 'soft' lecture about forgiveness right before he told me you were leaving."

"He said that? When?"

"A little while ago. He told me you'd stopped at his house to say good-bye and were heading out of Magdalena, destination unknown."

"Huh." She cocked a brow, eyed him. "Talk about a conniver. I never said that, and the last time I saw him was when we made pizzelles." She paused, added, "Several days ago."

They looked at one another, burst out laughing. "So, the Godfather of Magdalena really does rule this town and the people in it, doesn't he?"

Elise threw her arms around his neck and whispered. "I'd say he knows how to get results."

"I'd say we've got to invite him to the wedding."

"Absolutely."

That was the last word they spoke before Michael lifted his bride-to-be in his arms and carried her to bed, where he undressed her, planted kisses where her clothing used to be, and made love to her. Deeply. Honestly. Completely.

***

Michael sat in Rex MacGregor's office, one booted foot resting on his thigh as he waited for Rex to comment on the proposal Michael and Gracie worked out. He'd had a few more ideas late last night and called Grace...after Elise fell asleep in a bed covered in pink rose petals. Oh, but she'd sure liked those petals, cried when he told her how he contacted Mimi to switch out red roses for pink. Who knew a guy trying to please his woman in a nonsexual way would get rewarded in a very sexual way?

"What's got you smiling like that?" Rex's loud voice broke through his thoughts, shattered them to bits of nothing. "You thinking about that bride-to-be?" He didn't wait for a response, but plowed on, "'Course you are. No doubt about it, with a grin like that?" The nod said he recognized "in love" when he saw it. "I been married a lot of years and every now and again, somebody catches me with this silly grin on my face and it's always when I'm thinking about my Kathleen. I don't admit it, because you don't want to tell your plant manager you're still mooning over your wife of thirty-plus years." He shrugged and turned brick red. "But I don't mind telling you."

Michael folded his arms over his chest and nodded. "I just want to make it through the wedding and then I'll start thinking about the next thirty years."

Rex shook his head and laughed. "That girl is not going to stand you up a second time; you can trust me on that one. Why, news of you two is all over town, how you're a real love match, how you were all doe-eyed in Lina's Café, and little Lucy Benito couldn't wait to tell everybody your fiancée finally baked you those damn sugar cookies you wanted."

Oh, but those sugar cookies had tasted good, especially the ones Elise had hand-fed him…in bed…naked…

"There you go with that smile again." Rex pushed the papers in front of him aside, planted his elbows on his desk, and said, "I'm real happy for you, Michael. And I'd be pleased and honored to do business with you and your family. I read the proposal and I agree to the terms. Let's have our lawyers make it all legal so we can get started. Are you good with that?"

"Sure. My sister wants to meet you and Bree and plans to visit soon." He thought of Gracie and Bree together, two women forging ahead into a man's world. They'd both do just fine.

"Looking forward to it." He blew out a long breath. "Your old man would be proud. Bree's damn excited about the prospect of working with your sister on this."

"She surprised me," Michael said. "Bree has a real knack

for dealing with customers and vendors, and she's getting a handle on compromise versus being a pushover. She'll be okay." Who would have thought he'd give the thumbs up to Bree Kinkaid? Not him, but she'd proven herself and was eager to learn and actually excited about the damn cabinets! Her husband on the other hand, was just a plain jerk who didn't appreciate his wife. Rex's next words said he felt the same way.

"I'm real proud of Bree, but it's Brody I'm worried about. He's developed a mean streak and I swear it's aimed at my daughter. He's jealous is all, but I won't have it. If he doesn't straighten up, I'm calling him on it."

Michael rubbed his jaw, thought of Brody Kinkaid and his muscles stacked on top of muscles. "You don't think that will cause a problem for Bree?"

Rex's expression turned dark, his mouth pulled into a frown. "Hell yes, it will, which is why I haven't fired his ass before now. I don't know what to do about him." He ran a beefy hand over his face and sighed. "But what I do know is I want this deal signed and sealed, airtight, as soon as possible. It's the only way I can protect the people I care about, and keep this company safe."

"The Androviches are looking forward to working with you." He'd get a crew lined up, but he might need to travel here once a month or so in the beginning. If it were summer, Elise and the kids could come with him...

"I'll be stepping down as soon as the paperwork's in place, not that I won't come snooping around or serve as a consultant, but the day-to-day business will fall in Bree's lap." His eyes misted. "It's been a long time coming, and I have to admit, it's bittersweet. Part of me wants to walk out the door and spend more time with my wife, but the other part wants to sit right in this chair and help Bree along." He sighed. "I really do wish your father were here to witness our companies doing business together."

The old man would be proud. He'd died before his children grew into adults and made something of themselves. It had taken Michael longer than Nick and Gracie, but he was finally getting the hang of this "making responsible choices" and "behaving like an adult". Not that it hadn't taken him well into his thirties to achieve, but his mother had never given up on him. *Damn*, but he hoped Kevin didn't have a wild streak in him like Michael did. And he sure as hell hoped Sara didn't. That could be a disaster *and* a headache. Elise would be a good influence; she'd settle them down like she'd settled him down. She would make them believe in hope and possibilities...

Rex cut into his thoughts, pulled him back. "If there's ever anything I can do for you, just say the word."

Michael rubbed his jaw, gave him a slow smile. "Well, there is one small thing."

***

"Relax. She'll be here." Nick threw Michael one of his big-brother-knows-best looks and said, "And stop fidgeting. You're driving me crazy."

Michael cleared his throat, fought down the mini spurts of panic shooting in his gut. "I'm fine."

"Yeah, sure you are. Trust me, every guy who's ever stood in your place shifts into panic mode right about now."

But not every guy was marrying a woman who'd no-showed the first time. Michael squashed that thought, concentrated on the trees in front of him, the scent of pine and bark around him, the blue sky above. This was his heaven and Elise had been the one to suggest Rex MacGregor's land as a place to get married, not St. Stanislaus with its stained glass, organ, pews, and priest. He smiled at that. But who better than Mimi Pendergrass, the Mayor of Magdalena, and the owner of the Heart Sent to marry them? He'd expected his mother and Dominic Pentani to have a thing or two to say about a nonchurch wedding that wasn't "blessed", but neither said a word. Maybe because they were so relieved for another chance to get this right, they didn't care about the how or the where. Yeah, he got that and he felt the same way, too.

"Look at Mom," Nick said, leaning toward him. "Who would have thought a blue-jean wedding in the woods would make her smile like that? She looks happier than she did when Alex walked down the aisle and you know she was ecstatic then."

Michael shrugged, fixed his gaze on their mother, who sat next to Gracie, Rudy, and their brood. "Maybe I'm the favorite, ever think of that?"

Nick sliced him a look, scowled. "No. Never." He adjusted his black vest, said, "She's just happy you're getting your sorry ass settled down before you hit forty."

"Funny. You'll be there before me."

"Don't remind me." And then he turned serious. "I'm really glad for you and Elise. You're great together."

"Thanks." It wasn't like Nick to get all soft on him, but after the last wedding fiasco, maybe his big brother thought he needed to hear the words. Michael glanced at the gathering of family and friends who had come to witness their wedding. Pop Benito sat in the second row, looking dapper in a navy suit, pink shirt, and matching bow tie with some kind of funky hat on his head he called a fedora. Rex and Kathleen MacGregor were beside him, with Rex looking casual in jeans and a pink button-down shirt, his wife decked out in a purple dress that made her red hair glow. And there was Lucy Benito and her "friend" Jeremy Ross Dean, both dressed in pink shirts and jeans. Further back, he spotted Bree and Brody Kinkaid, their kids between them, again in pink. He'd met Elise's new friends and their husbands, the

Desantros, the Reeds, and the Casherdons, and recognized the Desantro man as the one who had been in Lina's Café with Lily the first time Michael met her. Lily's mother sat next to him; someone told him the woman could carve a mean bowl and he might just have to find out about that.

The pink shirts were Elise's idea. Michael offered to wear the monkey suit again, promised he wouldn't complain about it, but she'd said no, said she preferred a more "Michael" look: blue jeans, pink shirt, and black vest. Where the hell she got the idea that he would *ever* wear a pink shirt was plain crazy, because he'd never owned one and never planned to own one. But here he was, wearing a pink shirt, a black vest, and jeans. She'd asked the men to wear pink shirts in honor of their commitment to their women, and when she put it like that, what guy wasn't going to do it?

The gathering was small, the seats folding chairs resting on a makeshift wooden floor. There was no organ, no violin or fancy music, nothing but a guitar, a keyboard, and a soloist. Nobody cared, least of all Michael. All he wanted was for Elise Pentani to say "I do" to the rest of their lives. When the music changed, everyone turned to find Mimi Pendergrass, the Mayor of Magdalena, walking down the aisle with a bible in one hand and a bouquet of pink sweetheart roses in the other. It was fitting that Mimi officiated over the ceremony seeing as she had a part in getting Michael and Elise together again. On either side of her were his children, Kevin and Sara, each carrying a ring on a pink satin pillow. He could see their smiles from here. As the music shifted yet again to a softer note, Lily Desantro appeared, pink dress flowing to just below her knees, hair done up in flowers and ribbons, carrying a bouquet of pink sweetheart roses. Her mother told Elise that Lily hadn't been able to sleep a full night since she and Michael asked her to be the maid of honor. Her smile was even brighter than

Kevin and Sara's and spread past him, to the trees and the sky.

And last, his bride appeared. She wore an ivory dress that flowed to the ground and reminded him of an angel. *His angel.* Nick squeezed his shoulder, a silent assurance that this time, Michael would get his bride. Elise moved toward him on her father's arm, not a run, but not a meandering pace either. Power-walking? A half jog? Dominic had a hard time keeping up with her, his short legs making an honest, if impossible effort. As she grew closer, her face turned brighter, her hair sparkling with jewels and flowers, her eyes glittering with hope. And love. So much love. When she smiled up at him, he smiled back, his heart filling with real joy. Minutes later, Elise Pentani made him the happiest man on earth—*she said yes.*

Epilogue

Bree slipped the black nightie over her head and smoothed it into place—what there was to smooth. Gracious, there were more dips and curves to this nightie than a roller coaster she'd ridden years ago. Brody loved roller coasters. She looked at the scooped neckline in the mirror. He would love this, too.

It had been three days since Elise and Michael's wedding, and word had it Mimi donated an extra three nights of pink rose petals for the honeymoon suite. Oh, but those days seemed so far away. There had been a lot of tears shed at that wedding, most of them happy, some sad, others full of longing, still others, hope. She guessed people like Pop were remembering their partners, wishing they were still by their side, carrying on the day-to-day business of life. Other people like Lucy Benito might be wondering if Jeremy Ross Dean might be her one and only, the key to her heart, or if they would never be more than friends. Michael's mother had a sadness around the eyes and mouth that said she knew loss, same with Miriam Desantro. Then there were the people whose faces shone brighter than a full moon: Christine and Nate, Gina and Ben, Tess and Cash, and the Androvich family—Nick and Alex, and Gracie and Rudy. Nick and Alex had an extra reason to shine, because secret of secrets, Gracie had told her Alex was pregnant! And dear, sweet Lily sparkled, her smile so bright it made Bree want to cry. Maybe Lily was the lucky one; she gave her heart without expecting anything in return and accepted people for who they were, not who she wanted them to be.

Bree pasted a smile on her face. Brody had only danced with her once at the wedding and that was after Pop made a big to-do about her not having a partner for the first slow dance. Shoot, she almost wished she'd flung her arms around Pop and danced with *him*. Her husband had been halfway through a bottle of beer and would have preferred to finish it first. It hadn't bothered Michael or his brother, or Nate, or Ben, or Cash, or any of the other men to hand off their beers to dance with their women. But not Brody Kinkaid. He had to pout and fuss, like he'd run out of oxygen if he didn't get that last sip. It had been downright embarrassing and a bit humiliating. Pop had snatched Brody's beer and given him the "evil eye" and a nod at Bree that said more than five hundred words could. Brody had taken her hand and led her to the wood-constructed dance floor where they shared a slow dance like they used to, her head resting on his big chest, his hand at the small of her back. Gliding, like they used to...off in their own little dream world.

It was time to make new dreams, lots of them, starting tonight. She took one last look in the mirror, grabbed her bathrobe and eased into it, tying the belt tight. Some surprises were best enjoyed slowly. And tonight she had a delicious surprise in store for her husband, one that would make him feel twenty again.

Ten minutes later, Bree swiped at a tear and stared at her husband. How could everything have turned so wrong so fast? She'd only asked him to pick up a few groceries on his way home from work tomorrow because she had a meeting with her father. Could he really not buy a gallon of milk, six bananas, and a four-pack of strawberry yogurt? She sniffed, forced her breathing to even. Maybe she should have waited until *after* to ask about the groceries, but the thought popped in her head and she wanted to get it out there before she forgot...and before Brody told her he had somewhere to go that did not include straight home from work. Why couldn't she ask him to help out? He should want to, like Cash and Ben, and Nate.

"Brody, we need to talk about this. It isn't healthy to get all mad and storm around." She squared her shoulders, pretended she wasn't half-naked, and said, "If you don't stop this anger, you'll head to an early grave like your Uncle Stu." And then what, she wanted to ask? He'd leave her with three babies to raise and no husband? The very thought sucked the air from her lungs, stole her logic, and made her spit out words she should have held back. "Don't you care about me and the kids? Don't you want to be healthy for them?" Pause. "For me?"

"Bree, will you just lay off? Dang, but I feel like you're suffocating me." His gaze honed in on her, his expression hard. "Why does everything with you have to be so much darn work?"

Breathe. Breathe. She stood in the middle of the room, her bathrobe clutched against the low neckline of the black nightie she bought this afternoon. A few minutes ago, she'd pictured a night of sharing kisses, making love, whispering tender words and promises that would make her soul open up. Bree had pictured recapturing the past, being in love and being loved—like it was before years of marriage, three children, and a miscarriage changed it all. But it was more than that, even if she didn't want to acknowledge it. Brody didn't like that her father had brought her into the business and wanted her to run it when he retired. No, her husband believed *he* should be in charge of the company, should be in charge of her work schedule, too, her comings and goings, how many babies they had, when they bought a new car, took a vacation, when they made love. Brody Kinkaid believed he should be in charge of *her*.

Bree swallowed hard. "Brody." She kept her voice soft and even, inching toward him. He felt that way because he was afraid of losing her; she saw that now. She'd show him how much she needed him, that he was still her "number one" and even if she ran one company or ten, he was her life partner, as in always and until they drew their last breath. If she'd neglected him lately, well, that would all change. Pronto. Friday night she'd make reservations at Harry's Folly and if her mother could babysit, maybe they'd drive to Renova and stay over in the fancy hotel that just went up. She'd ask Mimi for a bag of rose petals, too, just like they had on their honeymoon. She would get things back to the way they were, the way her husband liked them.

"Don't be angry." She smiled up at him, stroked his arm. So strong, so much muscle. "Let's talk, baby." If he wanted to make love every night, she'd do it. He'd only touched her once in four weeks, a sure sign he was not happy with her. Bree leaned on tiptoe, sprinkled kisses along his jaw. Who cared where they went on vacation as long as they went together? And a car? He could have that new truck he wanted, even though they wouldn't all fit in it. If it made Brody happy, then she wanted him to have it. "I'm sorry I haven't been available." She unbuttoned his shirt, slid her fingers inside to touch his chest. Nobody had a chest like Brody. "That's all going to change. You'll see." If he needed a little reassurance, she'd give it to him.

"Bree—"

"Shhh…quiet. This is your night, Baby. Whatever you want." She ran her tongue over a nipple, sucked. When he groaned, she did it again, then eased her hands along his belly, settled her fingers on his belt buckle. "Whatever…" Her fingers worked the buckle open, started on the jeans. "You…" Next came the zipper…slow and steady. "Want." Laughter spilled from her as she coaxed him to the bed. "All night," she whispered, seconds before he fell onto the bed with her on top of him. When he clasped her face between his hands and burned her with a look that branded her his, she almost cried. *Yes*, she wanted to shout, *I am Mrs. Brody*

Kinkaid. The kiss came next, hard, deep, needy. *This* was the man she'd so desperately missed. *This* was the man she would grow old beside. When his big hands gripped the front of her nightie and ripped it down the middle, exposing her breasts and belly, Bree smiled. "Yours for the taking."

They would make love now, a frantic joining with so much passion she'd cry. His voice would crack when he asked if she was okay, wiping tears from her cheeks, her chin, planting the softest kisses on her eyelids. And then, as he held her, he'd whisper "The Promise" in her ear as she drifted to sleep. What a beautiful pledge to their love, one she held close to her heart and carried with her, even during the cloudy patches of their relationship, especially lately. But the dark clouds were drifting away, she could feel it, and in their place would come bursts of sunshine. Her heart swelled and she recited her husband's pledge. "'The promise I make this day. Means my love is here to stay. In all the months—'"

"Stop it!" He tossed her off him and flew from the bed, fastening his jeans with jerky movements.

"Brody?" Bree knelt on the bed, nightie gaping open around her stomach. "What's wrong?"

He snatched his shirt, pulled it over his head. "What do you want from me? I'm not a machine that can perform on command." His eyes narrowed on her, his lips a slash of anger. "Just because you're gonna be the boss at work doesn't mean you're the boss in the bedroom."

His words pummeled her heart, tore at her soul. "Don't say that."

"Why?" He sat in the chair across the room and yanked on his socks. "Because it's true or because you want me to pretend it isn't?"

Why was he saying such horrible things? "It's not true." She scrambled off the bed and ran to him, ignoring the tattered nightie that exposed her half-naked body. "Please don't talk like that." Bree knelt at his feet, looked up at him. "Tell me what you want." The tears started coming, and she swiped at her cheeks. "Anything, just say it so we can get back to the way things were."

"Anything?" Brody's jaw twitched, the muscles in his neck bulged. "Well," he said, a gleam in his eye, "for starters, you can tell your daddy you're quitting."

"What?" He wanted her to leave *now*, when she'd finally gained enough knowledge and confidence to stay?

"Yeah, I want you to quit." His lips pulled into a smile, but there was not a lick of kindness in it. "Tell your old man you want to stay home and take care of *your* old man." That made him laugh, his mouth open wide enough to reveal his molars. "And," he continued, pulling on a boot, "it wouldn't hurt for you to put in a good word for me. Say you think I'd do a great job; say I'm better suited to it, being a man and all."

Was he making fun of her? Trying to make her feel puny and insignificant? "Why are you doing this?" Her gaze narrowed on his hands as he laced his boot. Strong hands, hands that had held their babies, touched her where no man ever had...

"Why am I doing what?" He stood and stepped around her, headed for the dresser, and grabbed his wallet and keys. "Should I sit around, quiet like a mouse, and wait for you to toss me a crumb or two of attention? Should I throw you a party because your old man is handing you a title that should be mine? I'll bet you'd like that, and I'm sure the guys in the shop would get a good laugh at my expense." He shoved his wallet in his back pocket, clutched his keys tight. "I did not sign up for this, Bree, not this."

Where was the man who'd called her Honey Bee, who wrote her a poem, and rubbed cocoa butter on her belly to battle stretch marks? That husband had never raised his voice to her, had insisted there were stars named after her, maybe planets, too. That husband wanted to unwrap her like a present when she wore new lingerie, fix her juicy steaks, and swing her in the air, clinging so tight it made her breathless and dizzy.

Where was that husband and how could she get him back? She needed that man, needed him so bad she could hardly take a breath. "Okay," she said, desperate to do whatever it took to get him to think of her as his Honey Bee. "I'll quit."

The smile he gave her this time was real. "Good. That's real good, Bree."

She eyed the keys in his hand. "Are you going out? It's late." *And I thought you'd want to be with me... I gave you what you wanted. I made you King.*

Brody glanced away, cleared this throat and settled his gaze on her. "I need a drink. Maybe two." He smiled again, long and slow, like he used to when he looked at her. "I like what I'm hearing, I sure do. I knew my girl wouldn't disappoint me." Then he crossed the room, gave her a peck on the cheek, and whispered, "I'll see you later, Honey Bee."

***

Pop folded his hands across his lap and studied the portrait of his wife. *This* was his Lucy, her eyes bluer than a robin's egg, skin as soft as a rose petal, and a smile that could heat the darkest soul. This Lucy had long since replaced the memories of the one who had spent her last days on this earth, frail and eaten by the cancer, her cheeks hollowed out, lips worn thinner than his mustache, skin bruised and beat up. God forgive him, but if she hadn't breathed her last breaths when she did, he might have broken down and found a way to end her pain. But the good Lord had stepped in and taken over because forty-two minutes later, Lucy Benito, love of his life, mother of his son, left this world. Now she lived in his heart, shared his oxygen, invaded his thoughts. She was everywhere. "Thank you, God," he whispered and made a quick sign of the cross.

Then he smiled and said, "What do you think, Lucy? We did good with that Androvich boy, didn't we? Boy, but he was some work. Stubborn as they come; I'd put him right up there with Nate and that's saying something, isn't it?" He shook his head and thought about how Michael Androvich had not believed there was forgiveness in his heart and then when it mattered most, he'd learned there was. And that had made all the difference in the boy. Who would have thought a body could get a smile out of him? A real smile, not one of those stretched-lip imitations that don't mean a dang thing but "take my picture." Elise Pentani knew how to make that boy smile, and Pop would bet Michael Androvich would be doing a heck of a lot of smiling with that new wife of his. And if Pop were a betting man, he'd wager there'd be a baby by next year.

Babies made him think of their granddaughter. "Lucy will be having the baby soon. Can you believe that belly? It's the size of one of those seedless watermelons that you always said were too expensive." He chuckled and rubbed his own belly that looked like a cantaloupe from Sal's Market. "The jury's still out on that Dean boy she's been bringing around the house. He might know how to cook the best penne in town and whip up rolls that melt in your mouth, but what's that tall drink of water know about a baby? And what's he expect from our Lucy?" He sighed, rubbed his jaw. "I suppose I'm gonna have to have a girl talk with her, though it's kinda late for that, seeing as she's already done more than talking. But we might as well get it out there in the open so there's no repeat performance until she's got herself settled."

Pop snatched the notepad and pencil from the table and started reading the girl's names he'd selected for his great-granddaughter. "Alfonsia, Cosima, Vincenza, Rafaella." He paused, repeated the last one again and let it settle on his lips. "Rafaella. Hmm. What do you think of that one, Lucy? Doesn't it sound like a princess? Rafaella Benito. Kind of catchy." He thought of a few more names that ended in vowels and added them to the list. If they rolled off his tongue with a purring sound, he put a star next to them. Pop was so busy adding stars and names that he didn't hear the knock on the door, until it turned into a pounding.

"Hold on, hold on!" He set the pad and pencil down, hefted himself out of the chair. Dang, but his foot had fallen asleep and he had to shake it as he made his way across the room like he was doing a jig. Pop opened the door and squinted. "Ben?"

"Hi, Pop. Do you have a minute?"

"Sure. Come on in." The boy was dressed in his police uniform, looking sharp and polished, but Ben Reed could look good in a recycle bag. Wonder if he'd look so good once the baby came along. "You and Gina pick out a name for the tyke yet?"

Ben shook his head. "Nope. We're toying with a few, but nothing for certain."

Pop took a seat and motioned for Ben to sit in the chair next to him. "I been working on girls' names for Lucy's baby. How about I give you a name or two to throw in the pot? I could work on boys' names, too, since you don't know if it's a he or a she."

"Uh...sure. Thanks." Ben Reed cleared his throat and said, "Look, Pop, something's happened and I need to talk to you about it so maybe you can help with damage control."

Pop sat up straight in his chair, leaned toward Ben.

"What is it?" The boy had come in police garb and now he was talking about damage control. Whatever was coming next could not be good. "Is this official business?"

Ben Reed's blue eyes turned dark. "I'd say it's official unofficial business."

"Ah. Official unofficial business." Pop tilted his head, rubbed his jaw. "Did you find out who stole my garbage can lids? I'll bet it was the Carlson boy, wasn't it?"

"No, this is about Brody Kinkaid." He cleared his throat again, met Pop's gaze. "He had a massive heart attack. We got the call from the Renova police. Rudy's heading over to Bree's and then to Brody's mother."

Massive heart attack? Renova police?

"He's dead, Pop. They tried to revive him, but it was too late."

"Oh, good Lord." Pop made the sign of the cross, blinked hard. Brody Kinkaid was a young man with a family. Poor Bree. She'd loved that boy more than just about anything on this earth, except for her little girls, and now he was gone. A hurt like that might never heal. And then, something Ben said tickled his brain, made it synapse and formulate a question that didn't sit right. "What was Brody doing in Renova?"

Ben Reed's gaze darted from Lucy's picture to the ceiling, the floor, and the arm of the chair, like a fly that's trying to find an open window. Finally, it landed on Pop. "That's what I need to talk to you about."

"Oh."

"Once the news hits, stories will start flying around," he paused, wiped a hand over his face, and continued. "Bad ones. Some of them could be true."

"How bad?" He had a feeling and it wasn't a good one.

"Bad enough to destroy Bree and the girls. People listen to you, Pop. If you tell them to leave it alone, they might, or at least they won't be so opinionated with their assumptions and accusations."

"Hmm. You know, Ben, there's not many things that can destroy a man's wife and children. I'm thinking of a big one, but the words aren't coming out of this mouth unless I'm right, and I ain't gonna know I'm right until you say it." Pop leaned in, met Ben Reed's clear gaze, and said, "So say it."

Ben opened his mouth and spit out the truth that Pop might later call a lie. "Brody Kinkaid was at the Renova Hotel with another woman. She's the one who placed the 9-1-1 call."

Pop shook his head, his heart heavy, his soul sad. "Damn fool idiot," he murmured. "Poor Bree's heart will never heal, not in ten thousand years." He swiped at the tears. "I'll do my darnedest to keep the truth from boiling over into this town. On my unborn baby granddaughter's soul, I swear I will."

The End

Many thanks for choosing to spend your time reading *A Family Affair: Winter*. I'm truly grateful. If you enjoyed it, please consider writing a review on the site where you purchased it. (Short ones are fine and equally welcome.) And now, I must head back to Magdalena and help these characters get in and out of trouble!

If you'd like to be notified of my new releases, please sign up at my website: *http://www.marycampisi.com*.

Want to take a peek at the secrets inside Gloria's notebook? Go to http://www.marycampisi.com/glorias-notebook/

About the Author

Mary Campisi writes emotion-packed books about second chances. Whether contemporary romances, women's fiction, or Regency historicals, her books all center on belief in the beauty of that second chance. Her small town romances center around family life, friendship, and forgiveness as they explore the issues of today's contemporary women.

Mary should have known she'd become a writer when at age thirteen she began changing the ending to all the books she read. It took several years and a number of jobs, including registered nurse, receptionist in a swanky hair salon, accounts payable clerk, and practice manager in an OB/GYN office, for her to rediscover writing. Enter a mouse-less computer, a floppy disk, and a dream large enough to fill a zip drive. The rest of the story lives on in every book she writes.

When she's not working on her craft or following the lives of five young adult children, Mary's digging in the dirt with her flowers and herbs, cooking, reading, walking her rescue lab mix, Cooper, or, on the perfect day, riding off into the sunset with her very own hero/husband on his Harley Ultra Limited.

If you would like to be notified when Mary has a new release, please sign up at

http://www.marycampisi.com/book/book-release-mailing-list/

Mary has published with Kensington, Carina Press, and The Wild Rose Press and she is currently working on the next book in her very popular Truth in Lies series, the A Family Affair books. This family saga is filled with heartache, betrayal, forgiveness and redemption in a small town setting.

website: marycampisi.com
e-mail: mary@marycampisi.com
blog: marycampisi.com/blog/
twitter: https://www.twitter.com/#!/MaryCampisi
facebook: facebook.com/marycampisibooks

Other Books by Mary Campisi:

Contemporary Romance:
Truth in Lies Series
Book One: A Family Affair
Book Two: A Family Affair: Spring
Book Three: A Family Affair: Summer
Book Four: A Family Affair: Fall
Book Five: A Family Affair: Christmas
Book Six: A Family Affair: Winter
Book Seven: A Family Affair: The Promise
Book Eight: A Family Affair: The Secret (TBA)
Book Nine: A Family Affair: The Wish (TBA)

That Second Chance Series
Book One: Pulling Home
Book Two: The Way They Were
Book Three: Simple Riches
Book Four: Paradise Found
Book Five: Not Your Everyday Housewife
Book Six: The Butterfly Garden

The Betrayed Trilogy
Book One: Pieces of You
Book Two: Secrets of You
Book Three: What's Left of Her: a
The Betrayed Trilogy Boxed Set

The Sweetest Deal

Regency Historical:
An Unlikely Husband Series
Book One - The Seduction of Sophie Seacrest

Book Two - A Taste of Seduction
Book Three - A Touch of Seduction, a novella
Book Four - A Scent of Seduction

The Model Wife Series
Book One: The Redemption of Madeline Munrove

Young Adult:
Pretending Normal

CPSIA information can be obtained
at www.ICGtesting.com
Printed in the USA
LVOW04s1505271015

459955LV00021B/810/P

9 781942 158042